PENNY WISE

Susan Moody

FAWCETT GOLD MEDAL • NEW YORK

A Fawcett Gold Medal Book
Published by Ballantine Books
Copyright © 1989 by Susan Moody

Library of Congress Catalog Card Number: 88-92209

ISBN 0-449-13236-6

Manufactured in the United States of America

First Edition: March 1989

For Kym Horwood

1

THE CLEAVER CAME DOWN SUDDENLY. NO WARNING. ONE moment the woman was caressing the long dark-skinned body, the next she'd decapitated it. The head gasped reflexively. So did Penny Wanawake. Blood oozed. The woman smiled. Her lips worked soundlessly, the head dangling from her fingers.

'So you'll go,' Lady Helena said on the other end of the phone.

Penny blinked. 'Go?'

'Instead of me,' said her mother. 'Take a few notes, look involved. You'll enjoy it.'

'I'm not going, Mother. I already said. 'Sides, Costas Kyriakou is a royal pain.'

Her mother breathed reminiscently. 'You didn't know him as a young man.'

'Life can be a real bitch.'

'If I drop out, Costas will take it as a personal slight.'

'Oh, my heavens.'

There was a shrugging sigh at the other end of the telephone. 'All right. I expect I'll find something else. Because Costas will cancel the Delhi job he just offered me, if I insult him by not turning up. He's like that.'

'I don't blackmail easy,' Penny said.

She watched the woman slit the body from neck to abdomen. Guts spilled out. They looked faintly greenish. Under her permanent tan, Penny felt it.

'Blackmail?' Her mother gave a laugh that didn't quite reach carefree. 'You make me sound like a common criminal.'

1

'Common, Helena? With your background?'

'Ah well,' her mother said. There was a quaver in her voice now. 'If you won't go, you won't. Maybe Costas will understand. Though I doubt it.'

So did Penny. From what she knew of him, understanding didn't figure on Costas Kyriakou's resumé. None of that mercy-seasoning-justice crap for him. He was the sort of rich man who would pass a needle through the eye of a camel without even blinking. From his headquarters in Athens, he controlled a business empire that stretched from Beijing to Bombay. The long way round. His reputation as an implacable enemy was boosted by the many stories of former business rivals reduced to scrabbling through trash bins after getting across him. If you can always tell a gentleman by the company he keeps, then Costas was one in spades. So far, he'd kept every company he'd ever acquired.

'If a man orders a classy interior designer in white, he's liable to object if they send him a six-foot shutterbug in aubergine,' Penny said.

'Why on earth should he? A beautiful girl like you?'

'Bet you're just saying that.'

'This is only a preliminary meeting. I don't think he's got all the financial backing he needs yet. He'll probably spend most of the time on his boat.'

'Mother, you know how I feel about boats.'

Lady Helena wasn't listening. 'Odd, the romantic ideas people have about themselves,' she said. 'Costas sees himself as a cross between Odysseus and Captain Ahab.'

'Just the pair I'd pick to go sailing with.'

'You'd love it,' Lady Helena said firmly. 'Did I tell you Irene Lampeter's also been invited?'

'Quel coincidence,' Penny said. 'Her programme's on the TV right this very minute.'

'What's she making?'

'Fish.'

The woman on the screen shoved the body to one side. With a sharp knife she chopped mushrooms silently with garlic cloves. She added prawns, taking them in handfuls from a white bone-china saucer. She put

2

several in her mouth, giving the cameras a guilty little moue. It was the sort of gesture that had endeared her to millions. Why her food programme consistently made the Top Ten ratings. She reminded men of Mom. She reminded women that there was life without aerobics. She put one hand on the top of the blade end and moved the knife in a quick circle. Shredded parley ensued.

'Irene's related to Costas by marriage,' Lady Helena said.

'How come?'

'She had an affair with Costas once, when she was much younger. A very passionate one. Until he introduced her to his cousin, James Lampeter.'

'What happened?'

'Coup de complete foudre, my dear. Irene took one look and the next thing we knew, she and James were married.'

'Costas must have loved that.'

'Like a tooth abscess. He was *raging.* But then he always was a bad loser.'

'James Lampeter died young, didn't he?'

There was a pause. Then Lady Helena said, 'You can't *possibly* be suggesting . . .'

'Just asking.'

'Even Costas wouldn't go that far.'

'Who knows how far anyone would go, given enough motivation?'

On screen, Irene Lampeter clove lemons in half. She poured cream from a wholesome jug and massaged the dead fish with oils from bottles that contained sprigs of greenery. Under the lights, the studio kitchen seemed painted in child colours. Dead white saucer, acid yellow fruit, bright green parsley. She lifted the fish and laid it in orange earthenware. She opened an oven door of black glass and put the dish inside.

'Alexandra will be there too,' Lady Helena said.

'Aaargh,' said Penny.

'What's the matter?'

'My jugular,' Penny said. 'Someone just sank their teeth in and won't let go.'

3

'You remember Alexandra from school, don't you?'

'As someone I'd swim through cesspits to avoid.'

'From what Costas tells me, she's grown into an extremely nice young woman.'

'She was not an extremely nice young girl.'

'People develop.'

'So does herpes.'

'You're being very prejudiced. Alexandra's a grown woman now.'

'Can a leopard change its spots?'

'She must be well past the spotty stage,' said Lady Helena. She did some more deep breathing. 'Goodness, you are lucky.'

'Why?'

'Costas's island is so beautiful. The views. The scent of pine. That amazing sea.'

'Mother, if you've finished with the Michelin guide, I do have friends here.'

'And the food!'

'Mother, I'm not going.'

'Is that your last word?'

'Definitely.' Why did she feel that that wasn't destined to be the most accurate statement she'd ever made?

'In that case, I won't bother telling you who is working as Costas's PA right this very minute.'

Uh-oh. Penny instantly recognised the change in her mother's voice. As though someone had wrapped a cosh in a cashmere sweater.

En garde, Wanawake.

'Good,' she said.

The television screen showed Irene Lampeter moving across the studio floor to a table laid for two. A celebrity of some kind awaited her. Penny recognised him as the presenter of a TV series on Historical Sites Nobody Ever Heard Of. Something like that. He was dinner-jacketed, with hair that looked as if it had been freeze-dried and reconstituted. Penny had only caught his programme once. She had no wish to catch it again. TV wasn't the ideal way to see historical sites. He was wearing a shirt with eyelet frills outlined in navy. Snappy

4

dresser. No man in eyelet frills was worth the kind of culinary effort Irene had just made.

'Uh—who?' she said. No will power, that was her trouble. No moral fibre. She hated herself for asking. She knew she'd regret it.

'Who is what?'

'Knock it off, Mother. Is Kyriakou's PA?'

'Theo.'

'Theo *Schumann*?' She was right. She regretted it.

'Yes.'

'Theo is a friend of *Alexandra's*?'

'So I heard.'

'I thought he had better taste.'

'I understand from Costas that Alexandra wants to marry the boy.'

'How does the boy feel?'

'Ask him when you get to Greece.'

There was a short silence. On screen, the celeb grinned at the studio audience and held out a chair for Irene with extravagant gestures. He removed a rose from the crystal vase in the centre of the table and offered it to her with a bow. Penny's cleaning lad appeared from the right, dressed as a waiter, and handed him a menu. He handed one to Irene. He went away.

Penny put her hand over the telephone. 'Was that it, Lucas?' she said. 'We sat through all those fish guts for one and a half seconds of you?'

'There's more,' the cleaning lad said. He sat on Penny's white sofa, his arm round his pregnant wife.

'I thought the fish looked fascinating,' Barnaby said. He raised his glass at Penny. Beaded bubbles winked below its brim. Well below. 'I've never seen a horizontal phallic symbol before.'

'I hope you don't expect me to believe that,' Penny said.

'Do you think I overplayed it?' Lucas said. He turned to his wife. She shook her head, looking serious.

'Not a bit,' she said. She had to be having him on.

'I based the part on Denholm Elliott in *Trading Places*,' Lucas said to Barnaby.

Barnaby nodded solemnly. 'I could tell.'

5

Penny spoke again into the phone. 'When is this trip scheduled for?'

'Ah,' said her mother.

'*Not* that I'm capitulating or anything.'

'Your father and I were in the U.S. when Nixon resigned.'

'And?'

'I know capitulation when I see it.'

'Just the date, Helena. Save the smarts for your New York parties.'

'Next month. Twelfth of May.'

'Right.'

Penny put down the phone. She and Abe Lincoln. Not controlling events but controlled by them. Shit.

In the TV studio, Irene Lampeter turned in her chair and looked behind her. A hand offered her something and she took it, speaking directly to the audience. Some kind of plug. With the sound off, it was difficult to tell what for. When she'd finished, she pulled on a pair of oven gloves shaped liked giant lobsters. She opened the oven and pulled out a dish. She showed it to the camera. It bubbled and heaved. Different oven, different dish. You couldn't fool Penny. The credits came up. When the last one had rolled over, Penny said, 'Where's the more?'

'Don't say you missed it,' said Lucas.

'Missed what?'

'The hand,' said the pregnant wife. She'd been a dancer before she married Lucas. Once she'd produced Lucas's child, she hoped to be again. 'With the menu. That was Lucas.'

'Your agent must have been inundated with offers,' Barnaby said. He poured more champagne.

'They remake *The Hand*,' said Penny, 'they'll know where to come for the name part.'

'You can laugh,' said Lucas, laughing. 'Just wait till I'm making pots at the National.'

'Lucky Potts,' said Barnaby. 'Whoever he is.'

'What did your mother want?' Barnaby asked later, his hair dramatic as a marigold against the black pillows.

6

'Me to take her place on some business conference she'd agreed to go to,' Penny said. She lay on her stomach on the bed. Naked. Long tall Penny. Six foot of her, being backrubbed by the man she loved.

'Where?'

'Greece.'

'And of course you turned her down.'

'Of course. Who wants to go to tacky Greece, anyway?'

'Yecch,' said Barnaby. 'All that sun. All that wine-dark sea.'

'All that wine-dark wine.'

'What kind of business conference?'

'Ever heard of Costas Kyriakou?'

'The millionaire? Who hasn't?' Hands curved around Penny's shoulder blades, Barnaby said, 'Not a very suitable companion for your mother.'

'Turns out they're old friends.'

'Your mother is old friends with just about everybody.'

'Seems he's hoping she'll help him take England by storm.'

'No one's managed it since 1066. What's *his* gimmick?'

'Hotels.'

'Didn't he already take over some cheap Brit chain last year?'

'We're talking upscale here. I mean, like palatial. None of these anonymous plastic hotel rooms and one-cup packets of instant plastic coffee. The man's promising something different. Something with a touch of class.'

'Lady H providing most of that, presumably.'

'Once the hotels have been built, the idea is to sell off individual suites to the big corporations. Saves the harassed executive from checking out the Tourist Information booths the minute he hits town. My mother claims the multinationals are already forming lines to buy.'

'It's a good idea,' said Barnaby.

'I can think of others.'

'So can I.'

'Want to swap one of yours for one of mine?'

'Nothing like a full and frank exchange of views.'

They were still exchanging them when the Literary

7

Gent came home. Along with Miss Antonia Ivory, the tenant sitting in the basement flat, he'd been part of the fixtures and fittings when Penny bought the house in Chelsea. One of Britain's leading novelists, the Literary Gent was at present suffering from writer's block. Somewhere between brain and typewriter, the latest leading novel had disappeared. Most of the advance had long ago gone on cheap gin. With the rest he'd bought a new pair of Hush Puppies.

Coming home involved several tries at the keyhole. Plus some Anglo-Saxon language. As he lurched up the stairs they heard him intimate unmusically that little things meant a lot.

'A lot of what?' said Penny.

'Comment in the locker room,' said Barnaby.

'Your thing isn't little.'

'You should be grateful for small mercies.'

'Thank God I don't have to be.' She touched a large one. Barnaby smiled at her.

'This bed thy centre is, these walls thy sphere,' he said. 'You going to turn over?'

'Consider it Donne.'

'Could I ask you a personal question?' Barnaby said.

'Sure.'

'Ever thought of getting married?'

'Yeah.'

'And?'

'If it ever happened,' said Penny, 'it'd be to you.'

'Meanwhile?'

'Take these chains from my heart,' Penny said. 'And set me free.'

Barnaby moved his hands over the sides of her breasts. He touched the base of her throat, holding a finger against the pulse there. 'Oh Jesus, Penny,' he said.

'I know,' said Penny.

Barnaby drew in a deep breath. He let it out again. In the quiet, they could hear faint electronic beeps from the basement. Miss Ivory playing Space Invaders on the computer she'd bought with what she'd made out of reselling her British Telecom shares.

'When does your mother want you to go to Greece for her?' asked Barnaby.

'In three weeks. 12 May.'

'Go.'

'Why?'

'Because I'll be away.'

Penny stiffened. 'Where?'

'In South Africa.'

'Doing what?'

'Something illegal.'

'How unusual.'

'And maybe dangerous,' Barnaby said seriously.

Penny pulled away from him and sat up. Lamplight slid over the rounded surfaces of her body. It took Rolls Royce seventeen coats of paint to achieve the same sheen. Penny used baby oil. 'What kind of dangerous?'

'Moderately.'

'What're you getting mixed up in?'

'So far, not much. My guess is we're all going to get mixed up in it soon. Things have gone too far out there. The trouble is, someone thinks I'm already mixed up in it, and I'd like to find out why. Also, there's some personal business I'd like to clear up before it's too late.'

'Family business?'

'Maybe. It might be a good idea if you weren't around.'

'I liked your other good ideas better than that one.'

'So did I.'

'Got any more?'

'Here's one I clean forgot to mention.'

He mentioned it. While he did, Penny thought about him going back to the country of his birth. Although his father still lived out there, growing rich on diamonds and other people's sweat, Barnaby himself hardly ever visited. Partly because he hated the place. Partly because the authorities considered him a subversive element. If they knew he was coming, they certainly wouldn't bake a cake. Most they'd do would be to polish up a handcuff, maybe sweep out a cell. South Africa was dirty pool. She knew. She'd spent time there herself, a while ago. She hadn't enjoyed it. If you white, you all right.

9

But if you black, brother, get back. To the townships, because you can't live where we live. To the kitchen, where we can't see you. To the end of the line. South Africa was big on insights, if you were black. Like Penny.

Once, Barnaby had been just another run-of-the-mill jewel-thief and catburglar. Then he made the mistake of catburgling Penny's *apartement* in Paris. He had never been the same since. She told him that his education was incomplete. She offered to complete it. She persuaded him to turn his considerable brain to the problems of the Third World. Like starvation. Like disease. Like death. The R.H. Domestic Agency was born, fronted by the impeccably antecedented Miss Ivory. Not only was she first cousin to a horse, she lived right there on the premises. Very convenient. Very lucrative. Especially for the Third World.

Once, she had been just another rich girl, daughter of Dr Benjamin Wanawake, Permanent Ambassador to the UN from the Republic of Senangaland. Her mother was Lady Helena Hurley, whose family stretched back over six centuries of English history. After school in England, she'd gone to L'École Internationale in Switzerland before spending a year at the Sorbonne and another at Stanford. When she wasn't vacationing at the California beach house, or partying in the New York apartment on East Seventieth, she had lived at Hurley Court, the ancestral home of her mother's family. Black had been what you put your chips on if you didn't like red.

Then she'd gone to Africa, and everything had changed.

'Does your business involve diamonds?' she said.

'It might do.'

'Does it involve your father?'

'Possibly.'

'Will you be carrying a gun?'

'Do I get a kewpie doll if I answer five in a row?'

'You got one already, hot stuff.' Penny reached out and switched off the light.

2

GATWOCK. 6 A.M. ACRES OF HIGHLY POLISHED FLOOR. CAVernous voices issuing from the ceiling. People in warm British clothes pushing baggage carts about and shivering in the air-conditioning. The departure lounge atmosphere was as thick as bogwater. Fear of flying fought it out with squirts of Je Reviens from the duty-free perfume counters. It was gut-squeeze time.

Penny looked around for Irene Lampeter. Although she had never met her, she knew a lot about her. So did anyone who read the Sunday supplements and owned a TV. Irene was a triumph for the pre-menopausal woman cast suddenly into the business arena with no marketplace experience. If your definition of success included money, Irene was one. Widowed at forty-two, her only skills had been domestic, her only assets a heavily mortgaged manor house of Cotswold stone, and two sons. The eldest had been destined for the Bar but was forced to give it up when Irene could no longer support him. The Law's loss was the world's gain. Tim Lampeter proved to be a financial whizz kid. Within a few years, he had turned his mother's abilities into a million-pound enterprise.

With clever packaging, designed by the second son, the Lampeters had successfully tapped the gypsy in the soul of every urban muesli-eater. Irene brought out a book called *Lovesome Things*, half cook-book, half herbal, and lusciously illustrated with backlit photographs taken by the second son. Sales of Lampeter products soared.

11

After an appearance on breakfast television, Irene began to feature on *Any Questions*. Robert Robinson got her to *Stop the Week* with him. It was a short step to her own food programme on TV. *Pick and Choose* was now into its third series. National recognition came when her round face and citrus-coloured smocks were lampooned on *Spitting Image*. Fame at last.

In no time at all the Lampeter Group had launched into hedgerow beauty, producing a line of cosmetics which leaned heavily on weeds. Next, they branched out into rustic fabrics with matching wallpapers. An elderly film-star did out his French farmhouse in them. Famous people were photographed eating Lampeter goodies amid Lampeter furnishings. Lampeter outlets appeared all over England. The Lampeter Group acquired a swarm of helicopters to ferry the family from opening to opening. Branches were launched in New York and Paris. Financial editors on the serious newspapers whispered of expansion into the catering business. It was success, 1980s-style.

Penny's flight was announced. The passengers shuffled aboard. In the small first-class section of the plane, the wide executive seats were styled to fit wide executive hips. Plenty of room for the hand-made alligator shoes and the hand-held computers. If you were sitting down. Penny wasn't. She found herself trapped between two seats, braids brushing the stowage compartment above, while a thickset geek with red curls hassled the flight attendant about a blanket for his fat wife's knees. Wife didn't look like she wanted a blanket. Not for her knees. Not for anything else, either. Except possibly to throw over the geek's head and smother him.

'Hey, guys,' Penny said after some minutes of this, 'how about we sort this all out later, huh?'

The man looked at her as if she'd been scraped out of a colostomy bag. 'Were you addressing me?' he asked. He obviously thought that, if so, she had one hell of a nerve.

Penny looked down at the top of his head. 'Yeah,' she said.

'Do you know who my wife is?'

'No. Does she know who I am?'

Who *was* his wife? Penny tried to sneak a look but the fat woman kept her big red face turned away, as though afraid people might scream if she hit them with the whole thing at once. Her husband had a black beard shaved to mitred corners of his face. It didn't match his hair. It made Penny feel antagonistic. It was probably meant to.

'Please,' the wife said, 'do sit down, Hector.'

'Not until we get a blanket,' Hector said.

'If you would just sit down, sir, someone will bring . . .'

'I don't *want* a blanket,' said the wife. Was it Irene Lampeter? Head down like that, Penny couldn't be sure.

'Darling, you will,' her husband said, 'Just wait until we take off. The temperature always drops, isn't that right?' He stuck out his jaw at the attendant.

'All our cabins are fully—'

'Refrigerated,' the man said. 'I'm not going to let you get cold, love. You've only just got over bronchitis.'

'It was a cold,' Love said wearily. Sounded like an old argument.

'Bronchitis.'

'I'll bring you a blanket as soon as the passengers are seated, sir.'

'I want it now.'

Time to muscle in on the act. 'I want doesn't get,' said Penny.

'What did you say?'

Penny was getting pretty steamed. 'You want me to stand in the aisle the whole damned flight?' she said.

'I'm sorry if you're inconvenienced, but my wife is—'

Penny pushed him. Arrogant little twerp. She used her hip and some force. He fell into a seat. 'Heavens,' she said. 'I'm sorry. I must have tripped.'

He didn't believe her. She could tell she hadn't made a fan.

Her seat was great, even though she was right across the aisle from Hector and wife. So was the bourbon she ordered once she was in it. The detective novel she'd brought to while away the hours was a bit of a wash. The hard-boiled PI hero not only murdered with impunity and then spent pages justifying his personal ethic of violence, he also fancied himself a gourmet. Gaahd. There were lots of things you could call a man who put together salads that contained among other things both seedless grapes and pickled gherkins, but gourmet wasn't one of them. The other things included honey.

She tried to sleep. Mainly in order not to think about Barnaby in moderate danger. It didn't work. She'd spent a lot of time in the past few years in more than moderate danger herself. Big deal. That was the difference between the You and the Other. You never even thought about it when it was You. You couldn't stop when it was the Other. And the Otherness of Barnaby Midas, antique dealer and art thief, was terrific. Had been, ever since she first found him in her Paris *apartement*, trying to liberate her jewellery. He'd pretended to be the gasman. She'd pretended not to care. Later, when she saw him con Cartiers out of one of their diamond rings, she stopped pretending. She never told him where she hid hers.

It didn't matter that he operated on the shady side of the law. Nor that as well as Eton his education had included nine months in Parkhurst Prison. She loved him. It was that simple. And she didn't want him to go back to South Africa. If the authorities got hold of him, the best he could hope for was house arrest. She didn't fancy her chances of locating him if she heard that he'd 'gone away.' Not with her kind of tan. Nor did she fancy her chances of getting through the rest of her life without him. She shifted in her seat. Crossed her legs. Closed her eyes. Opened them. In Africa she had seen the great divide between haves and have-nots. She'd seen people die of starvation, while Europe paid millions in storage fees to house its grain surpluses. It was then that the girl with the Gucci luggage had metamorphosed into the Camera with a Conscience, as one reviewer had described her last photographic exhibition at the Photographers Gallery.

14

Barnaby. Panic milled about inside her. Only way to stop it was to apply the Scarlett O'Hara principle. Think about it tomorrow. With any luck, tomorrow never comes.

Better still, close your eyes and tune in on the conversation across the way.

'You look so terribly tired,' Hector was saying.

'Do I? I don't *feel* tired.'

'You look it. Those BBC people don't seem to give a damn about you. I had a word with your producer about it, actually.'

'Oh, Hector . . .'

'I said he was working you too hard on this new series. I told him he should remember you weren't a young woman.'

The wife was silent. Penny wondered if he meant to be cruel, or was just insensitive. He looked several years younger than the wife. Who, from what he'd just said, surely had to be Irene Lampeter. Penny half-opened an eye and snuck a look. They said television distorted, not that it rendered almost unrecognisable. She saw Irene put her hand on Hector's and smile at him.

Hector stared straight ahead. 'Also, that you aren't in the best of health,' he said.

Irene pulled away from him. Briefly closed her eyes. 'Hector,' she said, 'there is nothing whatsoever wrong with my health. There never has been.'

Hector, on the other side of Irene, turned his head. He looked deeply at her. Even through her own slitted eyes, Penny could see that it was the kind of look that went well beyond eyes and straight into souls. 'Irene,' he said. For a moment, he shone. His voice was warm and sincere. 'You know that's not entirely true.' Moving his head slightly, he caught Penny's eye. The light in him went out.

Penny hoped he'd think she was asleep. She shifted around like someone dreaming of wood-boring insects. For a moment, she'd seen in Hector the power on which charismatic movements are founded. Wowee. It was heady stuff. Seemed there was more to Hector than immediately met the eye.

'I've been so much better lately, darling,' Irene said.

'But you still get breathless when you go upstairs.'

'That's because I'm much too . . .' she stopped.

Fat, Penny thought.

A year ago, Irene Lampeter hadn't been so fat. Plump, yes. It was part of her charm. Now, she must weigh in at three stone heavier than she had during her most recent series. Three stone was forty-two pounds. How could anyone get that fat? Penny wondered. She imagined all the drooping flesh, the pendulous breasts, the chafing thighs.

'Anyway, I told him,' said her husband, 'you'd be taking your holiday in May, whether he agreed or not. I said—'

'Hector, he already *had* agreed. I told him all about it, as soon as Costas invited us. There was no need to speak as if he had me tied down at the studio with a ball and chain.'

'—I said I just hoped you lasted that long without a serious physical breakdown.'

'Hector, see if you can get me something to drink, will you? I feel terribly thirsty.'

'I said, if anything happened to you, I'd hold him personally responsible.'

If anything happened to Irene. What was likely to happen? Penny did some more shifting. She gave the kind of moaning little sigh that sleepers make as they turn in their dreams. When she squinched her eyes open again, Hector was staring straight at her.

She tried to remember what her mother had said about Irene Lampeter's newest husband. Something on the Stock Exchange? She couldn't remember. Except that he was ten years younger than his wife. At least.

Also a bit of a jerk.

Great.

One thing about queuing in jungle temperatures, you got time to catch up on your sweating. In the past twenty minutes, Penny had done a lot of that. Not as much as Irene Lampeter, who was standing in line be-

16

hind her. Considerably less than her husband, Hector. Squat as a trash-can, he looked as if he'd just stepped out of a fridge.

Nobody went and nobody came. The passengers from the plane had been herded into a wire-fenced enclosure with a concrete hut at the end. The purple-blossomed vine thing growing over it did nothing to disguise the fact that it lacked architectural dignity. They were watched over by a soldier in army fatigues and the latest thing in lethal weaponry. After half an hour, he cleared his throat. People jumped. One woman screamed. He seemed to be guarding them. Hard to see from what. Behind her, Hector told his wife the locals ought to take a leaf out of England's book. He said that back home they didn't keep you hanging about for hours, it was just a question of a stamp on your passport and Bob was your uncle. Penny hated a bigot. On the other hand, bigots were made, not born. Bigot-wise, standing in line for twenty-five minutes under a baking sun was probably a fertile breeding-ground. Ahead of them, the concrete shack crumbled slowly into the ground. It was pretty exciting stuff. Like watching your fingernails grow.

There were a lot of things Penny would rather be doing than hanging about at the edge of an airfield in Greece. Swallowing a long iced drink undoubtedly came top of the list. Followed closely by swallowing a second. Heat shimmered on the tarmac. A goat whined behind the hut. The plane that had brought them from Gatwick wallowed on the runway, gleaming hotly in the sun.

Irene Lampeter said she was desperately thirsty. Further back in the queue, a man was talking about his necklace. It was fashioned from heavy twists of gold. 'I never take it off,' he said. 'Never.' His wife, blonde in a woollen turquoise pant-suit, agreed. 'Never,' she said. Penny wondered why not. For luck? Anyone who could afford that much gold didn't need any more.

There was a stir far off in the heat haze near the gate. The soldier straighened up and adjusted the strap of his weapon. The queue rubber-necked. A Mercedes in silver and garnet appeared. It stopped in front of them and a hunk got out. He was the sort of person Helen of Troy would have stuck around for. He wore cut-offs and suntan and thick-soled Ocean Pacific toe-ins. He hooked his fingers over the fence.

'Hey, Pen,' he said.

Penny walked over to him. 'Theo Schumann,' she said. 'I'll be darned.' She couldn't help smiling.

'Looking for a good time, babe?' Theo said.

'You fixing to give me one?'

'Why else you think I came?'

'Hoped you might be the rescue squad.'

'What're you talking about, rescue? I'm the guy who gets to beat the prisoners' teeth in.'

'Write down what you want me to say and I'll sign it,' Penny said. She rolled her eyes. 'Anything to get out of here.'

'Cool it,' Theo said. His eyes were extraordinary, pupilled like a cat's, and the colour of bottleglass. Penny remembered them from when he used to visit his sister, Roxanne, at school in Switzerland. The same school Alexandra Kyriakou had attended. 'Just try to act normal.'

'How do you mean, act? I *am* normal. Or I was. Frying my brains out here in the sun hasn't done them any good.'

'The passport guys are probably on their lunch break,' Theo said. He looked over the other passengers. 'Hey, I'm supposed to pick up someone called Irene Lampeter. Seen her?'

'That's her,' Penny said. 'The—uh—not very slim lady.'

'She looks kinda nice.'

'Can't say the same about the husband.'

'That the guy with her?'

'Yeah.'

'Love the beard,' said Theo.

'I'll go tell her you're here.'

Penny went back to her place in the line. 'Hi,' she said. 'I'm Penny Wanawake.'

'Helena's daughter,' Irene said.

'Yes, ma'am.'

'I should have realised. She said you were visiting the Kyriakous in her place. I'm Irene Lampeter.'

The stocky husband raised his eyebrows, disapproving as a swan. 'Irene *Oakley*,' he said.

Penny was trying hard not to look anywhere but at Irene's eyes. Irene saw her doing it. She smiled. It was a sad smile. Penny could tell that until recently there'd been a lot less of Irene than there was now. Both by the fear in her eyes and by the baggy dress she wore. Fat may well be a feminist issue, but long-term fatties learn to live with it. They walk tall. They dress stylishly. Short-term ones buy medium-control girdles and pray a lot. Irene looked like she had calluses from pressing her palms together.

'Of course. I mean Irene Oakley,' she said. 'I'm so used to being introduced as Lampeter.'

The husband put out his hand. The thousand-watt bulb lit up behind his eyes. Not for long. It wasn't worth wasting energy consumption on someone like Penny. He switched it off again. 'I'm Hector Oakley,' he said.

Penny screwed up her eyes. 'Oakley?' she said. 'The guy who rescued all those people?'

'Which people?'

'My husband,' Irene said. Her eyes were on their knees, begging Penny to like him. Her face was blotched with red patches. Sweat had broken out on her upper lip.

Penny nodded towards the fence. 'That's Theo Schumann, Mrs Lampeter.'

'Mrs Oakley,' Hector said.

'He's come to pick us up once we've cleared passport control.'

'Control,' said Hector. 'I shall tell them what I think of them.' Some of his vowels were Northern. 'Keeping us standing about in this sun. It's not good for my wife, all this heat.'

Irene smiled at Theo.

'Hi there,' he said. 'Welcome to Greece.' His teeth shone in his dark-tanned face.'

'You're so like your mother,' said Irene.

19

For a moment Theo's face changed. The light, almost pupilless eyes turned the colour of steel. Looked like Irene just trod on the kind of territory angels steer clear of. Then he smiled. 'I'm glad.'

A door in the concrete hut opened. A waft of urine-soaked air emerged. Oakley said something unpleasant about Mediterranean drains. Irene shushed him. Beyond the wire fence, Theo chewed grass.

It was another hour before the passengers had been stamped and allowed to pass into the grandeur that was Greece. The grandeur consisted of the other side of the wire fence. There was an empty space in the grandeur where the bus to pick up the passengers should have been.

Theo opened the door of the Mercedes and helped Penny and Irene in. Penny felt closer to Helen of Troy than she would have thought possible. Their fellow passengers watched them drive off without speaking. They looked downcast. The man with the gold chain seemed to have run out of luck.

Oakley rode in front with Theo. That didn't stop him turning round several times to check that Irene hadn't started fitting or contracting pneumonia. Irene smiled at her husband a lot. She touched him sometimes, leaning forward to put a hand on his shoulder. He told them all that she had just recovered from bronchitis. She said it was a cold. He said bronchitis.

The road rose sharply towards a rocky peak between olives and grey stones. Beehives stood here and there. They passed wayside shrines made of rusted metal with blanched plastic flowers inside and photographs of bearded saints bleached by sun to the colour of glaucoma.

From time to time, Theo caught Penny's eye in the driving mirror. His hair was tiger-coloured, his body burned to the colour of sherry. Words like 'Adonis' and 'young god' kept popping into Penny's head. She made them pop right out again. At the top of the hill they looked down on to the sea.

'What colour is Greek wine?' she said.

'Red,' Theo said. 'Or white. Depends what colour you ask for.'

'But not grey?'

'Never grey.'

'So how come the sea's always called wine-dark?'

'I read about that somewhere,' Oakley said. He turned round from the front. He told them all about it. His voice was deep and full of chords. You listened despite yourself. The voice was bigger than the man. When he'd finished he asked his wife how she was. She said she was fine.

At a primitive jetty waited a cream-painted launch. Several men with copious hair leapt about on it with ropes. Undoing them. Doing them up. Tying knots in them. Theo helped Irene on board, with Oakley fussing along behind reminding her of her gammy leg.

'It's not gammy,' Irene said.

'Arthritis,' Oakley said.

'Oh, Hector. You make me sound like some decrepit geriatric,' said Irene. She pressed her hand suddenly to her chest and breathed deeply for a couple of seconds.

Oakley didn't answer. The implication hung above them. Irene *was* a decrepit geriatric. Or pretty near. Penny couldn't make it out. Why did Oakley act as though this was Irene's last outing before she took permanently to her coffin? Anyone could see that if she was ill it wasn't with a wasting disease.

On shore a young woman in a white skirt appeared with an octopus in one hand. She started beating it against the harbour wall. Purply-white tentacles flopped and slopped on the stone. After a while, she began smearing it onto the jetty. Long-legged, long-bodied cats gathered quietly. Theo came and stood beside Penny at the rail as they cast off.

'There must be easier ways to die,' Penny said.

Theo laughed.

Further along the deck, Oakley was trying to force Irene to sit down. From the expression on her face, it was obviously easier to do as he said than to argue. When she was seated, he kissed her forehead. The way

21

a spider might kiss a fly already trussed up ready for the evening meal. She smiled radiantly back. Not in the slightest like a trussed fly. It must be sex. Personally, Penny thought square beards were an even bigger turn-off than salads featuring gherkins. Oakley looked up and saw her watching him. She looked away.

'How do you like that guy?' said Theo.

'I don't,' Penny said. 'But she obviously does.'

'She must be crazy,'

'Love is the sweetest thing.'

The launch curved round the lee of an island which rose sheer from the water. Theo pointed to a hazy shape that appeared on the horizon. 'That's Kyriakou's island,' he said.

'I thought no one was allowed to own bits of Greece,' said Penny.

'Onassis and Kyriakou,' Theo said. 'They were the only two. And Onassis is dead.'

'Are you going to be in on this business meeting we're supposed to have?' Penny said.

'You bet.'

'Think these discussions are going to be the fruitful kind?'

'Bound to be, with Jason Jackson taking part.'

'Don't think I've met him.'

'What a treat you got ahead, hon.'

Kyriakou's island came nearer. They saw pines and cypresses. Midway between sea-level and the summit, against a bluff of grey rock, red pantiles gleamed amongst the trees.

'Hear you and Alexandra're getting kind of tight,' Penny said.

Theo put his arm round her waist. 'Kind of,' he said. 'No more than that.' His voice sounded odd. 'I'm more interested in getting tight with her father, at the minute.'

'Does she know that?'

'Does she hell. Think I want to get a reputation as a gold-digger?'

'The money your father's got, no one's going to think that.'

'Way I figure, if I want Alexandra, I got to get Kyriakou first.'

'And you do want her?'

Theo looked up at the sky. He smoothed the skin of his throat. 'I don't know,' he said. 'He hates to let go of his possessions.'

'She's his daughter.'

'Same thing.'

The island came nearer, rocky where it touched the sea, then densely covered in green. It pushed upwards out of the water, like Mount Ararat before the rains finally engulfed it. Men in white clothes were waiting to tie the *Alexandros* up. The passengers loaded themselves into jeeps and were carried uphill to a house of honey-coloured stucco looking over the Ionian Sea. Nothing much was happening out there except the sun glinting and a heat haze making the islands mysterious and beautiful and Nature being memorable. No boys on dolphins. No conch-blowing tritons or tridented sea-kings. Boring, really.

3

IF THEY EVER MADE A MOVIE VERSION OF HIS LIFE, COSTAS
Kyriakou would have been a natural for the name part.
He was big. He was burly. Penny hadn't seen him for
several years. She'd forgotten just how much of both he
was. Standing at the door and watching him wrap his
arms around Irene, she made an instant decision not to
let him wrap them round her.

'Irene!' he said. 'It's been so long.'

'Much too long, Costas, dear. Not since James died.'

Ooops. James clearly wasn't Costas's favourite name.
Hearing it produced a frown. 'Yes,' he said. He un-
wrapped Irene. Plump as she was, Costas made her look
frail. He held her away from him for a minute. Without
smiling, he said, 'You haven't changed.' He was lying.

Hector Oakley stood behind them. 'Introduce us, Irene,'
he said.

Irene broke away. The two men shook hands. The
Greek's size emphasised Hector's lack of it. Until he
switched the lights on again. Lit up, he was irresistible.
If he'd started handing out Kool-Aid'n'cyanide cock-
tails, Penny would have drunk one without question.

'This is an enormous pleasure,' he said. He sounded
as if he'd been working towards a meeting with Kyriakou
all his life. Maybe he had.

The little frown again creased the Greek's forehead.
His face went cold. 'And this is the man you have
chosen, Irene?' he said.

'Yes.'

'Ah.'

Amazing what a lot you can do with a simple ah. What Kyriakou did was make it clear he didn't think much of Irene's taste. Especially when her former lover was still around. It was easy to see why he might feel that way. Kyriakou was the stuff cartoonists dream of, from his thick black hair and silver eyebrows to the gold-headed ebony cane and the slight limp. The wound that had caused it was never spoken of, but nearly everyone who came in contact with him received the same subliminal image of a young Kyriakou, a sweaty rag tied round his head, handling a machine-gun, or possibly a machete, with ferocious intent. Some added a rocky landscape full of vague insurgents with knives between their teeth. Others saw a mother and sisters cowering, the youthful figure their only protection against rapine and pillage. This, despite the fact that Kyriakou had no sisters, and no one in their right mind would have wanted to rape his mother. In fact, although he seldom mentioned it, his boyhood had been impeccably middle-class and included several years at an English public school.

Normally featured in evening dress, today he wore buff-coloured slacks and a pale blue golf shirt. His shoes were two-tone docksiders, worn without socks. One of the tones was pink. He held his arms out as Penny came towards him.

'Beautiful Helena's beautiful daughter,' he said richly. 'Come.'

Penny sidestepped. Jeez. With arms like that, a person could spend the summer with her ribs in plaster. 'Hi, Mr Kyriakou,' she said. 'How's tricks?'

He told her. He was somewhere in his sixties and still full of vigorous blood. Hector listened, one arm keeping his wife at his side. Every now and then, Kyriakou looked at Irene. Once he shook his head as if he couldn't believe what he was seeing.

Behind him, a woman was standing by the sliding glass doors that led out on to a cantilevered terrace strewn with terracotta pots of geraniums and fuschias.

25

Although she was in the room, she implied that she was somewhere else. Her mouth yearned.

'Alexandra,' Kyriakou said, without turning his head. He tapped once with his cane.

At the sound of the first syllable, the woman straightened. She came forward, smiling. She was slim. Anorexically so. Her linen dress of navy and oatmeal hung like a tunic from her shoulders, the heavy material swaying as she moved. She held out her hand to Hector. 'I'm Alexandra Kyriakou.'

Hector took it. He lit up again. 'Hello there,' he said. He hadn't smiled like that at Penny.

'Hello, Penelope,' Alexandra said. 'Do you remember me?'

'Of course she does,' Kyriakou said. He didn't look at his daughter.

Penny wanted to say, no, she didn't. The girl she remembered had been overweight and arrogant. Fierce black eyebrows had met across a dominating nose. Where the other girls happily swopped sweaters and nail-polish and books, she hated anyone to touch her stuff. She had been very unpopular. A marathon away from this poised woman with the sad eyes fixed on an invisible horizon. Even the eyebrows had changed.

'Of course I do,' she said.

'I'm glad you were able to come.' Alexandra glanced at her father. He was watching Irene. Tentatively she smiled again at Penny.

Kyriakou tapped his cane on the marbled floor again. 'I wish to smoke,' he said. His daughter brought him a box of cigarettes. While he made a big production out of finding an onyx holder and stabbing a cigarette into it, she stood at his side with a lighter. When he was ready, she snapped it into flame. Kyriakou lit up and drew in. The smoke from his first drag floated straight into his daughter's face. Must have been accidental.

'And what exactly do you do, Mr Oakley?' he said.

'I'm a businessman,' said Hector.

Kyriakou stared at him in a way that Penny couldn't wait to practise. The cocked eyebrow, the faintest of smiles, the impression of well-bred astonishment were an object lesson in onedownmanship. Hector wasn't a quick study. He didn't seem fazed. Kyriakou turned on the pressure a little, blowing smoke up at the ceiling and producing a quizzical expression.

'Business?' he said. He leaned contemptuously on the word. Business was something the Kyriakous of the world conducted. The rest weren't even also-rans.

'Yes,' Hector said.

Irene's hand tightened on his sleeve. One of those marital devices for shutting up a spouse before he said something he might regret. Why? Hector was unlikely to admit to insider trading or fraudulent real-estate deals, even if that was his line.

Kyriakou didn't ask. Maybe he didn't care. Maybe he too had noticed Irene's warning touch. Instead, he pressed his cane to a spot on the floor. 'How long is it that you've been married to my cousin, Mr Oakley?' he said.

'Three years,' said Hector.

'I ask, because the ceremony, if you remember, was conducted in such secrecy that none of Irene's family were even notified,' said Costas.

Hector's chin said he could field whatever was thrown at him. 'As I understand it, you're not actually related to Irene,' he said. 'Except as a cousin of her former husband.'

'A first cousin.' Kyriakou blew smoke towards Irene. She was looking like someone wondering who had cast the first stone. 'And once a very good friend of Irene herself.'

Nuances abounded.

'Private was the way we both wanted it, wasn't it, Irene?' Hector said.

'Well, I would quite have liked . . .'

'My wife is something of a public personage in England,' Hector said. 'If the date had leaked out, we would have been inundated with reporters.'

'It was probably best kept private, in that case,' Kyriakou said. 'How frightfully sad I would have been to learn that my cousin had been lynched by a mob of

27

screaming photographers. Or, for that matter, my dear Oakley, that you had.'

If Hector believed that, he was nuts. 'Cousin by marriage,' he said. You had to admire the way he refused to wilt. 'Once Irene's first husband died, there was no real connection between you and her. Though Irene told me the two of you once had a bit of a fling.'

The cane tapped sharply. Alexandra stepped forward. Penny wondered how long the fling had been. If she hadn't already known that Costas wasn't the forgiving sort, she'd have realised it from the way he smiled at Irene.

'How about a swim before lunch?' Alexandra said. 'There is a pool at the side of the house, or there's the sea.'

'My wife won't,' Hector said.

'Hector. Of course I will,' Irene said. 'What are you talking about? I'd love a dip in the sea.'

'Salt water's so much more invigorating,' said Kyriakou.

'Isn't the sea round here supposed to be polluted?' Hector said.

Kyriakou frowned.

Alexandra put a hand on her chest.

Irene coughed nervously. 'I'd love a drink of water, if possible,' she said.

'What the hell,' said Penny. She was beginning to feel a knot of tension in her shoulder. 'We all consume a peck of dirt by the time we die. Or so they say.' She popped her dimples in and out. Now is the time for all good folk to be the life and soul of the party.

'That may be true,' said Hector. 'I just don't want to swallow it all in one go.' He raised jokey eyebrows at Kyriakou. Kyriakou didn't raise any back. He turned and started down the steps leading from the patio to ground level.

'Hector!' hissed his wife.

'What's the matter?' Hector said.

'Costas is our host, for heaven's sake. You insulted him.'

'How?'

28

'By saying the sea round here is polluted.'

'So it is. As a matter of fact, I read somewhere this is some of the most heavily polluted water in Europe,' said Hector. 'I think you ought to use the pool.' He placed a tender arm about her shoulders. Irene sighed.

They all met up again at lunch-time. The dining-room was long and cool. Semi-circular like a wine cellar, it had been driven straight back into the hill. One long wall was rock; opposite it, a huge saltwater aquarium provided most of the light. At the open end glimmered the sea.

A man was watching it. He turned as they came in. His hair was slicked straight back towards his neck, Gatsby-style, above a dead-white face. Dressed in a black jumpsuit with the zipper pulled down to his navel, he gave Penny's white one a hard stare.

'Do you know Jason Jackson?' said Alexandra.

'No, she doesn't,' Jackson said. 'But her mother does.' He touched Penny's sleeve with one finger. 'Fiorucci,' he said. 'So's mine.'

'We look like a double act,' said Penny.

'The Black and White Minstrels?' He had the mid-Atlantic accent of a popstar or a fashionable hairdresser.

'I play a mean ukelele,' Penny said. 'How's your tap-dancing?'

Although Jackson quirked his mouth as if amused, he wasn't. He seemed to be struggling with some in-depth anger. Penny's tonsils started to swell.

He was in his mid-thirties, and hoping people wouldn't take him for a minute older. At first glance he appeared to lack every single quality that might have seemed necessary in one who had bought a small country house in the Cotswolds and in less than ten years turned it into a byword for luxury. That was at first glance. At second, you took in the eyes, as round and blank as Orphan Annie's. Behind them must be triple-strength steel, since the Rockingham Hotel was not only booked solid throughout the year but maintained a considerable stand-by list of would-be patrons ready to drop everything to stay there should the chance arrive.

'Your mother's a very charming lady,' he said.

'She certainly charmed me,' said Penny. 'Only reason I came.'

'Thought you only came because I did,' Theo said. He took her arm.

From the rippling blue-green shadows, Alexandra watched them, enigmatic as a statue. When everyone was seated, she went to a door and called through it. She took her place beside her father, though her eyes were at the bottom of the long table where Penny sat with Theo.

Near her, Hector Oakley began a number about some pills. 'Here you are, darling. Twice a day before meals,' he said to his wife. He swung a small brown-glass bottle between thumb and forefinger. He tapped a couple of pills on to the palm of his hand. 'Don't let's forget to take them, after all that fuss this morning.'

'Fuss?' said Costas. He displayed interest on the level of a man enquiring what kind of rope his noose was made of.

'Yes,' said Irene. She glanced brightly round at them. She popped some pills into her mouth and drank off a glass of Perrier water. 'I forgot them this morning so Hector insisted we'd have to go back. And just as we were about to make a U-turn and start back home, Christopher—that's my second son—appeared. He'd found them and come tearing down the motorway after us. Wasn't that nice of him?'

They all agreed that it was.

'I must be senile or something. We had dinner at Jason's the night before last, didn't we?' She turned to the owner of the Rockingham, who nodded briefly. 'And I forgot them then, too. It's lucky we live close by so Jason could drop them off at our house the next morning.'

'What are the pills for?' Costas said.

'High blood pressure,' said Oakley. 'Very dangerous in a woman of Irene's age and . . . age.' He didn't say size. By then, he didn't need to. He smiled at his wife. Costas watched him, his eyelids occasionally drooping like a bird of prey's. Irene seemed mortified. Kyriakou began to tell them that he would be taking the whole party sailing on the following day. Penny repressed a groan.

Theo held a dish for her. 'Listen,' he said *sotto voce*, as she helped herself to stuffed aubergines, 'my dad's arriving any minute.'

'So?'

'You gotta protect me.'

'What's the problem?'

'Dad's new wife,' Theo said. He poured purple wine into Penny's glass.

Penny laughed.

'It's not funny. Man, she is really gross. Always coming on to me, feeling me up. I mean, what's a guy supposed to do when his own stepmother's trying to jump his bones before he can get out of bed in the morning?'

'Warm-hearted kinda gal, huh?'

'That's the funny thing. She's colder than a lemming's nest. Looks like she's gonna snap in two when Dad tries to cuddle up.' Theo forked food into his mouth and at the same time shook his head. He swallowed. 'Poor old Dad,' he said.

'Maybe the lady's in love with you.'

'Sure,' Theo said sourly.

'Better watch your step, Theo.'

'I'm too busy watching my ass.'

'Only I seem to remember someone called Phaedra tried the self-same trick. Far's I recall, things didn't work out too well.'

'I saw the movie.'

Penny chewed. Then she said, 'Last time I saw you, your stepmother was some goofy hat-check girl who couldn't spell her own name.'

'What the hell *was* her name?' Theo snapped his fingers. 'Jodi? Or was she the one before?'

'Not Jodi,' Theo said. 'Definitely not her because I was still in school when Jodi got her call-up papers. And no one sorrier than me to see her go, I may say.'

'To see her was to love her,' Penny said.

'And I did.'

'Who came after Jodi?'

'Barbara,' said Theo. He rolled his eyes. 'Barbara the Barracuda. Boy, was she ever a mistake.'

'The others were successes?' said Penny.

'Compared to Barbara, Lucrezia Borgia would have been a success. The trouble Dad had, getting her out of his hair.'

'The amount Marty's got, should've been a cinch.'

'Don't you believe it,' said Theo.

'Where's this latest wife from?'

'Hollywood. At least that's where Dad met her. Apparently she's been playing bit-parts on the daytime soaps for years.'

'Marty goes to Hollywood. Sounds flaky.'

'His accountant advised him to look at movies as part of a tax shelter plan,' Theo said. 'When he came back East, Sibylla—my new stepmom—came too.'

'What'm I supposed to do to keep you out of her clutches?'

'Act like we're a number.'

'Wouldn't Alexandra do a better job?'

'Stick around a while and you'll see just how much time off she gets. He practically makes her clock out to go to the john.'

'He?'

Theo lifted his chin towards Costas.

At the other end of the table, Hector Oakley raised his voice. 'Avrios,' he said. 'That's what it's called. It's a tiny island, completely deserted, but it does have a rather beautiful shrine, dedicated to Athena.'

'This is most extraordinary,' Costas said. 'All my life I have lived in Greece. I have never heard of this shrine.'

'Isn't that always the way,' Irene said, bright as Brasso. 'I lived in London once for five years and never went to the Tower.'

'Nor of this island,' Kyriakou said.

'That doesn't alter the fact that it's there,' said Oakley. 'Look on the map. Though it's so small it's not shown on some of them.'

'So how is it you know of it?'

Oakley looked down at his plate. 'I read about it somewhere,' he said. 'And I've been there before.'

'I would be glad to know your country as well as you know mine,' Costas said. Hostilely.

'I have relatives over here,' Oakley said.

'Where?'

'Oh.' He gestured towards the windows. 'South of here.'

'That would make it on—uh—Kefallinía,' said Costas, rocklike. 'Or do you mean on the mainland?'

'Somewhere like that.' Oakley obviously wasn't planning to give them a run-down on his family.

'Athena,' Jason Jackson said. 'Isn't that the name of your new venture, Costas?'

'It is.' Kyriakou swivelled his eyes away from Oakley. He seemed puzzled. Big fish don't usually get talked back to by little ones. Yet this particular minnow didn't even seem aware that size-wise he was way out of his league.

'I'm looking forward to hearing much more about it,' said Jason.

'When Marty Schumann gets here, we shall discuss the matter extensively.'

'It's a little inaccessible, but I understand it's well worth a visit,' came Oakley's voice. 'It's dedicated to Athena Parthenos. The Virgin. I read somewhere that's an unusual personification for the goddess to take in this part of Greece. I would very much like my wife to see the place, Kyriakou, if you're able to put in there. Not that there's a harbour, of course.' He showed teeth that owed hundreds to the orthodontist. 'But that's no problem. Just anchor off-shore, load up the dinghy, and Bob's your uncle.'

The big Greek could have come straight off Easter Island. He didn't speak. His silence managed to convey that of course his yacht could put in any damn place he ordered it to. Also, that while he was in several minds about ordering it to do so for this crass person he was far too refined ever to come right out and say so. Also, that whoever's uncle Bob was it wasn't his.

A small crone dressed in black came in and bent towards Alexandra's ear. Alexandra stood and went out with her.

'It's right on top,' Oakley said. He put his hand over his wife's. She flinched slightly.

'What is?' she said.

'This shrine. Fountain, really. If you drank the water from the sacred spring you were supposed to be blessed with wisdom.'

'Why?' said Kyriakou.

'Athena is the Goddess of Wisdom,' Oakley said. The rich texture of his voice was threaded with scorn.

'Too bad Hector didn't swallow some, last time he was there,' Penny said quietly to Theo. 'Costas is looking mad.'

'It's one of his specialities,' said Theo.

'Did I not understand you to say that your wife had some trouble with her leg?' Costas said courteously, smiling over at Irene.

'No,' she said, shaking her head.

'Yes,' said Oakley.

'Hector, there is absolutely nothing wrong with my leg.'

'That is not true, Irene. You can't hide it from me. I'm your husband, you know.'

'I know.' Absently she rubbed a hand over the area above her heart. Sweat appeared on her upper lip as she drew in several rapid breaths.

'If, as you appear to believe, your wife has some small medical problem,' Costas said, 'dragging her up a hill in the heat to see a possibly non-existent shrine . . .'

'Of course it exists.'

' . . . would seem both a difficult and unsuitable activity.' Costas didn't add what everyone round the table was thinking—given Irene's weight, it might even be impossible.

Alexandra returned, silent as a shadow. She sat down again. When her father finished speaking, she told him that the Schumanns had arrived, that she'd shown them to their rooms, that Marty was having coffee, and his wife was taking a shower.

Kyriakou listened without moving. Also without meeting his daughter's eyes. 'We shall, of course, stop at Oakley's shrine,' he said. He nodded at Alexandra as though she were an aide-de-camp. His gaze remained on the sea beyond the semi-circle of glass. 'Where is it?'

Hector went into detailed explanation.

'If we get off to an early start tomorrow,' Alexandra said, looking towards Theo, 'we ought to get there just before lunch.'

'Excellent,' said Costas. 'We can eat aboard the yacht, and then—uh—Oakley . . .'

'Hector,' Hector said.

' . . . can guide us up to this temple of Athena . . .

'Fountain, really.'

'Which I, for one, have never heard of, and would therefore be delighted to visit.'

'Personally,' said Theo quietly to Penny, 'I shall probably remain on board. It'll be far too hot to do anything but lie about naked in one's cabin. Grab some zzzs. Possibly with something long and cold. What about you?'

'Are you asking, or suggesting?'

'A bit of both.'

'I may be long, but I'm not cold,' Penny said.

'Cool,' said Theo. 'I meant cool.'

Kyriakou drank from a small coffee cup. He pulled the butt of his last cigarette from the holder and dropped it into a piece of Steuben glassware. He fitted another and lit it. 'Since Marty Schumann is here, perhaps, Irene, we should make a start on some of the business we have to get through,' he said.

'Can't it wait?' Oakley said quickly. 'We've only just arrived—'

'Darling, *please*.'

'—and my wife isn't very strong.'

'Strange,' Costas said. Smoke seeped slowly from his mouth. 'For a weak woman, she has achieved so much. Always so fit, always so well. Is that not right, Irene?'

35

'I still am,' Irene said. She smiled at her husband and nervously swallowed more water. 'Hector takes such good care of me.'

'Darling,' Oakley said. He bit his lip. 'Your blood pressure . . .'

'How in the world did Irene come to get hitched to a mother-hen like that?' Theo asked under his breath.

'Perhaps she was lonely,' said Penny. 'Successful people often are.'

Theo stared down the table at Costas. 'Are they? I haven't had a chance to find out.'

'Penelope, my dear,' Costas called. 'Will you join us? Since your mother was so unfortunately not able to be here, it might be helpful if you listened to our discussions so you can tell her about it later.'

'It might be as well if I were there too,' Hector Oakley said.

'That won't be necessary,' said Costas.

'My wife's concerns are naturally my own. And if I can ease some of her burdens, obviously I must do so.'

'Hector, dear. I don't have any burdens.'

'Except Hector,' Theo said softly.

'We discussed all this the other day on the telephone,' Hector said. His mouth smiled.

Costas raised one manicured white eyebrow. 'My business was with Irene herself,' he said.

'I'm concerned that my wife doesn't overtax herself. Whatever she likes to think, she isn't as strong as she imagines. She needs someone to look after her affairs, take some of the worry from her.' Hector turned to Irene and deepened his voice. 'I hope I'm the one,' he said. He switched on.

'Oh Hector . . .' You could almost smell Irene melting.

'But if you'd rather I didn't sit in on your meeting, of course I won't.'

'*Hector.*'

'Irene managed her own affairs with extreme competence for years before she met you, Oakley,' Costas said. 'There is no reason why she shouldn't go on doing so.'

'I'm sure it won't matter if Mr Oakley is present,' Alexandra said quietly.

For the first time, her father looked at her. He nodded. 'Very well.'

'Those two are a terrific team,' Theo said. He sent a smile in Alexandra's direction.

'How'll he take it when she tells him she's getting married?'

'She already has, several times.'

'What happened?'

'He bought or frightened them off.'

'Poor girl.'

'She's a woman,' Theo said. 'Not a girl. She wants some babies. We both do. And she's getting kinda desperate. Not that he's noticed.'

'Why don't you tell him?'

'I'm too young to die,' Theo said. And laughed.

4

PENNY FOLLOWED THEO ALONG A ROUGH-CAST WHITE PAS-
sage of arctic chillness while the others collected the
kind of equipment they felt germane to a business discussion. They passed through a door on to a large terrace bright with refracted sunshine. It faced out over
pine-trees and sea towards the mainland peaks. There
was still snow on the highest of them. Comfortable lounging furniture in heavy white basketwork stood to one
side, set round a couple of low tables. There was a
serving table against one wall. In the middle of the
terrace was a green-tiled swimming-pool. In the middle
of the pool was Marty Schumann.

'Hi, Dad. Glad you could get here.' Theo waved at his
father. So did Penny.

Marty took a cigar out of his mouth. 'Hi, kids,' he
said. 'Hey, Sibylla. Here's Theo.'

'I noticed.' The woman who sat in one of the cush-
ioned chairs looked up at them. Her hair was as straight
and heavy as lampshade fringing. Set in it was the face
of a beauty-contest winner: high cheekbones, full mouth,
big teeth. Sibylla Schumann was somewhere around thirty-
five, icily chic, smoothly blonde, very very classy. Penny
didn't have the Social Register handy, but she'd have
guessed the class was recent, even though, the way
Theo had told it earlier, Sibylla liked people to believe
that half her forebears came over in the Mayflower,
while the other half was already on the beach to greet
them. She was dressed in keep-off sherbert colours:

38

melon and peach and mango. Her clothes were as loosely structured as her accent, which was semi-English, as though to emphasise her Dissenter origins. She went with Marty Schumann the way a pearl goes with swine.

Her hands were busy with a complicated piece of embroidery involving roses and froths of leaves. She nodded at Theo. She apparently couldn't see Penny. She looked down at her roses again. But not before Penny had registered that the lady didn't breathe through her mouth. Behind the pretty face were more brains than the rest of Marty's wives had between them. Most of them had barely been able to read until it came to the fine print on a divorce decree.

Marty Schumann wiped his mouth with the back of his hand. 'Hey, Theo,' he said. He spoke in the intriguing kind of voice the Fawkes guy must have used when outlining his plans for November the Fifth. 'You kids done good. Real good.'

'Think so?' Theo said. He looked over his shoulder at the door.

'Best move of my life,' Marty said. He moved his head up and down a couple of times.

'What was?' asked Theo.

'Sending you to that fancy business school they got at Harvard. Plus the time you done in the Swedish hotel.'

'Swiss, Dad,' Theo said.

'Aw hell. Swiss, Swedish, what's the difference,' said Marty. He floated in the pool like a clumsy water-lily. Nobody had ever called Marty Schumann glamorous. His stomach was the result of more business lunches than most people had hot dinners. The hairless scalp testified to the worry of a thousand dodgy deals. Those boiled-potato eyes could spot the let-outs in a contract faster than the average corporation lawyer could snap open the combination lock on his lucite briefcase. Definitely not glamorous. In spite of which, the overall effect was pleasing.

On the wide tile ledge beside him were two stacks of papers. Their edges were curled. He reached out and sucked in half of an ice-cold Martini. He looked at the papers. 'Real good,' he said again. He looked at his wife. 'They covered just about everything, good as I coulda done myself,' he said.

'Is that right?' the Snow Queen said. She pushed a yellow-threaded needle through her embroidery.

'Finance, building projections, union negotiations, in-house domestic labour, everything,' said Marty.

'What about allowance for possible cost over-runs?' Sibylla said.

'You name it.' Several decilitres of martini joined those already lapping at the inside edges of Marty's belly. He gazed fondly at his son. 'I wanna tell you I'm real proud of you. Matter of fact, never would of thought you'd turn out so smart.' He looked over at the sixth Mrs Schumann. 'He was kinda erratic there for a while. Guess it came of not having a mom.' He thought about it. 'A real mom,' he said.

'There were probably other women in his life,' Mrs Schumann said, lifting her eyes to stare hugely at Theo.

'Sure,' said Marty. 'His sister, for one.'

'I wasn't thinking of her,' Mrs Schumann said. She moved her gaze up and down her stepson. Marty, sluicing martini, didn't notice. Penny did.

'Hi,' she said. 'I'm Penny Wanawake.'

'Sibylla Schumann.' The smile that came with the name could have unblocked drains.

'Her mom's Lady Helena Hurley,' Marty said. He vanished unexpectedly beneath the water. Bubbles rose. So did the cigar. When he surfaced, he was spluttering. 'Jesus,' he said.

'You shouldn't try to do so much,' his wife said.

'You know me,' Marty said. 'Like to keep busy.'

'Most men would concentrate on either drinking or smoking while they're swimming,' Sibylla said. 'One or other. But not both.'

'Last time I saw Helena,' Marty said, 'was in Washington. Wearing some kind of a black velvet bikini and playing the saxophone slap bang in the middle of the British Ambassador's swimming pool. Musta been around the time I pulled off that Barbados deal.' He shook his head. 'I was kinda green in those days. Never even seen a bikini before. Beattie would never've . . .' He stopped.

'Sounds like mom,' Penny said. She sat down on one of the loungers. Beattie. Theo's mother. Who'd died when he was around five. She tried to remember how. She wasn't sure she'd ever known.

'Whaddya think, then, kid?' Marty said.

'What about?' Theo had walked around to the other side of the pool. As far from his stepmother as he could get.

'This project of Costas's. Athena or whatever. Kind of a fancy name, but I guess it's a fancy operation. Could be a real smart deal for me, you know. It's time we moved upscale, got out of the cheap chains and into some class.'

'You think the Athena project's got class?' Theo said.

Marty looked troubled. 'Doesn't it? Maybe class izza wrong word,' he said anxiously. 'That's the trouble with Costas. Give him one lousy hotel as part of one lousy takeover, and suddenly he's making Conrad Hilton look like a B & B landlady.'

'It sounds way over the top to me,' Sibylla said.

That was Penny's impression too. Not that anyone had asked for it.

'Wait'll you hear what else he has in mind,' said Theo.

'Hey, kid.' Marty lumbered through the water towards the steps of the pool. A wake formed. He lowered his voice again. 'Tell me something. Did you know about this Athena project when you set your own deal up?'

Theo smiled. 'What do you think, Dad?'

Marty chuckled. 'Hear that, Penny?' he said.

Penny nodded. 'Couldn't help but,' she said.

His grin rippled the top of his naked head. ' "What do you think, Dad?" the kid says.' He looked up at his son again. 'Here's what I *don't* think, son. I don't think it was just one of those coincidences which I personally never had much time for.' More chuckles. 'Wouldn't put it past you to've snuck a look at whatever Costa's got going down here. Bet that's one of the first things they

41

taught you at Harvard, huh? How to get one up on the opposition.'

'For chrissake, Dad,' Theo said. He checked the door leading to the rest of the house. 'Watch it, will you? Costas hears you, there'll be hell to pay.'

'Well, I guess you know by now tangling with that guy can be dangerous. But I'll tell you this for nothing. When Costas finds out about this scheme you're cooking up, he is not going to like it. Fact, I'd say he is definitely going to hate it.'

'So don't tell him,' said Theo. He helped his father heave himself out of the pool. With a peach-coloured towel, he dried the water from Marty's back and shoulders. Drops fell on to the papers at the pool side. Theo bent to wipe them off with a towel. He picked up one of the piles. 'If this is my proposal, for Pete's sake keep it away from him.'

'Yeah, yeah,' Marty said. He chuckled some more. 'But I tell you this, Theo. Knowing what you kids been up to behind his back, I'm going to enjoy this vacation more than I've been able to enjoy anything for a helluva long time.' His gaze moved to his wife. 'Not since they fixed my prostate, matter of fact,' he said.

Costas came in. Behind him was Jason Jackson, followed by the Oakleys. Alexandra brought up the rear.

Sibylla dropped her embroidery. Bending to pick it up flushed up her cheeks. Her face was suddenly blanker than a Noh mask. She began nibbling at her lips, pulling the top one into her mouth and biting it with her lower set of teeth. When Marty introduced her as his wife, she shook hands, keeping her face half-turned away. Perhaps she was afraid people would start clamouring for autographs. Nobody did.

They gathered round the tables. Alexandra served coffee. In front of Irene Lampeter she set a glass and a bottle of mineral water which Irene immediately opened and poured from. She produced notepads set inside leather covers with an owl logo embossed on the front. She produced pens. She sat down beside her father and stared into the centre of the pool. Penny wondered what she saw there. Power? Freedom? Babies?

Costas cleared his throat. 'This is, of course, merely a preliminary discussion,' he said. 'Exploratory. At this stage, I'm more interested in hearing your comments on my proposal—which I hope you've all had time to read—than in coming up with definitive ideas.' He looked round at them. He was not entirely at ease.

Neither was Sibylla. She kept tapping her pen against her teeth, her eyes flicking from one to another of the group. Theo was sitting next to Hector Oakley. They stayed longest on him. Which figured.

Costas outlined his proposal for a five-year plan. Also the five-year plan that would follow it. His idea was to startle provincial Britain with a chain of satrapally luxurious hotels. Not that provincial Britons would stand much chance of being startled, since the luxury would begin with prices set at a level that only millionaires and international conglomerates could afford. The clientele would be so exclusive that 99.9 per cent of the people alive in the world today would never qualify. Not even if they were elected Queen, Pope and President all in one. Not even if they were as rich as Croesus and as popular as Mahomet. The other point one per cent would need to be put down on the admissions list at birth before they'd have a hope in hell of getting through the doors.

There would be no one-night stopovers, Costas said. No casual trade. No catering to family parties or mere holiday-makers. This was strictly the luxury end of the market. People would be queuing all round Europe for a chance to stay in one of his palaces. And to pay through the nose for the privilege. He had already made approaches to concerns who might be interested in coming in on the project, and hoped that a cartel of international businessmen, perhaps headed by Marty Schumann, would put up the bulk of the cash. Helena Hurley would design the interiors, Irene Lampeter would create an exclusive new range of coordinated soft furnishings. The best chefs in the world would be poached from their present positions by offers of twice their current salaries. And Jason

Jackson, proprietor of the well-known Rockingham Hotel, would be asked to serve as a consultant.

Jason didn't look as if he'd willingly serve as anything except executioner. 'I'd be a bloody fool to accept such an offer,' he said. Something was coming to the boil just above the zipper of his jumpsuit.

'A big name to draw in the customers,' said Costas. 'On top of all the other big names.'

'Including Saarino & Aahlbeck as architects, I see,' Jason said. 'Which means, if everyone agrees to come in on the deal, that you'll have reproduced exactly the combination of talents that put the Rockingham at the top of its class.' His eyes bugged.

'The Rockingham is only one hotel,' said Costas.

'But you'd be setting up in direct competition to me.'

'Unique, of course,' continued Costas, as though Jason hadn't spoken. 'And perfect of its kind. But we're talking about a chain, not just a single unit.'

'I should make it clear right now,' said Jackson hotly, 'that the Rockingham is absolutely not for sale.'

Costas's white eyebrows angled towards each other like a sad clown's. 'Whoever suggested it was?' he said.

'Just so you're quite sure about it,' said Jason.

'My father has already checked that the market will bear a new luxury-class hotel,' Alexandra said.

'Guess who did the checking,' Theo said, speaking close to Penny's ear. 'And very informative the two of us found it.'

Costas glanced at him. 'The market will bear considerably more than one,' he said. 'We are on the threshold of a new age, the age of leisure. Not only are the rich getting richer but there are more of them. People will be willing to spend on luxury outside the home, because they will already have all they want inside it. Jason relies on his superb cuisine, his superb antiques, his superb decor.' He smiled at Irene. 'I shall be offering something different, a luxury based not on a perceived notion of the first class, but on the esoteric. Jason's appeal is particularly English in that it offers the lower members of his caste-ridden society a chance to live for a while as they believe their betters live, to ape the aristocracy. But I shall be catering to the imagination. My appeal will be international. After all, everybody dreams.'

'What do the rich rich dream about?' said Penny.

'Harems. Chinese emperors. Louis Quatorze.' Costas tapped his cane.

'South Sea islands,' Alexandra said. 'Hollywood. Roman orgies.'

'I've never dreamed of Louis Quatorze in my life,' said Penny.

'Read Costas's brochure, and you will,' Theo said.

Alexandra smiled slightly. 'My father has very vivid dreams.' The smile changed to sad. Or was it envy?

'As long as the Rockingham isn't one of them,' said Jason. 'Anyway, how do you know I'm not planning to expand myself? In which case, throwing in with you is the very last thing I'd be interested in doing.'

'Expanding?' Costas said. 'My dear Jason. You must be in a better position than . . .'

'Than what?' Jason's white face began to darken.

'Than I realised,' Costas said with the kind of smoothness that called attention to itself.

'That's not what you were going to say, is it? You've been prying into my affairs, haven't you?' Jason's voice rose. So did he. 'I *knew* it. That so-called oil baron who arrived a couple of months ago, said he came from Dallas. He was about as much a Texan as I'm Wyatt Earp. Who was he? A financial analyst? One of those Wall Street types you go in for, checking out my costs? Don't think I wasn't on to you years ago, Mr Bloody Kyriakou. Mr High-Class-Rip-Off-Artist.'

'Rip-off-artist?' Costas tapped his cane. 'What does that mean?'

Alexandra leaned over her father's shoulder. 'Thief,' she said. Penny couldn't help noticing that she enjoyed saying it. 'I imagine Mr Jackson is accusing you of stealing his ideas.'

'Jason,' Irene said. She put out a hand.

'It's been going on for years,' Jason said. He stamped

over to the edge of the pool. 'Jesus. Every time he stays with us, my manager has strict orders to check the inventory, just to make sure he hasn't walked off with something.'

Costas didn't like that. He frowned. 'I don't care for the implications of what you are saying.'

'You seem to think you can just muscle in and duplicate the Rockingham in a matter of days.'

'Of course I do not,' Costas said. 'Which is precisely why I invited you along as a consultant.'

Jason turned. 'What is this, the kiss before the big betrayal scene? As if it didn't take years to build up a place like mine.' He folded his arms across his chest and set his feet apart. Penny watched the triangle of sunshine that glittered between his legs. 'Years of smarming to the aristos, making contacts, smiling at greasy Somethings-in-the-City, dancing attendance on fearful old harpies inch-thick in make-up and glitter eyelashes, kissing their horrible wrinkled hands that always smell of dying dogs. And then you have the unbelievable nerve to try and keep me sweet by offering me a so-called consultancy. Well, thanks a lot, Mr Iscariot, but no bloody thanks.'

'Why doesn't he come straight out and say he doesn't like Costas?' Penny said to Theo, dribbling the words out for his ears only.

'Sounds like he's been mulling over this for weeks,' Theo said, using the side of his mouth.

'And every time he's mulled, he's come up with the same answer.'

'Takeover?'

'Check.'

'Costas wouldn't dream of doing what you're suggesting,' Irene said.

'Irene, dear,' said Jason. 'We've been friends a long time and, believe me, when I gave you that money after James died it was truly intended as nothing more than a gift and I didn't for a single minute expect you to pay it back. But quite frankly, dear, even though I'd be the last to deny you're a dab hand with the quince jelly, you are one of the most stupid people I've ever come across in my life, so would you just keep out of this?'

'Ooh, the bitch,' murmured Penny.

Irene gasped.

'Look here,' Hector said. 'Do you mind?'

'I think you are a little overwrought,' said Costas. He tapped twice with his cane.

'Overwrought, am I?' Jason said shrilly. 'Christ. I'll say I am. The only reason I came here was I hated to miss out on a week at your expense, let alone the chance of an early-season tan. Plus, of course, your chef, who I must admit on his good days makes Anton Mosimann look like a short-order cook, even if his bad days are simply *dire*.' Jason's adrenalin was flowing now, the injections of malice adding a sparkle to his rounded eyes, a lift to his slicked hair. Seen against the sunlight, he seemed as insubstantial as a shadow. You couldn't miss the way his shoulders were shaking. Everyone except Hector Oakley seemed mesmerised.

Costas lit a cigarette from a pack Alexandra handed him. The amount of business involved, it really needed a bigger audience. 'Calm yourself, Jason,' he said. 'You will alarm your friends.'

'Well, I just hope you aren't including yourself in that category,' Jason said. 'Don't think I don't know who's behind the staff troubles I've been having lately, or the way the interest rates on that private loan I took out last spring have suddenly been jacked up.' He leaned above Costas who stared up at him as though watching the dance patterns of a gnat. 'And doubtless I've also got you to thank for the fact that one of my backers has decided to get out of the hotel business and wants his investment back.'

'If I didn't know you better, Jason, I would suppose you to be on drugs.' The smile on Costas's face was made up of blandness and indifference, with a strong dash of contempt. It was a smile that made Jason's fists tighten together. Someone drew in a sharp breath.

'Looky here, Jase,' Marty said. 'You're getting kinda

47

steamed up. Wouldn't you like to sit down and talk this thing over a bit, huh?'

Jason shook his head. 'No, I wouldn't,' he said. In the bright watery light, his hair gleamed like treacle. 'What I *would* like to know is what gave Costas the idea that I'd go along for a single solitary moment with his bloody arrogant schemes. Consultant! I mean, I might be a bit reckless sometimes. I might sometimes be a tiny bit foolish. But *that* incredibly naive I am not. The only kind of consultants whose expertise Mr Kyriakou would think of paying for charge in guineas.'

Irene made a noise like two pieces of Velcro being torn apart. 'It was me who gave him the idea,' she said. She gave Kyriakou a merry little glance. 'After all, Costas dear, you're not a real hotelier, are you?'

'How exactly do you mean?' Costas frowned.

'Hotels are only *one* of your interests,' Irene said.

'My dear Irene,' Kyriakou forced a laugh. Penny's spine shivered. 'Not a *real* hotelier?'

'Not like Jason,' said Irene. She could tell she'd pressed the wrong button. She hadn't yet worked out why.

'There I must agree with you,' Costas said. 'I've been accused of many things in my time. Being like Mr Jackson has so far not been one of them.' His expression could have shattered light-bulbs.

'I suggested you, Jason, after what we were discussing the other day,' said Irene. 'Also, I thought it would mean some extra money coming in, with all the financial troubles you've been having lately . . .'

''Oh, you *dear* thing,' cried Jason. Fresh fury was gathering beneath the surface of his cheeks.

' . . . which could help with your new hotel . . .'

'A new hotel?' Costas said.

'You been holding out on us, Jase,' said Marty.

'You utter *cow*, Irene.'

'How dare you speak to my wife—'

'The Coalport, was . . .' continued Irene. '*What* did you say?'

Jason's face had reverted to white. 'I can't tell you, ducky, how touched I am by your concern about my

48

financial position,' he said. 'I mean, my *God*, I might just go bankrupt or something, if you and your precious son weren't *gracious* enough to keep your eye on me. I mean, I haven't managed to run my own affairs all these years, have I?'

'Jason!'

'And naturally, when I tell you something in the *strictest* confidence, I want you to broadcast it ten minutes later to the entire Greek nation. I mean, obviously, if you let your hair down over a bottle of wine with someone you *thought* was a friend, you run the risk of her taking out a full-page ad in the paper and letting the whole world in on it. I mean, that is a risk you just have to take.'

'Fa chrissakes,' said Marty.

'That's bloody rude,' said Hector. He tried to get up out of his low chair.

'But Jason. We *are* friends,' said Irene. Tears came into her eyes. 'Aren't we?' She put a hand on her chest and began to take deep breaths. Her face reddened.

'Hey now,' Penny said.

'Your pills, Irene,' said Hector. 'I left them in the dining-room.'

'I don't want my damn pills,' Irene said. She looked round the table. 'You all hate me, don't you? All of you.'

'Irene, for heaven's sake.'

'Mrs Lampeter,' Penny said. She stood. She went round and put her hands on Irene's shoulders, pressing down. She could feel the air squeezing in and out of the lungs beneath.

'It's true,' Irene said.

'Come on now, honey.' That was Schumann. 'Ain't nobody here hates nobody else. Ain't that right, folks?'

'Of course they don't,' Alexandra said, looking at her father.

'Depends on your definitions,' said Sibylla.

Ask Penny, whichever way you hacked it, Marty was out of sync. Watching the others, Penny wondered by how far. Because one thing was clear. There was a lot more in the room of almost anything than there was of brotherly love. Everywhere you looked, tensions sprouted like mould on old bread.

'You're all against me,' said Irene, neurotic as a hurricane. Her big face crumpled. She began to weep. Tears fell down her broad red cheeks. Marty Schumann put his hand on her arm. His wife didn't notice. She was too busy concentrating on her embroidery. Against a full-blown red rose, her needle trembled ever so slightly.

'Please don't cry, Mrs Lampeter,' Penny said. She took hold of Irene's wrist like an old-style doctor asking a patient what seemed to be the trouble.

'Oakley,' sobbed Irene. 'I'm Mrs *Oakley*.'

Was that the trouble? Or just part of it?

5

THAT EVENING PENNY AND THEO WALKED TOGETHER along a stone-edged path down by the beach. Close-crowding greenery hung over them, backlit by crimson light from the day's-end sun. At the water's edge, brown seaweed hugged the big rocks. Patches of clear water here and there showed white sand, cross-hatched with fish movement.

Irene's outburst had been a hard act to follow. If nothing else, it had lessened the impact of Jason's. Shortly afterwards the business discussion had broken up with nothing conclusive said. Irene herself had been tidied away into her room. Costas reminded the rest of the party that he would take them sailing the following day and went away, followed by Alexandra. Marty Schumann looked unthrilled at the prospect. Penny felt it. Gaahd. It was a good thing she'd been raised to be a dutiful daughter. A person who hadn't might have been tempted to rebel. Might have thought there was a limit to how far she was prepared to go for her mother. Not Penny. No sir.

She'd spent some time beside the pool along with the Schumanns. Sibylla didn't speak. She seemed preoccupied with something more than yellow roses. After a while she put her embroidery back in its bag. She got up and left, saying she must try her call to New York again.

Round his cigar, Marty sighed. He was back in the pool. His swimsuit did less for him than its designer in his worst nightmares could have imagined.

'I kinda hoped she'd have a good time, coming to Europe and all,' he said. 'Thought she'd enjoy looking up those high-class ancestors of hers.'

Penny rubbed oil into her legs. Didn't seem much point saying Sibylla behaved like she wouldn't know a good time if she found one in bed with her. 'Where's she from?'

'Detroit,' Marty said. 'Her folks adopted her. Guess that might explain things.' He didn't say what things.

'She's probably just suffering from jetlag.'

'Tell you something, Pen,' said Marty. 'You meet the right guy, you hang on to him.'

'I frequently do.'

'What I mean, something happens to him, don't go trying to find him again. Not the way I did. It don't work.'

Hell. Sounded like Theo was in line for a new step-mother any week now. 'I'll remember that, Mr Schumann.'

'Tell you something else. Sometimes I still cry about my Beattie. Ain't that a stitch?'

'Not really.'

'I hear a song. Smell a perfume. Real tears. Boy. That'd give those Brooks Brothers preppie types in my boardroom a real kick, see Marty Schumann crying his eyes out over some dame's been dead twenty years.' Marty splashed about. His costume seemed about ready to float off his buttocks. He tugged at it with one hand, causing himself to nosedive.

'What was—uh—Beattie like?' Penny said, when he came up, minus the cigar.

Marty turned over on to his back and thought about it, floating on the green water. 'Strong,' he said. 'Real strong. Not so much in the body, I don't mean. She was kind of a little lady. But strong in the—in the heart's what I'm trying to say.'

'Like Roxanne,' Penny said.

'Sure. Just like my Roxy.' Marty smiled. Pieces of his cigar floated on the waves he made as he kicked his legs. 'Say, you know she's got three kids now?'

'Tell me,' Penny said.

*   *   *

The path was dark and grassy, winding between bushes. Penny and Theo reached some flat terraced steps leading up to rocks. As they started up them, Hector Oakley appeared at the top. He was agitated.

'Oh—uh—hello,' he said. His lips scarcely moved. He stood above them as they climbed towards him. The red curls seemed clamped to his head. He moved on past them without stopping.

'Would I be wildly off beam if I said something's upset that guy?' Theo said.

'He looks like he just met a gorgon,' Penny said.

'They the chicks with snakes growing out of their heads?'

'Right. Turned you to stone as soon as look at you.'

The path veered round to the left, past small yews and some box. They rounded the corner. Ahead, the path widened into a look-out point at the top of a fall of rocks. The islands grouped together on the far edge of the sea, vague as half-remembered dreams. A stone bench faced out over the water. On the bench was Sibylla Schumann. Her embroidery lay beside her. She was watching the sunset, her mouth open, her hands clenched, each thumb perfectly symmetrical across the fists they made.

Theo stopped. 'Now that's a lady turns me to stone without even opening her eyes,' he said under his breath.

'If we're talking stones, how many does your father have to look under to come up with the specimens he does?'

'Finding's one thing. If only he didn't keep marrying them.' Theo looked momentarily bleak. 'If my mom hadn't died . . .'

'I guess he feels safer that way.'

Sibylla Schumann turned towards them. Penny had seen excitement before. She recognised it instantly. Though the other woman was doing her best to contain it, she had the look of a brass bottle the instant before the genie leaks out in a clap of thunder. Her tamped-down ferment was so intense that Penny involuntarily

53

looked back over her shoulder. Could Hector Oakley possibly have been the cause? The answer had to be in the negative. A scrubbing brush had more charisma, except when he switched on. And just now he'd looked like the plug was terminally fused.

'Theo,' Sibylla said, 'isn't this a fantastic view? Come and sit next to me.' She patted the seat beside her.

'I can see it from here,' Theo said.

'I shan't eat you,' Sibylla said.

'You won't get the chance,' said Theo.

'You must learn to love me,' said Sibylla. 'I'm your mom now.' Laughter bubbled in the words. She grinned at him. She still had a problem with directional blindness. The direction being Penny's.

'Hi, Mrs Schumann,' Penny said.

'Oh. Hello.'

'We just passed Hector Oakley,' said Penny.

''Who?'

'The little guy. Irene Lampeter's husband.'

'Is that who he is?' Sibylla said.

'Yup,' Penny said. 'Hector Oakley. The guy who came in from the cold and swept one of the richest women in England right off her feet.'

'You can tell he's smart,' Sibylla said. She laughed aloud and turned her head on its long white neck. 'My God: he'd have to be. He sure as hell didn't grow up to be much of a looker.'

'All he looked when we saw him was sick.'

'Hardly surprising, coming from here,' said Theo.

'Now then, honey. That's not nice,' said Sibylla. Excitement squeezed out of her eyes.

'Did you talk to him?' Penny persisted.

'Yeah, sure. Exchanged a word or two.'

'What do you think of him?'

'If he was the only boy in the world, I'd shoot myself.'

'What did the two of you discuss?'

'What is this?' Sibylla said. She looked out at the red-soaked sea and laughed some more. 'Open day at the Spanish Inquisition?'

'Just interested,' Penny said.

54

'If you really want to know, we talked a bit about money.'

'Making it, or spending it?'

'Making, of course. I don't need any tips on how to get rid of the stuff.' Another laugh.

'Especially when you didn't have to earn it,' Theo said.

'Listen, kid. Don't give me any of that crap. Your father got value for money when he found me.'

Theo snapped his fingers. 'Remind me where that was exactly. On sale in the bargain basement?'

'Listen, you little jerk.'

'Cut it out, you two,' said Penny. To Sibylla she said, 'You talked about money?'

'Sure. Didn't you know he was a betting man? He gave me a hot tip for the Derby.'

Penny could believe it or not, just as she pleased. She could see Sibylla wasn't going to say anything else, and that what she had already said was probably not the truth. But there was one more question she wanted to ask.

Before she could, Jason Jackson appeared. He was in a navy blue tracksuit with a towel round his neck. If he felt any embarrassment at his earlier outburst, he wasn't letting on. He nodded at Penny and Theo.

'Mr Jackson,' Sibylla said. She stood up. 'Could we talk?'

Jason stopped. He seemed puzzled. 'Of course, Mrs Schumann,' he said 'Uh—what about?'

'I have a problem,' Sibylla said. 'And I think you could help.' Her eyes were shining.

'How?'

'I'll tell you,' said Sibylla. 'Just as soon as these two bozos leave.'

The two bozos weren't stupid. They could take a hint. They left.

6

PENNY NEEDED A SUNTAN LIKE CAESAR NEEDED ANOTHER stab in the back. On the other hand, it was cooler up top than below decks. She lay face down on the forecabin roof in the shadow of the jib, except when the occasional breeze blew up and they went about. Ionia pushed out of the water all round them, hazed in heat, cragged and pined, peopled with unseen satyrs and randy gods. Sometimes the little wind brought the sound of goat bells knocking the air; sometimes a thyme-sated bee thudded on to the deck for a moment. Otherwise, it was still, the boat hardly moving, the sea unrippled, opaque, except for sudden patches the colour of old glass.

Below her, Theo lay spread out on a towel. Oiled as a sten gun, he wore a swimsuit the size of a posing pouch. Maybe it *was* a posing pouch. The ends of his hair were bleached almost white. The sun was being pitiless up in a sky that didn't know the meaning of the word cloud.

Footsteps shook the fibreglass cabintop. Penny opened an eye and saw Sibylla Schumann sidestepping along the deck past her down to the flat area occupied by Theo. She shut it again. Uh-oh.

'Hi,' Sibylla said. Not to her.

Theo shaded his eyes, then opened them, screwing them up against the brightness of the sky. 'Hi,' he said. It didn't need an amplifier to make it clear he wasn't thrilled by the prospect of his stepmother's company.

'Mind if I join you?' she said.

'Yes,' Theo said.

She laughed. 'Don't be silly.'

'I mean it.'

'Want me to rub oil on you?'

'Penny did it earlier.'

'Bet she enjoyed that,' said Sibylla. 'How about you rubbing some on to me?'

'Ask Penny. She already has oily hands.'

'That wouldn't be any kind of fun for me, now would it?'

'Depends.'

There was silence for maybe five seconds. Then Theo said in an outraged whisper, 'Just stop that, will you?'

'I'm only trying to—'

'I know what you're trying to do.'

Almost asleep, Penny could hear Marty in the cockpit talking to Hector Oakley and Costas. ' . . . so, like I say, the guy comes up to me and offers me his sister. Swears she's a virgin, swears she's clean. Well, I mean, virgin, how many virgins you got left in Tijuana? Some kid just fresh out of the womb maybe, and even then I wouldn't trust them Mex doctors no further'n I could throw them. So I tell him, I sez, "Look here, my friend, you're talking to the wrong guy, I happen to be a married man." Course, I don't say I'm married for the fifth time . . .'

'I'm the sixth Mrs Schumann,' Sibylla said softly, somewhere near Penny's foot. Behind her voice was something as cold and hard as an ice-cube.

' . . . they're all Catholics down there and that kinda thing don't go down too good. "A married man," I sez, and do you know what that little jerk sez to me, no more than ten years old he was, and trying to sell me his sister for chrissakes, he sez, "She weel show you how to make your wife veree happee, señor, verree happee." Can you beat it? I just hope to tell you how happy my wife'd be, I give her a dose of the clap . . .'

'That'll be the day,' Sibylla said.

' . . . so I sez, "Buzz off, kid, I'm not into that kind of stuff, I got better ways to get screwed than by some hooker's probably been on the game since she was weaned.'' And do you know what the kid come back with?'

There was a silence. In it, Hector Oakley cleared his throat and said, 'I simply can't imagine.'

'I hope that was the only reason he turned the kid down,' Sibylla said, so quietly Penny almost missed it.

'That's my dad you're talking about,' Theo said.

'I know that, honey.'

'I happen to love him.'

'How about loving your new mom just a little bit, hmmm?'

'Bug off, Sibylla.'

Penny loved Theo's father too. Marty had only started marrying when his kids were grown. Before that, he stayed home and minded the babies, letting out rooms to occasional boarders. By the time Theo and Roxanne were in high school, Marty was negotiating for the fourth site in a chain of budget motels that would eventually stud all fifty states.

'I'm really trying to love you, too,' said Sibylla. '*Son.*'

'Might not've been too many Schumanns around in eighteenth-century Virginia,' Theo said, 'giving the Indians VD and TB and stuff. But he's more of a good guy than you'll ever be.'

'Well, I should hope so, Theodore.'

'Well, then.' Penny heard Theo roll over on his stomach.

'So what are you saying?' said Sibylla.

'I'm saying keep your goddam hands off me's what I'm saying. I wish I knew just why in hell you ever married my dad.'

'Would you believe I loved him?'

'Not even if hell froze over.'

'Perhaps you'd prefer to believe I married him for his money.'

'Now that has the ring of truth,' Theo said. Penny heard him sit up. 'Dad should have known that if you shop in flea-markets, you're bound to get bitten.'

'You don't know one damn thing about me, kid. And so far, you haven't made one single friggin' effort to find out. If you had, you might find I'm not so bad.'

'Get lost.' There was a thump as Theo turned over hard on his side.

'As a matter of fact, I've been thinking about you a lot lately,' Sibylla said.

'Keep your thoughts to yourself, OK?'

'I think we'd make a good partnership.'

'You're already married. Or had you forgotten? Besides, I have to tell you right now I don't go for older women.'

'I wasn't proposing marriage, Theodore. But you have a good business head, and so have I.'

'Thought you were some dozy fifth-rate screen actress out in Hollywood.'

'Second-rate, maybe. Not fifth. Your dad and I met when he came out to California and bought up some motels, including the one where I lived.'

'What were you, the resident hooker?'

'I owned it,' Sibylla said.

For a moment Theo was silent. Then he said, 'You don't have to work now you're married to my father.'

'I like working.'

'On your back?'

'Too boring,' Sibylla said.

At the wheel, Costas brought the yacht about, searching for wind. He fancied himself as a sailor although he kept a fulltime skipper on board to handle the tricky bits. He'd told them earlier that the crudeness of an Onassis-type luxury liner with its chandeliers and sunken baths, its fifty-man crew, wasn't for him. The *Alexandros* was only a forty-two footer but he liked the elemental feel of a small boat pitted against Nature's savagery. He said he was confident that if it came right down to it he was more than a match for Nature. It was a real shame that there was so little savagery in the Ionian Sea.

' . . . hadn't hardly got off the plane before this cab-driver's offering to take me to some high-class whore-house on the edge of town, sez the place specialises in the elotic, that's what he said, these Japs can't hardly pronounce English, see, the elotic, he sez, so I sez, "Look, buddy, I don't know what it is about me, but I'm just not that kind of a guy," so he sez . . .'

'I'm good at making money, Theo. Why don't you let me in on this deal you and whatsername—Alexandra—are cooking up?'

'How the hell did you know about that?' Theo said, his voice dangerous.

'I keep my ears open. And my eyes. And Marty talks. So how about it?'

'My dad's got all the backing money I'd need.'

Sibylla yawned. 'OK. But just remember that he thinks I'm a pretty smart cookie. One word from me that the enterprise didn't seem awfully sound . . .'

Alexandra called that lunch was ready.

'Thank God,' said Theo. 'I need a change of air.'

'Why don't you jump overboard, kid?' Sibylla said lazily.

Penny turned over and stood up. Sibylla lay below her, facedown, almost naked in an apricot bikini. The strings of her top were undone. There were brown freckles all over her back. Penny wondered if any of them were cancerous. A pack of cigarettes was tucked into the elastic of her bikini, a matchbook folded over the edge of the cellophane wrapper.

Theo got up. He held his towel against his body. For a moment he stared down at Sibylla. Then he sidestepped towards Penny and they made their way aft.

'Hey, your stepmother is really cute,' Penny said.

'My stepmother is pure Hammer horror.'

'You want to be careful, Theo.'

'I am being.'

'Maybe you're not handling the lady right.'

'Right or wrong, I'm not gonna handle her any way at all.'

Between them, Irene and the skipper had prepared a cold lunch. Down in the main cabin, Hector was fussing about. Whatever had upset him the evening before, he seemed fully recovered now. He was nagging Irene again. He said 'in this heat'. He said 'bronchitis'. She said 'cold'. He said 'overdoing it as usual'. She said that it was too hot to sit around for long, it made her feel ill. Besides, she liked having something to do. He shook

60

pills from her brown bottle and put it back on the chart table. He stood over her while she washed them down with wine, smiling up at him. He smiled back. She proceeded to drink a lot more wine. Costas watched them both.

While they ate, Costas talked about the Athena hotel chain. It was going to revolutionise the British hotel trade, he said. Jason Jackson just loved him saying it. You could tell by his sour look. Today he was got up in a black wrestling leotard that reminded Penny of photographs of her maternal grandfather, Lord Drumnagowrie, stepping into the sea off the west coast of Africa during his time as Governor. He was wearing just such an outfit, though his was baggier round the crotch. Not that she had been about at the time, but the camera doesn't lie. On the other hand, it can make you look a prat. Especially when it comes to baggy. Rogers, her grandfather's valet, always pointed out that his personal preference at the time had been for a bathing-dress rather better cut, rather more stylish, but, as Miss Penelope well knew, his lordship wouldn't be told. Thank goodness they didn't have video cameras in those days, Rogers often said. What a laughing stock we'd have been then. He pronounced it vid-*ay*-o.

As well as the black garment, Jason wore the expression of a man who'd never expected much and that was exactly what he'd ended up with. He looked as if it wouldn't take a lot to make him spit. Understandably. A man who bills his hotel as England's finest can't he expected to put on his dancing shoes and break into a boogie when someone tries to upstage him. Was Costas being insensitive about this whole thing, or was there some vital element that Penny had missed out on? She couldn't tell. Alexandra listened to her father, her face giving nothing away. When Costas paused, she filled in the blanks. Quiet efficiency. As Theo had said, father and daughter made a good team.

After coffee, Costas folded up the brochures and brought out a chart. He pointed to something on it. 'You want to

61

take us to this island here, do you?' he said to Hector Oakley.

Hector stared down at the grey lines. 'Uh—navigation's not exactly my subject,' he said.

'I'm not asking you to steer us there by the sun,' Costas said impatiently. 'Just to tell the skipper whether this is the right place. As you see, it's not named, but from your description I don't know what else it could be.'

'It certainly looks as if it ought to be. Yes. That's it. It was right in close to another small island.'

The boat gave a small shudder. 'Wind,' someone said. 'We have wind.'

They put up more sail. The *Alexandros* scudded towards a small hump of rock so close to a larger hump that for a long time the two seemed joined. In the distance, other sails triangled across the sea. A chunky white ferryboat moved purposefully from one side of the scene to the other.

As the island came nearer, they could see a narrow channel of water between the larger and the smaller outcrop.

'We shan't be able to go too close inshore,' Alexandra said.

'I find it hard to believe that the ancient Greeks would have been foolish enough to build a shrine up there,' said Costas.

'They probably wouldn't have believed a modern Greek would be foolish enough to build a house on your island,' Alexandra said. She tacked on a bar or two of nervous laughter.

Costas didn't answer.

The skipper manoeuvred the *Alexandros* as close as he dared, then dropped anchor. The tiny island was no more than a steep hill of scrub and boulder. At the top of the ridge was a sheer grey wall of rock some eighty feet high. The remains of a long-dry stream bed fell away from it, straight down for a couple of hundred feet, to end as boulders on the tiny white beach that lay directly in front of them.

Irene looked up at it. 'Where's the fountain?' she said.

'Just beyond the rocks,' Hector said. 'You'll see when you get up there.'

'Get up there?'

'Yes. It's much easier than it seems from here.'

'But it's so steep.'

'Think chamois,' Penny said.

'Go for it, Irene,' encouraged Theo.

'I don't think I really need to climb up there, Hector,' Irene said. 'Couldn't you just take photos and show me later?'

'You don't *have* to go,' Costas said. 'Now I've seen the place, I certainly don't intend to.'

'Irene.'

'Yes, Hector.'

'I want you to go.'

'Why?' asked Costas.

'Because it's there,' said Penny.

'It is plainly ridiculous, so soon after lunch, and in this heat,' said Costas.

'I want you to go.'

'I shan't make it, Hector.' There was real fear in Irene's voice. It wasn't fear of heights.

'Why not?'

'I shan't. I can't.'

'Why can't you?'

'Because I'm . . .' All their conversations came to this, Penny thought. Irene manoeuvred into a position where she had to shout out loud that she was too fat. Does he get a kick out of humiliating her? 'Because I don't feel like it,' Irene said, her voice louder than she intended.

Theo had gone over the side and brought round the dinghy. It floated below them. Irene looked over the side of the boat. 'Anyway, I can't possibly get into that,' she said.

'Nonsense,' Hector said. 'Isn't that nonsense, Costas?'

'It won't sink, if that's what you mean,' Costas said. 'But whether this is wise, in view of the circumstances . . .'

'I think I'm the best judge of that.'

'I think you got a hung jury,' said Penny.

'You don't know what it means for me for you to see that shrine,' Hector said to his wife.

'Mrs Lampeter,' Penny said. 'Are you OK? You look kind of—' She could tell Irene was going to have to come.

'I'm absolutely fine,' Irene said.

'Don't say I didn't warn you.' Costas stared at her. 'If you don't feel up to it, my dear Irene . . .'

'Come on,' Theo shouted from the water. 'Alexandra. Penny. First landing party going ashore. What about you, Dad?'

'Long as no one expects me to start climbing no hills,' said Marty. 'And remember, son, I don't swim too good, so don't go tipping me out or anything stupid.'

'I got my Lifesaver certificate right here in my pocket, Mr Schumann, don't you worry,' Penny said. She scrambled down the steps and reached for one of the rope handles in the dinghy. 'I'd rescue you.'

'Well, I just know you would,' Marty said. He adjusted his cigar. He wore a hat made of artificial straw with a black band round it. He walked to the stern and bent over to see Theo in the dinghy below.

'Dad,' Theo said. 'You trying for Best-dressed Tycoon, or what?'

'How d'ya mean?'

'That hat.'

'What's wrong with it? Man said all the best people were wearing them.'

'And you believed him?'

'Listen, kid. At that price, I couldn't afford not to.'

'What happened to that real panama Roxanne gave you last summer?'

'Aw hell, I don't know,' Marty said. 'Musta sat on it.' Truth was, he had looked too darn like his grandad in it, reminded him of the old man sitting out on a hard chair on the sidewalk in the steamy heat of summer in the Bronx, looking like what Marty himself never wanted to look ever again, like what he'd worked hard all his life so Theo would never be. Which was poor. He explained some of this as he clambered down the stern ladder and into the dinghy, staggering a little on the yielding floor of grey rubber. He didn't ask where Sibylla was. Costas came down the ladder and jostled in next to him. From above, the skipper reached down Costas's gold-headed cane. Theo rowed them ashore.

Close to, the idyllic little beach was covered in tar and plastic bottles. Jellyfish glistened just below the surface of the sea. The air was full of herb smells.

'I'll go back for the others,' Theo said.

'Watch out Miss Roving Hands doesn't seize the opportunity to rape you,' Penny said.

'Long as the opportunity's the only thing she seizes, I can cope,' said Theo.

They watched him pull back across the hundred yards between the boat and the shore. After a while, Irene Lampeter clambered heavily down the aluminium ladder, helped from above by her husband, from below by Theo. She made an awkward bulky figure in her long-sleeved flowered muumuu and big hat. Body language said loud and clear that she was unhappy. Hector Oakley followed her into the dinghy. Jason, with small black shorts pulled over his outfit, followed him. The skipper jumped over the side and swam ashore. He squirmed a bit when he hit the jellyfish.

It was extremely hot. High overhead, the sun blazed in a sky like a silver tray. Easy to see why the gods were always dashing about in disguise. A shower of gold or a white hart just had to be cooler than sticking around Olympus swopping insults with the gang.

Costas found some shade under an overhang of rock where he could dangle his feet in the sea. He said he would stay there and if anyone else had any sense, they could join him. Only Marty Schumann took him up on it. The skipper swam away round the point. The rest of the party started climbing. It was a fairly tough climb. In places the slope was almost perpendicular. Thirty feet up, they were looking down through spiky green pines on to the *Alexandros*, at anchor in the narrow stretch of water between the two islands. Sibylla was still stretched out on her stomach, narrow strips of apricot across her skin. She'd covered her blonde hair with a peach-coloured scarf. There was no other sign of human life in the entire area.

The path they took was no more than a goat track, following the easiest zigzag way along low stone walls where olives grew. Once they must have been cultivated. Whether two years ago or two thousand was impossible to tell. Bees whizzed about. Insects thrummed. Sometimes they could hear the soft musical thud of goat bells. The whole place looked as though someone had scattered a jumbo-sized packet of wildflower seeds around and kept them watered. The angle of climb was too extreme for anything but open-mouth breathing. Nobody talked.

After a while, Irene suddenly stopped. She said she couldn't go on. She was panting heavily, her face greyish where it wasn't red. Sweat stood out on her forehead and cheeks.

'But darling,' Hector said. 'We're almost there.'

Irene shook her head. Her eyes were closed and she clutched at her chest. The baggy dress was wet where it touched her.

'Hey, listen,' Penny said to Oakley. 'This trip'd better be worth it. Way you're hassling the lady, we're expecting a bit more than some dried-up rocks and a few tufts of grass.'

'A personal appearance by Athena herself, minimum,' Theo said.

'I'd settle for Cupid,' said Penny. She smiled at Irene.

'Trust me,' Hector said.

'Why should we?' said Jason. He craned his neck to peer up at the wall of rocks above them. 'And how do you suppose your wife is going to negotiate that?'

'You can see she's had enough,' said Penny. Irene seemed to be trembling.

'Yeah,' Theo said. It looked like mutiny. Lucky for Hector there were no lifeboats handy. A navy blue bug with white spots landed on Penny's arm for a moment, and flew off again quickly.

'Well,' said Hector, 'if you really want to turn back after we've come this far . . .'

'I think it would be wiser to return to the boat,' Alexandra said. She stood close to Theo. 'It's much cooler on the water.'

Irene opened her eyes. She looked at her husband. He looked back. He plugged in to his interior energy grid. 'Darling,' he said. 'Please.'

Irene shook her head. She pressed one hand against her heart. 'Just give me a minute,' she said.

They gave her several. Penny looked out across the sea to other islands on the horizon, at the juxtaposition of rock and tree and blue sky, at a red spider spinning tiny intricate webs inside a flower, at the sun. By her leg, ants were busily taking home lunch for the rest of the guys. Lunch was a green beetle and a couple of leaves. She could just see the *Alexandros*, a miniature in the vast seascape. She wondered why Costas had called his boat after a son he didn't have, instead of the daughter he did. She looked over at Irene, who leaned against a tree, fanning herself with her hat. Every now and then she brushed her hand over her lips as though they bothered her.

Penny went and sat down beside Alexandra and Theo. 'I'm worried,' she said.

'Do you think there is something wrong with Mrs Oakley?' Alexandra said.

'Yes. But I don't see what we can do about it.'

'She's too big to kidnap,' said Theo.

'We could all say we were going back down,' said Penny.

'Hector would make her go on to the top without us.'

Irene lurched forward. 'Let's go,' she said. Her voice was weak. 'Let's get this over with.'

Hector beamed like a lighthouse. 'I promise you'll love it up there,' he said. 'The view. The *atmosphere*.'

Irene looked at him. She smiled. Very slowly she sank to her knees then flopped sideways, clutching at her heart. 'Oh, Hector,' she said reproachfully . . . 'I think I'm dying.' She fell with her face on the ground, the big hat sliding forward to cover her head.

For a moment everyone stared. Then Penny stood up and ran over to where the body lay. 'Take it easy, Irene,' she said. Irene didn't answer.

She bent down and put her head on the big woman's back. It felt solid, as if her skin were full of meat. She listened. Inside Irene there was no sound at all. No heartbeat. No stomach gurgle or muscle creak. No lung fill. She turned Irene over and put her mouth on the flaccid lips. They felt slack beneath hers, unliplike. She breathed in steadily through her nose and out through her mouth. She felt air expand the chest under hers. She did it again. And again. She thumped the place above Irene's heart several times. After a while, Theo took over. Then Alexandra. Nothing happened.

She looked up at Hector, who was standing over her. His head was framed by grey leaves. Behind them, the bright sky gleamed. 'Irene . . .' he said. His face had gone greyish at the edges. 'Oh God . . . Irene.' He knelt down and put a hand towards his wife.

'I think she's . . . dead,' Penny said.

'Dead?'

'Yes.'

'Dead,' said Alexandra. She stood up. She brushed her hands together.

'Yes.'

'You *killed* her,' said Theo.

Somewhere, over on the other island perhaps, the unseen goats clanged. Then several more. Bells. Passing bells.

7

SOME PEOPLE HAVE IT. SOME HAVEN'T. TIM LAMPETER, for instance. What he did have was thin tortoiseshell glasses, a high shiny forehead and the look of a curate whose egg had been bad all through. Plus eyeteeth so sharp piranhas would have been green with envy. Definitely not Penny's kind of man. It was hard to think whose kind of man he would be.

She reminded herself that Tim Lampeter was a genuine financial whizz kid. It didn't help any.

It was six o'clock in the evening. The sort of time Penny broke out the Jack Daniels. Tim preferred tea. He sat in her Chelsea drawing-room, balancing a cup on his knee. His pale face shone like a missionary's, alight with zeal. Except he wasn't fishing for souls. Only heads. One head in the particular.

'He murdered her,' he said.

'That's not what it said on on the death certificate.'

'None the less.'

'No mention of poison. No mention of guns or strangulation or blunt instruments.'

'You don't have to stick a knife in someone's ribs to kill them,' Tim said.

'I seem to remember they plumped for cardiac arrest, aggravated by her poor physical condition, in the end.'

'Aggravated by murder,' Tim said.

Penny wasn't sure why she was arguing. She, too, felt Hector Oakley to be morally, if not directly, responsible for Irene Lampeter's death. Yet what had seemed a certainty under the bright hard sun of Greece seemed less of one here in England, with rain slicking the windows and the safe smell of buttered crumpets in the room.

'Just supposing,' Tim said, 'that you're a middle-aged charlatan of some kind, looking for a rich widow to marry. Women of my mother's age are easy prey. They're always vulnerable when they find themselves without a man.'

'Is that right?'

'You meet someone—if you're this adventurer I'm talking about—in a high-stress job. Someone who drives themselves too hard all the time. You notice she's high-coloured, a sure sign of high blood pressure. It's only a step from there to working out a way to get hold of her money at small risk to yourself.'

Penny uncrossed her legs and crossed them in the other direction.

'Then,' Tim said, swallowing tea, 'once you've married them, you nag and fuss all the time, pretending it's because of your deep concern for their well-being. Because you spend so much time on bodybuilding or tennis or whatever yourself, you put subtle pressure on them to join you in things that are highly unsuitable for their age.'

'You're May, are you, to this rich lady you've managed to snare's December?'

'Of course.' Tim's Adam's apple bobbed. 'Maybe ten years or so younger. On top of that, you encourage her to cook delicious little meals swimming in cream and eggs, which you somehow don't eat much of but which she does. Sooner or later, you're pretty well bound to kill her.'

'Murder by cholesterol's kind of hard to prove.'

Tim set his mouth in a way that made it obvious he'd been a stubborn little boy. 'I'd like you to try. That's my first reason for coming to see you. I know you've done some detective work in the past—that Roman Catholic prelate, for instance.'

'Monsignor Capet,' Penny said softly. She would never

70

forget him sitting here on the big swing at Hurley Court, the amethyst on his finger glinting like a wicked eye in the sun, the crown of thorns crazy over one ear.

'And that friend of yours up in County Durham,' said Tim.

'Poor Kendal.'

'The point is, there must be something we could pin on Hector, to prove foul play or undue influence or something. I want to hire you to look into his background, find out about him. Everything you can. Thinking about it now, I realise just how little we know about him. Where he came from, what he did before he met my mother, that sort of thing. Whenever anyone asked him, he somehow always managed to turn the conversation on to something else.'

'Why would Hector Oakley want to kill your mother?'

'For her money, of course.'

'And now she's dead, has he got it?'

Ever since he'd knocked on her door half an hour earlier, Penny had been looking for a likeness between Tim Lampeter and his mother. If Irene had passed on her warmth and jollity, it wasn't Tim who'd inherited. Over the rim of her glass, she tried again for a resemblance. No dice. Any more than there was a resemblance between him and his second cousin, Alexandra Kyriakou.

'Unfortunately, yes. But I'm telling you right now, my brother and I didn't work enormously hard for years, just so that some jumped-up bastard in a beard could walk off with the majority shareholding.'

'Off-hand, I'd say you weren't overly fond of Mr Oakley.'

'That's one way of putting it.'

'You hate his goddam guts.'

'That's a better way of putting it,' said Tim. He tilted his head so the light from the street caught his glasses. He poured more tea from the pot on the table in front of him. The lid almost fell off. Penny winced. She knew all about materialism and the meaninglessness of possessions. On the other hand, the set had been a hundred

71

years old when it was presented to Penny's great-grandfather, the first Lord Drumnagowrie, some eighty years earlier. Not that Tim could be expected to know that. It was just that she'd hate it to be damaged while in her care.

'What happened was,' he said, 'as soon as they were married, three years ago, he seems to have persuaded my mother to change her will, leaving him her controlling interest in the Lampeter Group. My brother and I hold the rest of the shares between us. When we met yesterday, for our usual monthly policy meeting, Oakley told us he intends to sell out.'

'Did he say to whom?'

'Costas Kyriakou. Ironic, isn't it?'

'Kind of.'

'Naturally the two of us—Christopher and I—offered to buy him out, but we can't match the Kyriakou bid. We pointed out that my mother couldn't possibly have wanted Kyriakou to get hold of Lampeter. She loathed him.'

'Why did she accept his invitation, in that case?'

'Hector persuaded her to.'

'Perhaps they were in it together,' Penny said. 'Maybe Costas said he'd help Hector to—uh—get rid of your mother, on condition Hector sold out to him.'

'That's just the sort of thing I want you to find out. Before it's too late. Because you don't need much imagination to see what would happen if Kyriakou gets his hands on us.'

'Pretend I haven't got any,' Penny said.

'For a start, he's got his fingers in any number of business pies. We've done well because we always remained a family-based operation. For another, Christopher and I, not having enough shares between us to produce a voting majority, would lose all control over production, design, foreign sales, etc. What the hell does a Greek know about the particularly English appeal of Lampeter-style designs? If Hector Oakley sells to Kyriakou, the Lampeter Group would effectively cease to exist.'

'And what do you think I can do?'

Not that she needed to ask. He thought she could waste a lot of time on a wild goose chase. Like everyone else, he had her tabbed as a sucker. A soft touch. Why was that? She couldn't figure it out. Especially when she worked her buns off trying to be a hard one.

'That's the other reason I'm here.' Tim gave a noiseless gulp. 'You can . . . I'd appreciate it if you'd . . . if you'd tell me about what happ . . . her last . . . exactly how Mother died.'

Penny was quiet for a moment, gathering the memories from scattered parts of her brain. Then she told him. The hot hillside had suddenly chilled for them all, with death lying at their feet. There was the unavoidable need for necessary change that death always brings, the desire for volcanoes to erupt, islands to sink into seas suddenly tempestuous, suns to hide, comets to slice the sky. Instead, there had been the appalling logistics of moving the slack heavy body down those steep angles through spiky bushes and loose shale. Lifting her aboard had been a nightmare. They had radioed for help from the boat, trying to find a doctor on one of the islands and failing. Using Kyriakou's pull, they'd got hold of one at a military installation further south, who had flown by helicopter to where they waited at anchor off the larger half of the island.

They'd known she was dead from the first, long before the doctor had been lowered down to examine her and make the official pronouncement. An officer had followed him, to attach a harness to the body and supervise its lifting aboard the helicopter. All this had taken hours. Penny didn't tell Irene's son that in the fierce heat his mother's remains had already begun to decompose by the time she was taken off the boat. Nor how the flowered muumuu had ballooned as the body rose into the air, offering those below a bizarre glimpse of white lace.

When she'd finished, Lampeter said fiercely, 'I'll probably never pin anything on Hector. I've only got suspicions. But since you were there when she . . . when it

73

happened, I thought maybe you saw something, heard something, might somehow be in a position to confirm them.'

'What're you looking for? The inquest made it clear there was no dirty business. And it was a while ago now.'

'I don't exactly know what I'm looking for. Which is why I've come to you. I've arranged to meet him in my office at ten o'clock tomorrow morning and I'd like you to be there.' Tim drank prissily, then set his cup down on the table. 'For all we know Hector might even have a criminal record. At least we'd have something to work with then. Something to hold over his head.'

'Sword of Damocles kind of thing.'

'Exactly.' Tim widened his eyes to emphasise the point. Suddenly he didn't look a bit like a missionary. More like a cannibal. A cannibal with the kind of unsteady hand that might drop any Damoclean swords it happened to be holding right into the skull of whoever was underneath. He sounded ominous. Lethal, even. And here she'd been thinking that some people were born to have sand kicked in their face.

'I know we'll probably never prove that he had anything to do with my mother's death,' he said. 'He could afford to take his time about it. It wouldn't matter much to him whether it was on a Greek island now or next year on the tennis court, as long as it was sometime. Meanwhile, he lived like a king at my mother's expense.'

'You wouldn't say that if their sex was reversed.'

'What?'

'You wouldn't make pejorative statements about a woman living at her husband's expense.'

'That's different.'

'Why?'

Tim clearly didn't want to discuss equal rights. 'Will you take on the job?' he said.

'My degree's in fine arts, not in crime detection,' Penny said. Even to herself it didn't sound like she meant it. Because the bottom line was that she was nosy. She liked things straight. She liked them right.

And if Oakley had deliberately set out to push Irene Lampeter into her grave, then she didn't want him walking about the streets unpunished. OK. Vengeance wasn't hers, it was the Lord's. She knew that. It was just that sometimes the Lord took His own sweet time about it.

'My mother didn't deserve to die,' said Tim. He looked down at his hands. She could see him blinking.

'I'm not sure I can help,' she said, knowing she'd have to.

The door of the drawing-room opened. Barnaby came in. He wore a DJ and looked rakish. He beat Danny Kaye as a riverboat gambler into a brass spittoon. The black morocco document-case he carried under one arm bulged. Almost certainly with money. In the dusk, his hair flamed like rowanberries.

'Ah,' he said. 'Crumpets.'

Not a remark to set the heart racing. Unless the heart was Penny's. Exhilaration'll do it every time. And exhilarating was what she found the contrasts Barnaby posed. Between the surface and the underneath. Between the Mayfair antique shop and the steel-lined vault full of stolen treasures below it. Between the Old Etonian accent of everyday and the thousand different voices he was able to assume at will. Between crumpets and high stakes. Because dinner-jacket plus money meant only one thing. Barnaby was spending the evening at Bucknall's. Gambling. Barnaby only played cards when he felt lucky, and when he felt lucky, he won.

Recently he had decided that betting on horses was not an entirely efficient way of maximising the profits from his extracurricular activities. Burglary from the houses of the vulgar rich yielded loot that burned with a hard gem-like flame. Barnaby's fence was efficient. Miss Ivory's knowledge of racing form was extensive. But recently the bookmakers had grown leery of taking Miss Ivory's bets. Which was pretty mean of them when you considered what a sweet old lady she was. And so entirely respectable. But the need for aid was crucial. In Africa, politics and warmongering were, as always, preventing supplies from reaching the needy. People were starving. Children were dying. So Barnaby was about to maximise the proceeds from the diamonds he'd just smuggled out of South Africa at the blue baize gaming-tables which were one of Bucknall's little idiosyncrasies.

Penny said: 'Have you met Tim Lampeter?'

Barnaby hadn't. 'But I met your mother a couple of times,' he said. 'Also your stepfather.'

Tim clamped his teeth together. 'I'm rather old for that kind of thing,' he said. Anyone would think he'd just been invited to play Oranges and Lemons.

'How do you mean?' Barnaby said.

'Stepfathers. It's a bit Mother Goose, isn't it?'

'Interesting,' said Barnaby. 'Off-hand, I can't think of a single instance of a stepfather in Mother Goose. Can you, Penny? Plenty of stepmothers, but no . . .'

'Whatever,' Tim said. 'I prefer not to think of Hector Oakley as any relation of mine.'

'Oh. Right.'

'When shall I see you?' Penny said to Barnaby.

'Late.'

'I'll be waiting.'

'I'll be in the mood.' Taking a crumpet from the dish in front of Tim, Barnaby left.

Penny stood up. 'I'll do it,' she said. 'But not for money.'

'For what, then?'

'Helicopters. The exclusive use of three of yours for six months. Out in Africa. And no publicity.'

'Why?'

'Locusts,' Penny said.

'As in the Bible?'

'Exactly. Except those were only one kind. Right this minute there are four different species chewing Africa to pieces. If they aren't stopped, they're going to finish off what the crop failures have already begun.' Penny looked bleakly at the Käthe Kollwitz on the wall. 'If the locust swarms can't be destroyed, the famines out there now will look like Thanksgiving, compared to what'll come.'

'How're helicopters going to help?'

'By spraying pesticides. On the breeding grounds as well as the swarms.'

'It would be awfully expensive to get three helicopters out there,' Tim said.

'That's my price.'

'And it will reduce our fleet rather drastically.'

'Tough shit.'

'We'd have to hire in to fill the engagements we've already fixed. Do you know how much that'll cost?'

'You came to me, Mr Lampeter. Not the other way around.'

'I'd like to be sure you're worth it,' said Tim. He couldn't have been anything but an accountant.

'Nice girls aren't cheap,' Penny said. 'I'll see you tomorrow.'

When he'd gone, she poured another Jack Daniels, considerably bigger than the first. She put a Mozart piano concerto on the CD player and turned up the volume. At the moment, she was working her way through the entire piano works. If there was ever a seat going begging at the right hand of God, she would gladly nominate old Wolfgang for the empty space. Humming along, she made a béarnaise sauce, poured wine, sliced tomatoes. She made a salad of cos lettuce and raw mushrooms. She added avocado chunks and kiwi fruit. Personally she wouldn't let a pickled gherkin within a thousand miles of one of her salads. When the grill was ready, she shoved a steak underneath for a count of fifty-seven seconds then turned it over for fifty-three more. Perfect.

As she ate, she speculated. Had Hector Oakley really engineered Irene's death? And if so, how exactly had he done it? Tim had suggested long-term murder, but what about something more obvious: Irene's pills? Would it have been possible to substitute the pills she took for her blood pressure for others that would cause palpitations or convulsions? You'd only have to put them into her bottle and wait for her finally to take a couple of the dangerous ones. Or, to make it even more certain, wait until the situation was right then shake several out on your hand and give her the wrong ones. And the situation was unlikely to get righter than it had been the day she died. Stuck, that is, on one of the slowest and most capricious forms of transport known to man. Hours from help.

On the other hand, there were a couple of points to be considered. Always supposing Irene's death to be unnatural, and the pills responsible. First off, would Hector have drawn attention to them so often if he planned to use them as a murder weapon? Second, it didn't have to be Hector. Anyone on board could have substituted something lethal for the real thing. The little brown bottle was there in the locker for everyone to see. Before that, it had been in the dining-room on Kyriakou's island. It could even have been doctored before Irene left England. The question was, who, apart from Hector, would stand to gain from her death? Or wanted her dead?

If Tim Lampeter was to be believed, Hector had no need to hurry things along. If he carried on stuffing Irene like a Strasbourg goose, the result was inevitable. Collapse of stout party. If she could find evidence that he suddenly needed large sums of money, that might constitute some kind of proof. But it could never be the conclusive kind. Not unless he confessed. If not Hector, who? Was the notion of Kyriakou killing for control of the Lampeter Group so absurd? Could Jason Jackson, maddened with rage at Irene's betrayal, have decided to bump her off? What of the Lampeter sons themselves? Would a man hire someone to find a murderer that was in fact himself? Such double bluffs might exist in the fictional world of crime novels. Not in real life. Anyway, she didn't want to think about matricide.

Instead, she thought about life and about death, and how very seldom people wanted to exchange one for the other.

The Lampeter Group's head offices were near Covent Garden. Smells of stale oranges still lurked there although the fruit market had long since departed for the suburbs. Penny walked through the airy arcades, stopping to watch a fire-eater, a break-dancer, a clown, and a woman playing two penny-whistles at the same time. Sulky girls flogged hand-knit scenic sweaters or ceramic eggcups wearing ceramic Mary Janes. Thin shivering men stood beside stalls of silver jewellery, trying not to catch anyone's eye. In the chilly wind that whistled below the glass roofs, tourists sat under gay umbrellas and pretended they were having a riotous time.

The ghosts of old courgettes lingered in the hallway of the Lampeter building. Penny climbed the brown-linoleumed brass-bound steps to the first floor. Here, all was cuteness and light. The reception area could have doubled as a townie version of a farm kitchen. The pine was stripped, the pattern willow. Lampeter products stood about, bursting with country goodness, among jugs of dried wheatstalks and Chinese lanterns. Strings of garlic hung from the ceiling, along with herbs and other country messes. Very bucolic.

Hector had already arrived and was in Tim's office. Like those Before and After photographs advertising hair transplants, the difference was considerable between the Oakley of four weeks ago in Greece, and the Oakley who sat across from her now. There were stains on the lapels of his suit. There were red rims to his eyes. The aggressive square-cut beard had lost its bold outlines. So had Oakley. He sagged now, as if his stuffing had leaked. Either he was genuinely grieving, or Laurence Olivier had had a lucky break when Oakley decided against the stage.

'I thought we ought to talk about the future of the Lampeter Group,' Tim said. He seemed smoother than yesterday. A force to be reckoned with. A force you hoped would be with you.

Oakley stared dully at the desk top. Hard to tell whether it was genuine or he'd been working on dull stares. Watching him from Tim's side of the desk, Penny couldn't be certain which.

'How can you think about the future at a time like

79

this?' he said. He must have been working on clichés, too.

'Because I have to,' said Tim. 'Like the show, the jam must go on.'

Oakley lifted his head. He seemed bewildered. 'The jam must . . .'

'Now that you've had time to think about it,' Tim said, 'what I really want to discuss is how you feel about staying in with us.'

Oakley looked at Tim as if he'd just suggested he voluntarily opted for house arrest. 'Staying in?'

'You can appreciate that selling out to Costas Kyriakou could constitute a major blow to the freedom of operation we've always enjoyed within the group. In view of your relationship with my mother, I can't . . .'

'Marriage,' Oakley mumbled. 'It wasn't a relationship, it was a marriage.'

'Of course,' Tim said, polite as a carpenter about to polish off a dozen oysters. 'As I say, in view of that, I can't believe you would seriously want to jeopardise the future of the company she spent so many years establishing.'

Hector straightened his spine. Almost visibly, he sidelined his grief. If that's what it was.

'I can't see why it should jeopardise anything,' he said. 'When Kyriakou approached me, he emphasised that nothing would change.'

'Kyriakou approached *you*?' Tim couldn't help sliding a look at Penny.

'Certainly he did. And as I told you last week I intend to accept his offer.'

'Is there any point appealing to your better nature?' Tim said.

'None.'

'That probably *is* his better nature,' Penny said.

'I'm afraid I haven't exactly worked out the delightful Miss Wanawake's function at this meeting,' Oakley said. 'A considerable ornament, of course, but, I should have thought, of little use.'

Screw you, too. 'You won't get anywhere, buttering me up like that,' Penny said.

'She's here as my assistant,' said Tim. '*If* you don't mind too terribly much.'

Hector smiled. Sarcasm didn't faze him. He'd obviously read the same book Penny had. The one where it said about sarcasm being the tool of the impotent.

'I repeat, although his wasn't the only offer I received, I intend to accept Mr Kyriakou's,' he said.

'In that case . . .' Tim began gathering papers together. It looked like the end of the show. Penny knew it wasn't. So far, they'd just had the curtain-raiser. Anyone who walked out now and started hailing taxis was going to miss the whole point of the play.

'Unless you can match Kyriakou's offer,' Hector said deliberately. He squeezed the knuckles of one hand with the other and stared at both in a downcast way, as though he'd just remembered he was bereaved. 'If you can come up with the same money, then I'll accept it and Bob's your uncle.'

A young man came in carrying a tray. 'Hector!' he said. 'Good to see you.'

Hector didn't answer.

'Penny,' Tim Lampeter said. 'Have you met my brother Christopher?'

'No,' said Penny. She smiled. 'You're the artist, aren't you?'

A scowl crossed the young man's face. Then he said, 'I was. At the moment, I'm presiding over the test kitchens while the lady who normally does it is away on holiday.'

Christopher's likeness to Irene was accentuated by the roundness of his face. His eyes were warm, as hers had been. Although Penny wouldn't have tipped him to win a Handsome Hunks contest, he was a lot better looking than Tim. Not that it was hard to outshine the competition when the competition was only 40 watts. It made you wonder what James Lampeter had looked like.

Christopher handed round a plate with some cookies

on. Each one looked as if it contained the average person's fibre requirement for the next ten years.

'These are the latest thing to come out of the ovens,' he said. 'It's a new recipe. What do you think?'

Tim sank his teeth into one. So did Penny. Sinking in was easy. It was pulling out that took the time.

'Great,' she said.

'What do you think, Hector?'

Hector couldn't be bothered to tell.

'They stick to the teeth,' said Tim.

'Too much treacle,' Christopher said. 'I thought so, as soon as I read the specifications.'

'I thought specifications were reserved for desirable residences,' said Penny. Her teeth felt like Wellington boots after a walk in a muddy field. 'Cookies used to have recipes.'

'Not when they're baked on an industrial scale,' Christopher said boyishly. Penny wondered how old he was. Twenty-seven? Twenty-eight? Maybe a little younger. No one could get away with boyish after twenty. Twenty-one, max. He bit into one and considered. 'Yes, these definitely need rethinking. Substituting syrup for honey was obviously a mistake. I've been digging into old Elizabethan recipe books, you see. I thought it could be a whole new line for us. It's worth a try, don't you think? With the trend towards nostalgia, and everything. Look at that Edwardian lady and her diary. If it caught on like that did, we could make a *mint*!'

Oakley looked as if he couldn't care less if they made a bouquet garni. He put his hands on his knees and stood up. 'Gentlemen,' he said, 'I have better things to do with my time than exchange culinary tips.' He looked at his watch and walked over to the door. 'I've told you my intentions. It is now up to you. The ball is in your court.'

'And you won't change your mind?' asked Tim.

'No.'

'But the price Kyriakou is offering is way over the odds.'

'I need the money.'

'What happens if Kyriakou withdraws for some reason?' asked Christopher.

Panic moved like a trapped wasp behind Hector's eyes. 'Uh . . .' he said. He smoothed a finger along the corners of his beard. 'Then I'd be forced to accept the other offer I mentioned. I'm more or less obliged to, I'm afraid. Sorry.' He shook his head, about as sorry as a man who's found a Rubens in the attic. A tad more refined than Nero throwing Christians to the lions, but only just. 'You know where to find me, if you wish to get in touch.'

He went out.

'It doesn't look too good, does it?' said Christopher.

His brother crashed a fist down on the desk. 'I knew he was only after her money,' he said. 'Right from the very first time Mother brought him home. I could see him mentally adding up what everything cost and coming up with a sum beyond his wildest expectations.'

Who knows what moves a financial whizzkid? It was pretty clear that when his mother had started in on the wedding-bell talk, this particular one hadn't gone racing out to bulk-buy confetti.

'You don't really think he killed her, do you?' Christopher said.

'More than ever,' said Tim. 'Look at the way he's behaving. He can't wait to get shot of the shares and have the money safely in the bank.'

'Do you both dislike him?' Penny said. 'Or is it just Tim?'

Tim gazed at her through his glasses. 'I wouldn't say that,' he said. 'I wouldn't say we disliked Hector. Would you, Chris?'

Christopher shook his head.

'Mistrusted,' Tim said. 'Resented. Loathed. Any of those. Not disliked.'

Penny felt momentarily sorry for Hector. It didn't come easy, being a step-parent. Cinderella was probably a pain in the ass, if the truth were known.

'How much of a chance did you give him?' she said.

'Plenty,' said Christopher.

'How did he meet your mother?'

Tim shrugged. 'I don't know.'

'She said it was through the company,' said Christopher. 'She told me he had his own business.'

'Did she say what the business was?'

'Something to do with the Stock Market, I believe. I know he used to travel up to London most days, until Mother got him on to the board of the Lampeter Group. After that they used to work mostly from the office at home. Maybe he sold his own company, though I know he still comes up to London a couple of times a week.'

'We knew so little about him,' Tim said.

'People tend to take other people at face value,' Penny said. 'Which is usually all they're worth.'

'The thing is, we'd left home and had our own flats. Well, house, in my case. We just accepted what Mother told us about him. We weren't that interested, if the truth be told. We resented him so much.'

'Is he still living in the family home?'

'For the minute. He's about to move out, though,' Christopher said.

'What did you think of him, Penny?' Tim said.

'He certainly looked like a man who's found the streets paved with gold.'

'Our gold,' said Christopher.

'Whether he looked like a man who planned the slow murder of his wife in the expectation of plenty is something else.'

'You don't *really* think he killed Mother, do you?' Christopher said.

'I'm convinced of it,' said Tim.

'Just for the money?'

'Yes.'

'What's your next move?' asked Penny.

'To hope,' Tim said, 'that you turn something up.'

'And if I don't?'

'I'll think of something.' Tim stared hard at Penny, daring her to notice that his eyes were floating in tears. 'He won't get away with this.'

'Always so harsh, Timbo,' said Christopher.

'I feel harsh,' Timothy said. 'I *feel* harsh.' He pressed his fingers against his temples and studied the desktop. 'When I think of poor Mother, besotted with that man, turning herself into a nervous wreck, trying to please him, when she was worth five thousand of him. When I think of all that weight she put on, and how much she hated it, and him making her jog and swim and play tennis, and how ill she sometimes got, and how frightened she was of losing him, and then trying to scramble up some mountainside just to . . . that heat . . . her heart . . . pain . . .' Tim's voice petered out. Penny saw a tear splash down.

'How will you stop him?' she said.

Christopher produced a big mirthless smile which made shallow dimples in his cheeks. He stretched his big eyes to the maximum. 'Murder him, if I know Tim.'

Another tear splashed. It made a tiny tapping sound as it hit the desk. Right now the only thing Tim Lampeter looked capable of murdering was a Kleenex.

PENNY HAD BEEN UNOBTRUSIVELY WATCHING OAKLEY FOR a week. So far all she'd got to show for it was a big fat zero. Watching him wasn't difficult. Staying unobtrusive was. The Lampeter house, an attractive place of honey-coloured Cotswold stone, stood at the edge of a village rural to the point of depravity. Nothing like Penny had hit it since the day a German parachutist dropped out of the sky and asked the way to Buckingham Palace. Even when she put on her white belted mackintosh, they didn't seem to get the message that she wanted to be alone, rather than followed by a crowd of gaping rustics. One in particular—dark-eyed and foreign-looking and curiously unrustic—was very persistent. Maybe she should have worn a felt hat too.

Oakley pottered a lot. Once he mowed the lawn. Once he weeded the roses. Once he went down to the village and posted a letter. Penny couldn't make out the address. He drove over to the nearby Rockingham Hotel one evening and ate dinner with Jason Jackson. Penny watched them through the window. She tried not to press her nose against the glass. Standing there in the dark, she felt like poor Sarah Crewe in *The Little Princess*. While Jason and Hector ate their way through the menu, she didn't even have a candy bar. She wondered if there was anything sinister in the two of them getting to-gether. Although they were drinking champagne, neither of them seemed in festive mood.

Once Oakley went for a walk along the river. In the

rain. Penny was right there with him, hating it. He didn't drop any letters into hollow oaks. He didn't rendezvous with any sinister strangers of unCotswold swarthiness. He didn't do anything the whole damn week.

She'd already checked out the wedding certificate. It gave nothing away. Hector was down as a bachelor, Irene as a widow. They gave the same address. She'd rung Christopher Lampeter and asked why he thought his new stepfather was on the Stock Exchange.

'Mother said so.'

'Did Mother actually say, this is my new husband, he's on the Stock Exchange?'

'No. She said this is my new husband, I do hope you'll be chums.'

'*Irene* said that?'

'Yes.'

'Chums?'

'More or less.'

'How did the business about the Stock Exchange come up?'

'Over dinner one night, I asked Hector what he did, and he said he was a businessman.'

'Just that?'

'Just that.'

'Businessman could mean he manufactured bidets or worked for Colonel Gadaffi or anything.'

'So I said, oh you mean like double-glazing or plastic doo-hickeys for the tops of vinegar bottles, do you?'

'What did he say?'

'No.'

'Communicative guy.'

'So Mother said, Hector's in futures, aren't you, dearest? And he said, yes. And then they both laughed together in an extremely exclusive way, and that was that.'

Penny checked out the Stock Exchange. She also checked out the Commodities Exchange, the Metals Exchange and the Currency Exchange. If any of them had heard of Hector Oakley, they weren't admitting it. She'd gone through Dun & Bradstreet. Zip.

She rang all the H. Oakleys in the London telephone directory. Several of them were single women. Of the rest, none was the Hector Oakley she knew and disliked. It looked very much as though Hector Oakley had deliberately obscured his tracks. If so why?

She'd rung him at the Lampeter house. She pretended to be a *Guardian* Woman's Page reporter looking for a story on Irene Lampeter. He immediately clammed up. 'I *never* give interviews,' he said. She asked Lucas, the cleaning lad, to ring him, pretending to be the cops. Lucas couldn't decide between Lestrade and Sir John Appleby. By the time he'd settled for something off *The Sweeney*, all calls to the Lampeter home were being monitored. No wonder Lucas spent so much time being an out-of-work actor.

Penny said the hell with it. She wasn't planning to waste the best years of her life on Oakley. When she telephoned Tim Lampeter at his London home to tell him so, the phone was engaged. She went back to Chelsea and got into a hot tub. If you needed to think, neck-deep in Dior bath crystals was the best way to do it. How did you track down a guy who seemed to have no past? She couldn't come up with any ideas. Above her head, footsteps stamped on the floor. She distinctly heard a voice shout, 'Dammitall.' Sounded as though Peter Corax, Literary Gent, literary drunk, had run out of gin. Too bad it was pissing down outside.

Wrapped in a white bath sheet, she padded into the kitchen and fixed her favourite meal. Scrambled eggs. Producing good scrambled eggs was the finest of culinary arts. It was one of the reasons she might just possibly break down one day and marry Barnaby. Nobody fixed scrambled eggs like he did.

She sighed.

Marriage. She was against it. She didn't want to be answerable. She just wanted to be her. And whichever way you cut it, marriage meant you were one of a pair.

On the radio, Michael Parkinson was asking a giggly actress which eight records she'd take with her to a desert island, assuming the place was wired for stereo. In between gobbets of biographical detail, she told him.

'And then two years ago, you got the big break,' Parky said kindly.

The actress giggled. 'Yes.'

'You got lucky,' prompted Parky. 'You were picked to play the lead in a revival of Pirandello's—'

'That's right,' said the actress. 'Except it wasn't luck.'

'No?' Parky said. You could tell he didn't want to come right out and ask about casting couches.

'It was predestined. I mean, I knew something big was going to break for me.'

'And how did you know that?'

'My horoscope . . .'

'You believe in horoscopes, do you?'

'Absolutely. I mean, I wouldn't go *any*where without having a reading. There's this marvellous clairvoyant in Maidstone I go to, and she tells me exactly what's going to happen. It's amazing.'

'Let's have record number five,' Parky said patiently. 'Why have you chosen this one?'

'Record number five,' said the actress. She giggled. 'I'd like "Bring on the clowns".'

'Why is that?' Parky did his valiant best to hide the fact he thought one already was on.

'Because it reminds me—'

Penny didn't wait to hear of what. She switched off.

With the scrambled eggs she ate some caviar. Fish was good for the brain, right? After it, she didn't feel any brighter, but she did have an idea. She rang Tim Lampeter's office.

'Before I quit,' she said.

'Quit what?'

'The assignment.'

'You can't do that.'

'Try me.'

'What about the helicopters? I've already made arrangements.'

'OK. Do you have your mother's business engagement diaries for the past five years?'

'I can find them,' Tim said. 'Why?'

'They might provide a clue as to where she met Oakley.'

'I'll dig them out for you.'

'I'll drop in.'

In the Lampeter reception area, she waited on a rural basketwork sofa heaped with Lampeter Design cushions while the receptionist found Tim. She tried not to think blasphemous, but could you really make jelly out of dandelions? And who wanted to wash their face with oatmeal, anyway? Someone showed her into Tim's office.

Half a dozen red-bound diaries sat on his desk.

'Here,' he said. 'I've worked back from a month before they got married, but I can't see anything. To be honest, I hadn't realised how small her involvement in the company had been around then. Look, you can see. She wasn't even here most of the time.'

Penny watched as he riffled through blank pages. Occasionally a name appeared, but Tim dismissed it each time. 'That's nothing to do with Hector . . . No, she couldn't have met him there because I was along on that meeting . . . That's the BBC; we know he doesn't work for them . . . No: Christopher went with her on that one.'

'And when you come right out and ask him what he does for a living, he simply avoids the question?' Penny said.

'Yes. Christopher asked him again last night. He gave one of those phoney sighs and said it was too painful to talk about, and his life had only really begun when he met my mother.'

'And you, of course, jumped in and said, where was that exactly, Hec?'

'Naturally.'

'And?'

'He came out with a lot of guff about the surroundings being unimportant because the minute they set eyes on each other they knew they must always be together. And when we pushed it, he said he couldn't quite remember.' Tim shrugged. 'He always manages not to tell you anything, however insistent you are.'

'What about your mother's personal diaries?'

'She didn't keep one. There were duplicates of these

at home, by the phone, but most of the time she forgot to fill them in.'

'How many of the present staff were here three or four years ago?'

'Most of them, I'd think. A few of the women have gone to get married or have babies. I've asked everyone if they remember anything relevant, of course, but no one does.'

'What about her own secretary?'

'Monica? She's still here. I'll get her to come in.' He talked into a box on his desk. 'She works for me now, actually. I asked her already but she couldn't remember anything particularly significant.'

Monica was somewhere close to ninety and looked as though she'd have a hard time remembering anything at all, relevant or not. A costume museum would have given half its annual budget for her tweed skirt. Her bottle-green sweater was knitted in some loose stitch that gave a casual observer plenty of opportunity to observe casually her pink rayon underwear. If she'd ever had a prime, she'd reached it sixty years back. But though she looked like what was left of the Colosseum, there was nothing wrong with her brain.

'Irene was going through a bad patch then,' she said, groaning into a chair. 'You probably didn't notice, Timothy, being a man.'

Penny resisted the urge to debate the point. 'Any special reason?' she said.

'I imagine she'd got sick and tired of being on her own, and working herself into the ground. She was getting older. The boys were grown and gone. She probably felt there wasn't any point left to anything,' Monica said. Freud in drag. 'Personally I've no need for men, but Irene wasn't like that. She missed her husband dreadfully. I think she felt lonely and isolated. So it was a real blessing when she met Mr Oakley.'

Monica drank firmly from a cup of coffee provided by the receptionist and pushed a plate with some of Christopher's cookies on it away from her. 'Those things stick to the teeth,' she said. 'People are all for something chewy, but not something that they'll need paint-stripper to remove.'

'Did Mrs Lampeter ever say where she met Mr Oakley?' Penny asked.

'No. I already told Tim. I asked her once, and she said they'd met over a business matter.'

'Christopher seems to think he was on the Stock Exchange,' Penny said.

Monica wrinkled up her face and smoothed out a bag in her skirt. 'No, I don't think he can have been,' she said. 'Why don't you ask him?'

'We've tried,' said Timothy. 'He doesn't answer.'

'Did you form any opinion yourself as to where he met Tim's mother, or what he was?' Penny said.

'Some sort of expert on something,' Monica said. 'That's all I can remember Irene saying. Every now and then, she'd say she had to leave for a consultation. Of course, looking back, I can see she was having sex with Mr Oakley. You know all that palaver women go in for when they're meeting a man. Clean underwear, shaved legs, special care over make-up. I couldn't be doing with it myself.' She blinked like a tortoise and slipped a hand into her sweater to twitch at her straps.

'Monica. Please.' Tim had flushed. Possibly because the idea that his mother might still be active sexually had not occurred to him. Possibly because he didn't know about sexual activity. Or felt Monica shouldn't.

'I speak as I find,' Monica said.

'Consultation,' said Penny. 'It's a doctor's word. You have them with Harley Street specialists. With architects.'

'With psychiatrists,' said Tim.

'With trichologists,' Monica said.

'Hector Oakley is a lot of things,' said Penny, 'but I'd bet my bottom dollar a trichologist is not one of them.'

'Anyway, Mrs Lampeter wasn't afflicted that way,' said Monica.

'Interior decorators,' said Tim. 'The upmarket ones. You have consultations with them.'

'Solicitors,' said Monica.

Penny groaned. She'd wear out a finger if she let it walk through all those Yellow Pages checking for Oakleys.

In the end, it was easier than that.

The average female postal worker probably doesn't sound as if she has an olive stuffed up her nose. The one Penny was imitating did.

'Bister Oakley?' she said.

'Yes.' The voice hated to admit it. Poised to take the Fifth Amendment, it wasn't giving anything away it didn't have to.

'This is the bain sorting office,' Penny said. 'We have a parcel for you sent on from your forber address. That *was* id Lundud, wasn't it?'

'Yes,' Oakley said, sounding wary.

'Good. We just wished to confirb that with you.' She knew that if Oakley stopped to think, she could whistle for it. The Post Office might occasionally check destinations but not intermediate points of departure.

'Where's the parcel come from?' he said.

'Greece,' Penny said. It was a shot in the dark but not a wild one. Hector had been there very recently, after all. And he'd said he had relatives there. The shot seemed to hit the target.

'Oh yes?' This time he didn't sound so much as though he were trying to beat the polygraph.

'You can appreciate, Mr Oakley, that we're a little cautious of parcels coming in from that particular locality,' Penny said, easing into the part like a kissogram girl into a gymslip. So genuine only the Postmaster General knew for sure. 'There've been several letter bombs recently, as you may have read.' If he had, he was taking a different paper from Penny.

Subtle stuff. It implied that Oakley was important enough to have a letter bomb sent to him. Would he fall for it?

Not quite? 'Why would anyone send me a letter bomb?' he said.

There were several answers to that one, none of them suitable for a Post Office lady to articulate. 'Weren't you married to Irene Lampeter? Public personae are always at the mercy of cranks,' said Penny.

'But why would they send it to my former address? I haven't lived there for over three years.'

Penny's problem precisely. Why *would* they?

'The Greek Ambassador has urged that we take every precaution,' she said. 'Which is why we're troubling to contact you personally.'

'Has he indeed?'

She could tell the Greek Ambassador was powerful medicine. But not powerful enough. She increased the pressure. 'We have to be especially diligent these days, Mr Oakley. The Post Office does have a responsibility to the public.' Oh, the power of officialdom. People seldom got mouthy with monoliths. Before this one could, she added swiftly, 'It's merely that we can't read the *number*.' There was silence. She thought she'd probably blown it.

'Ninety-two,' Oakley said.

Penny remembered the olive. 'Didety-*two*?' she said, with a hint of vinegar. 'That must be how we got confused. Now, if you could just confirm that street name to us. It looks like didety-seved, you see.'

If he saw that, he'd see that the holes in her story were big enough to drive a dray-horse through.

'92 Westl—Just a minute,' Oakley said. He'd seen. 'It couldn't possibly have been addressed to me there.'

'We'll send the parcel on as soon as it's been checked,' Penny sang.

'Is that you, Lampeter?'

'We appreciate your cooperation, Bister Oakley.'

'Don't think I haven't noticed your watchdogs hanging around.'

'Thank you so buch.'

'This kind of behaviour won't get you anywhere, you know.'

She put down the phone.

She took the tube to Tufnell Park. Westland Road, the only street in the A—Z beginning with those five letters, was a row of identical pink-brown semi-detached villas. On most of them, the bricks had been aggressively painted in white, the window surrounds carelessly painted in blues and purples. They testified to a fresh wave of landlords, ethnic minorities establishing themselves in their new-found-land on their way to assimilation. A woman wearing a gold-edged sari under a cheap cardigan pushed a baby buggy down the road. A thin black boy in a Rasta hair-catcher jigged along the pavement, occasionally pulling leaves off the dusty hedges and sniffing them. Two tiny Chinese children sat on a wall and played pat-a-cake as though it were chess. The air was a heady mixture of gasolene fumes and curry powder, dirt and soy sauce.

Penny liked the whole scene. She liked the acceptance, the urgency, the confidence that things were getting better all the time. She liked the hard workers, the corner shops open half the night, the cafés serving at all hours, the cramped houses full of people who still had a dream to come true.

Number Ninety-two had seen better days. So had the guy who opened the door. If he'd ever had a dream it had been wet and a long time ago. Closer to sixty than he'd ever again be to fifty, his torso was encased in a yellow T-shirt that showed his nipples off to disadvantage. Elasticised braces featuring teddy bears held up his trousers. Some amateur had recently dyed the top of his black hair yellow. He had the rueful mouth of a man who didn't take himself too seriously.

'Yes?' he said. One of his wrists was wrapped in a heavy leather band set with metal studs.

'I'm looking for a Mr Oakley,' Penny said. Behind her, traffic fought its way between cars parked solid on both sides of the street. Westland Road seemed to be a direct link between a major building site and a car depot. Dust-streaked lorries bearing cement mixers and forty-foot-long trailers ferrying ten autos at a time inched past each other at ten-second intervals. It wasn't easy to ignore the march of progress.

'You'll have to keep looking, dear,' the man said.

'There's no Oakleys here, more's the pity. We've got a Veeraswami, or some such. A couple of O'Briens. About nine Muhammed Alis. Two Charlie Chans.' He bent them off on his fingers. 'And Colonel Williams. Let's not forget him.'

'Would he be the lovable old buffer in the ground-floor flat who remembers everyone that's roomed here in the past two decades?'

'Make that five, dear, and you've got him bang to rights.'

'In that case, I'd like a word with him.'

'Except it's days, not decades.'

'Rats,' said Penny.

'Anyway, he's no more a colonel than I am,' said the man. One of his ears looked as if it had been pierced. Unless it was a blackhead.

'What *are* you, just as a matter of interest?'

'The Chief Rabbi. Can't you tell?'

'And I'm Gypsy Rose Lee.' Penny said. She held out her hand.

The man took it. He felt in his pocket and slapped 10p into it. 'What does the future hold for me, Gyp?' he said. His palm was streaked with dark blue paint.

'I see a tall dark stranger,' she said.

'Me too.' The man raised an eyebrow at her and passed a finger under one of his braces. 'The name's Fabian Sykes, by the way.'

'Are you serious?'

'Not terribly.'

A bus trundled by, followed by five or six revving lorries that pushed the carbon monoxide levels up to unacceptable. Penny could feel her lungs crumbling. 'How about inviting me in for a cup of tea?' she said.

'You've got a nerve,' Fabian said. 'I get enough stick from the neighbours for not decorating the outside as it is. If they think I've started letting to your lot, I'll be for the chop.'

'There's nothing as pushy as a man with his property values to lose,' Penny said.

'My God, yes. You don't know what pushy is until you've lived in a gentrification zone like this.'

He stood aside and let her into the house. Penny went into a hall dominated by a chest of drawers and half a bicycle. The floor was bare, sandblasted but unvarnished. Next to a pay-phone on the wall there was a cross-gartered board covered in red felt, stuck with envelopes from all over the world. The wallpaper looked like porridge. You couldn't help but be aware that the plumbing was indoor.

Fabian led the way to the back of the house. It got cosier beyond the remains of a green baize door. The kitchen was entirely navy, from the enamel sink to the glass rolling-pin on the windowsill. There were frilled curtains in a Lampeter print with a matching cover for the toaster. *Homes & Gardens*–type garlic hung tastefully here and there. A smell that was either marijuana or Earl Grey didn't hide the fact that something very major was suffering from wet rot.

Fabian filled the kettle and plugged it in. Penny pulled out a blue-painted bentwood chair and sat down. 'How long have you been here?' she said.

'Just about forever, dear. I was born here. Lived here all my life.' He raised dyed eyebrows. 'I hope you're not from the Social Security. Because if so, it's straight back outside you go.'

'Just making routine enquiries . . .'

'The *fuzz*?' His eyes widened. They exactly matched the blue of the saucepans hanging from the wall.

' . . . about this Hector Oakley.'

Fabian wrinkled his soft pink forehead. 'Have I heard that name somewhere?' he said.

'I'm talking three years back. At least.'

'Three years? With the kind of turnover we get here? What do you think I am, The Amazing Memory Man?' He thought about it, plucking at his hair. 'Actually, the cast list was more or less the same then as now. Fewer Muhammeds and more Chans, of course. Personally, I don't know how the Ayatollah can sleep at night. Driving them all into exile. I'm thinking of getting a sniffer dog, as a matter of fact. These days, you can't be sure they aren't up there making bombs and hiding Armalites under the floorboards when you think they're watching *Dynasty*.'

'No one else?'

'No.'

'Who had Colonel Williams's room then?'

'Colonel,' snorted Fabian. 'Conman, more like. You can always tell. Done time, I shouldn't wonder.'

'Who was in his room then?'

'Oh yes. I'd forgotten about Michael. Michael Ashe. Me and my friend, we usually keep the ground-floor room for the rather more upmarket guests.'

'Bet you get plenty of those.'

'You'd be surprised, dear.'

'Michael Ashe didn't wear a black beard, did he?'

'Practically the only thing I ever saw him wear was a dressing-gown sort of thing, like a monk. Frankly, it did absolutely nothing for him.'

'What did he look like?'

'Medium height. Curlyish hair. Greyish eyes. Poutyish mouth. Oh and if it's any help, he takes size nines. He borrowed a pair of my friend's shoes once to take some woman out to dinner and said they fit perfectly.' He turned the corners of his mouth down. 'Different friend then, of course.' He looked briefly sad.

Terrific. That narrowed the field to a few million. Eliminate everyone who took size nines who wasn't Michael Ashe, and eventually you'd be bound to come up with the genuine article. Would he turn out to be the same article as Hector Oakley? Suck it and see. Penny felt around in her handbag and brought out some pictures she'd taken in Greece. 'Was this him?' she said.

Fabian tutted. 'Whoever told him he looked good in a beard should be cauterised. And the collars on that shirt!'

'Never mind the fashion notes, Fabian. Is it Ashe.'

Fabian shook his head. 'I couldn't say, love. Not really.'

Penny showed him another snap. On this one she'd blocked out the beard. 'What about this?'

'Mmm,' Fabian said. He moved his head about like a person trying to think of something to say about the

98

latest de Kooning. 'Could very well be. Yes. As a matter of fact, I think it is. Yes. That's Michael, all right. But it'd've been nearer four years ago than three that he was here.'

Could this be the crock of shit at the rainbow's end? Because there must definitely be something not quite jake about Hector Oakley. A man with an alias is a man with something to hide. But what? The blue kettle boiled. Fabian took teabags from a blue tin and made tea in a blue pot. When he'd put out blue cups, and milk in a blue jug, he sat down again. He touched the doctored snap. 'Where's that taken, anyway?'

'On a yacht in Greece. Last month.'

'He must have come up in the world.'

'What was he doing here?'

'He wasn't much of a one for girlish chat over the coffee cups, but he did once say this was his big chance to fulfil a lifelong ambition.'

'To live in Tufnell Park?'

'Do you mind? We're on our way up here, you know. Actually, he never explained exactly what he meant.'

'Where was he from?'

'He didn't say, dear.' Fabian poured two cups of tea and passed one to Penny. 'Up North, I'd have said, from the vowel sounds. He hasn't done anything *wrong*, has he?'

'Want to cast the first stone?'

Above their heads, shouting broke out. There was the sound of breaking glass. 'Oops,' Fabian said. 'That's the O'Briens. Honestly, they put you right off marriage, those two. They fight about everything. Do you know, he actually put her into the hospital once, just for saying it was a nice day.'

'Did he leave a forwarding address?'

'God, how I wish he would.'

'Michael Ashe.'

'Oh, I see. No. As as matter of fact, he left without any warning at all. I'd popped down to the club one evening, and when I came back he was gone. Lock, stock and jockstrap. Owing a week's milk bill, I may say. Thank God I get the rent in advance.'

'Shucks,' Penny said. Had the trail back into Oakley's past gone dead that quickly? 'Any visitors?'

'Visitors? My God, they never stopped coming. Sometimes it seemed as though they were arriving every fifteen minutes, day in, day out.'

'What about mail?'

'Yes. A bit.' Fabian widened his blue eyes. 'Hey, I'll tell you what. I might still have a letter that came for him after he'd gone. I didn't have anywhere to send it on, and I didn't like to return it to sender. Might upset someone.'

He got up and went over to a big painted dresser. Overhead, something hit the floor with a joist-shaking crash. Mrs O'Brien, almost certainly, since it was followed by female screams.

Fabian scrabbled about in a drawer and brought out a handful of letters. He went through them, and pulled one out. 'Here. Bet you anything it's from his wife and he's left her. Which is why I didn't send it back. Much better to believe someone's a lousy correspondent than that they're never going to get in touch again.' He pushed fingers through his parti-coloured hair. He looked as if he knew what a bitch life could sometimes be.

'The wife's always the last to know,' said Penny. She pressed down her excitement. Perhaps Oakley was a bigamist. Already married when he got hitched to Irene. Perhaps she found out and threatened to tell. Or at least cut him out of her will. Perhaps Oakley had killed her before she could. Great theory. Except that trying to provoke a heart-attack/stroke/coronary/ whatever was a hit-and-miss way of avoiding exposure.

The letter was dated over two years ago. A small gold lozenge was stuck in the top left-hand corner. Mrs J. Parfitt, it said. With an address in somewhere called Aghia Eufonia. In Greece. 'Can't be his wife,' Penny said. 'The surname's different.'

'Unless he's changed his name more than once.'

'Did he ever talk about his past life?'

'Like I said, he didn't talk at all. Just that one remark about a lifelong ambition.'

Penny stood up. 'Thanks a lot for your help,' she said.
'Any time.'

'If you remember anything else, let me know.' Penny
gave him her telephone number.

Up in the hall they passed a fat girl with bad skin and
a black eye. She wore a sequinned denim waistcoat and
a pair of stretch jeans that needed to stretch a good bit
further. She clattered up the uncarpeted stairs carrying
four bottles of Guinness.

'Mrs O'Brien,' Fabian mouthed at Penny. His eyes
rested on the pay-phone. Snapping his teddy-bear braces,
he said, 'I wonder if Michael still gambles. He was a
proper terror in those days.'

Penny stopped with her hand on the door knob. 'Back
up the tape a little,' she said. 'Oakley—Ashe gambled?'
Possibilities raced through her mind. Hector deep in
debt, being hassled by an enforcer. Hector in desperate
need of ready money. Hector, meeting financially-sound
Irene, working out a way to eliminate her in order to get
his hands on her assets, so he could sell them to the
highest bidder.

'I'll say,' said Fabian. 'Dogs. Horses. Boat race. Rain-
drops down the windows. You name it, he was on the
phone to the bookie about it. More than ready for Gam-
blers Anonymous, we always thought.'

'Carry on.'

'Actually, I think that's why he moved out in the end.
Me and my friend, we decided he must have put next
month's rent on a dog with a wooden leg, and left before
we could ask for it.'

'A compulsive gambler, would you say?' The sort of
man who might woo a woman ten years older than
himself for the possible rewards? The sort of man who
might slip a ring on a woman's finger while already
planning her murder?

'Definitely. But I expect you knew that already, didn't
you?'

9

THERE IS A BASIC DICHOTOMY BETWEEN SHORTS AND THE roar of the crowd. Not many in the former can confidently expect the latter. Footballers, maybe. Tennis stars. The personality on-screen was neither. Without much enthusiasm, Penny watched him clamber around a pile of stones in a pair of khaki ones. Every now and then he brushed at his hair as though it had been invaded by killer gnats.

Penny recognised him as the man who had been Irene Lampeter's special guest on her own TV programme. He appeared beneath a tumbled arch. Behind him glowed the Aegean. The camera panned to a lizard standing on someone's boot. 'As early as 784 B.C.,' he said. It wasn't gonie-grabbing stuff.

Lady Helena watched from the sofa. There was a glass of whisky in her hand. Ash from the cheroot she was smoking fell on to the white carpet. The celeb scrabbled in some kind of trough. The cameraman moved in close to fill the screen with khaki butt, then moved away again. The celeb showed his invisible audience a piece of yellowish dirt. His eyebrows momentarily lost their suave. 'Fine example of pre-Cumaean,' he droned. Beyond him, Penny could see more sea, girdled by islands. To the left, a hazy outline lay close to the water, like a cat settled by the fire. To the right was a two-piece island. The main chunk was large. The other, from this distance, appeared no more than a pyramid of tumbled rock.

'That looks just like the place with the ruined shrine,' she said, 'where Irene died.'

'And so we leave,' the personality said. They watched him turn his head and give a long tragedian's gaze across the Homeric sea to the double island. Odysseus forced to quit his sea-girt Ithaca because of the flighty creature who'd run off with Paris, or Priam, mourning his dead sons, couldn't have been more eloquently sad. It was moving stuff. The shorts killed it.

'You see one shrine to Athena, you've seen them all,' said Lady Helena. There was ash on her suede blouson. She brushed it away. 'The trouble with Greek ruins is that they're so . . . *ruined.*'

'You see one messy smoker, you've seen one messy smoker,' Penny said. 'Just how much longer are you planning to visit?'

Lady Helena stubbed out her cheroot in the Daum crystal ashtray. 'Why do you ask?'

'Because if there's one thing I hate worse than a smoker, it's a messy smoker,' Penny said.

'I am not in the least messy.'

'There was ash in the souffle you made last night.'

'I have to stay until at least the middle of the month.'

'Who says?'

'My stars. Look.' Lady Helena waved a magazine at Penny. 'It says right here. "After mid-month, talk over your insecurities with those closest to you." With your father away, that means you, darling.'

'I knew about your securities. First I heard you'd got insecurities too.'

'The way you nag at me, I'll certainly have some by mid-month.' Lady Helena tapped the horoscope she'd been reading. 'I hope you noticed this bit about my magnetic charm doing wonders for those nearest me.'

'You don't really believe all that stuff, do you?' Penny said.

'In a limited fashion, yes. Lots of perfectly sane people do. I know for a fact that Cornelia Falklend and her husband can't get out of the bath in the morning without a daily forecast from their palmist.'

103

'Their skins were scarlet but their hands were read.'

'More or less.'

'No one could possibly call the Hon. Cornelia perfectly sane.'

'All right. What about that Greek actress?'

'Melina Mercouri?'

'No. The one that only does black and white. You know. Not Garbo, but like that.'

'Tasso?'

'Yes. I know for a fact she visits a clairvoyant. So does Jason Jackson. He told me so, last time we worked together.'

Penny pretended not to notice her mother brushing ash off the coffee table on to the white carpet. She often disapproved of Lady Helena. Love went without saying. And admiration. It must have been disconcerting to find how completely her only child took after its father. Not that Penny's colour had ever closed doors. International high society, particularly the non-distaff side, had always been fond of Lady Helena, and was more than prepared to be equally fond of her daughter.

'Anyway, I'll be leaving sooner than you think,' Lady Helena said. 'Costas Kyriakou is in England and wants to set up another of his business discussions. He's holding some kind of promotional reception at the Rockingham, since the Schumanns are staying there. I shall motor up tomorrow, though I have to leave early.'

'Why?'

'I did tell you. I'm flying out to join Jan Hendriks—'

'That's the loony Dutch professor, isn't it?'

'—so I'll go straight from the Rockingham to the airport.' Lady Helena crossed her elegant legs. 'Jan happens to be one of the world's authorities on Homer.'

'Does he know Kyriakou?'

'Heavens, no. Jan couldn't be less interested in that type. He often says that the very rich are probably the most boring race on earth. The only thing that turns him on is Odysseus. And,' said Lady Helena modestly, 'me.'

'Is Hector Oakley going to be attending this party?'

'Costas mentioned him. I suppose he will.'

'The Lampeters don't live far from the Rockingham Hotel,' Penny said.

'I know.' Surreptitiously Lady Helena rubbed ash into the carpet. 'I expect that means the Lampeter boy will be there. I shall feel bound to talk to him and I really can't like him, though God knows I've tried. I suppose it's not really his fault he doesn't take after his parents. I mean, he could hardly expect to.'

'Why not?' Penny was on her knees with the dustpan. 'Mother, look at this mess. You really are a pain.'

'Because he was adopted. Still, you'd have thought some of it would have rubbed off, wouldn't you?'

'Adopted, huh?' Was the fact in any way significant? Penny couldn't tell. For the moment, she backburnered it. Later, she'd see if it meant anything. 'How about letting that magnetic charm of yours do wonders for me?' she said.

'How exactly?'

'Get me invited along tomorrow.'

'Simple. Costas will be delighted to see you.' Lady Helena sighed and reached for another cheroot. 'Change and decay in all around I see.'

'I hope you're not looking in my direction.'

'I mean Costas. As a young man, he was absolutely riveting. So much energy. He almost seemed to give off sparks. Did I ever tell you about the time he and I went to a ball at the French Embassy in Athens?'

'No. And if you think you're going to now, forget it.'

'Dressed as flamingoes,' Lady Helena said. 'Oh, he was marvellous in those days. Positively pinging with ideas. Now, I'm afraid, there's something about him that's slightly, well, *dubious*.'

'It's called power,' Penny said.

'Maybe dubious isn't a strong enough word. Last time I dined with him, I swear he actually threatened me. Not that he came right out with it, of course.'

'Why should he threaten you?'

'It's this Athena project of his. He more or less implied that if I turned the job down, he'd hang me up by my thumbs until I changed my mind. The frightening thing was the way he seemed to feel he had a *right* to be violent.'

'Listen, Lady H, don't go down any dark alleys with the guy, will you? Just because you drop ash all over my white rugs doesn't mean I want anything to happen to you.'

'Very touching,' Lady Helena said. She lit her cheroot. 'I wouldn't give Costas's stupidity a second thought, except that there was a rumour once about some ex-mistress of his.'

'If you set up as a mistress, rumours go with the job.'

'I can't remember the circumstances exactly, but they were unpleasant. I seem to remember she died rather mysteriously.' She closed her magazine with a snap. 'And guess what: all of us Leos are warned to be careful as there is danger around the third week of the month.'

'Never mind that rubbish. Give me some maternal advice.'

'Oh dear. Must I? It's never really been my forte.'

'I know. But—'

'The thing is, in one's time one has been and done all the things one ought to be advising one's child not to be and do. So it really does seem a frightful cheek on one's part to start handing out precepts and sermons, don't you think?'

'I'm not asking for a sermon, Mother. Or a precept.'

'What, then?'

'Just your advice on this.'

'On what?'

Penny held up the letter she had been given by the soi-disant Fabian Sykes.

Ash fell from the end of Lady Helena's cheroot. 'What is it?'

'Someone else's mail.'

'And what's the advice you want?'

'Should I open it or not?'

'Is it going to help you find anything out about Irene Lampeter's death?'

'Maybe. Maybe not.'

'It's not addressed to you?'

'No.'

'And you came by it more or less illegitimately?'

'Less, probably.'

'Then obviously there's no question about it. You have absolutely no right whatsoever to open it.'

'Agreed.'

'I wouldn't hesitate for a moment, if I were you.'

'I love you when you're maternal,' Penny said.

She examined the outside of the envelope. Might as well try to be professional. Semi-educated writing. Basildon Bond envelope. Pale blue biro. She handed it to her mother.

'What do you make of that, Watson?'

'Not an enormous amount, quite honestly,' Lady Helena said. 'Except rather horrid snobby things.'

Penny slit open the letter and unfolded the single sheet of lined paper inside. The only address was Eufonia.

Dear Bill, [she read]

Well, we finally made it, after all these years of talking about it, and so far we've got no regrets, it's like a dream come true. It's funny after all this time to find Eufonia just the same as it was before, I hope we can make a go of it I really do Bill. Jim seems ever so much better even after only a month, you will come and see us Bill, won't you, it will always be 'open house' for you. You know that.

I don't like to nag you, Bill but if you could see you're way to letting us have some of the £600 back it would be a big help, even over here it costs a fair bit to set yourself up, but if you can't, I suppose we can wait a bit longer, we're used to being a bit tight, aren't we, you and I Bill?

I hope things look up for you soon, Keep Smiling, eh, Bill?

Love from Joan

'Good grief,' said Penny. 'Bill must be another of Hector's identities.'

'Who do you suppose Joan is?' asked her mother.

Penny reread the letter. 'She doesn't sound like a wife.'

'An ex-wife perhaps? Though that reference to the past makes her sound more like a sister to me.'

'Which would mean Hector didn't commit bigamy when he married Irene.'

'Does that matter?'

'Just a good theory gone west. I wonder why this Joan used the name Michael Ashe on the envelope.'

'*I* wonder whether Hector paid back the £600. They sound as if they needed it. Do you think they made a go of it?'

Penny leafed through an atlas for a map of Greece. Eufonia was a small dot further down the coast from the postmark town of Port Faros. 'I may just have to fly out there and see,' she said.

The Rockingham Hotel had once been a Victorian country house, built for a newly rich manufacturer of a patented letterbox guaranteed to leave the mailman's hand on the end of his wrist. Attempts to establish a pedigree had resulted in a letterbox-manufacturer's idea of class. The woodwork was baronial, the fireplaces cathedral-like, the decor heraldic. The grounds spread in all directions, encompassing rose gardens, paddocks and croquet lawns. Beyond lay Cotswold country, rounded and greened with early summer. The gardens were one of the Rockingham's strongest selling points. No one knew how Jason had acquired the capital to purchase it but he had substantially improved the property, adding tennis courts and swimming pools and restoring the small maze that had been allowed to grow wild.

Penny parked her Porsche between a Rolls and a Daimler. It was already growing dark. Above ancestral leaves, the sky had turned school-uniform grey. Most of the house's windows were lit, sending a pinkish glow across lawns and shrubs and mock-Tudor brickwork.

Costas's reception was in full swing in what had once been the ballroon. The room was elaborate with chinoiserie, half-full with one of those crowds that consists of people watching each other watch each other. Calling it motley would be like saying Imelda Marcos was a bit of a spendthrift. Many of those present were shiny-chinned men with small shoe sizes. They were complemented by women in dentures and elaborate spectacles. Moving among them like butterflies round a herd of warthogs was a fair sprinkling of pretty girls with long free tresses which bounced when they walked. There were a lot of City types, balding for the most part, their patrician shirtfronts protestingly white in the sea of maroon and pale blue dress-shirts. Beside them, their mates laughed carefully, in dresses that did nothing for their upper arms. The room smelled rich. Stinkingly so.

Lady Helena, elegant in a dinner-jacket and diamonds, was flirting with a man in a burnous. Costas was talking to Hector Oakley. Penny was too far away to hear what about, but it certainly didn't look like he was asking Hector for a date. Hector was trying to talk him down. Neither of them appeared to be in sunny mood. On Costas's other side, Alexandra stood, faintly smiling, her dark eyes on Theo as he crossed the room to greet Penny.

'When does the fun crowd get here?' Penny said.

'Forget fun,' said Theo. 'Tonight we only got the money crowd. The *serious* crowd.'

A girl with breasts that could have been used to perforate teabags went by with a tray of filled champagne glasses. Penny took two. So did Theo. He stared down the front of her strapless Vicky Tiel.

'How in the world does that thing stay up?' he said.

'That's what I'm always asking Barnaby,' said Penny. She looked round the room. 'Does Costas really need financial backing from this lot?'

'Need doesn't come into it. He just likes to spread the load,' Theo said. 'If anybody's fingers get burned, it's never his.'

'The Mediterranean's answer to JR.'

'Costas makes JR look like Bambi's mother. Only a guy with an ego the size of a barrage balloon would be

109

tin-cupping this particular crowd. At least a dozen of them've already come out on the losing end in deals with Costas.'

'And still remained friends?'

'And still come to his parties. Not the same thing. Would *you* turn down free caviar?'

'Certainly wouldn't.' Penny looked around. 'Where is it?'

'The thing with Costas is,' said Theo, 'he genuinely doesn't give a shit about other people. Listen, I spent the last three months working for the guy—I've seen how he operates. Far as I know, he doesn't tie girls to buzz-saws or hang people out of tenth-storey windows by their ankles, but he's pretty damn unscrupulous. All's fair in love and business: I must've heard him say that a hundred times. And if business includes a little fooling around with someone else's wife, or bribing away someone's best R & D man along with the latest blue-prints, or harassing folk who won't move out to make way for his latest redevelopment scheme, so what? He genuinely believes that when he ends up the winner, he's actually won. That his opponents think he's pretty sharp.'

'What happens if he ends up the loser?'

'Trouble.'

'How often does that happen?'

'Almost never.'

'He seems a bit antsy about this Athena deal. My mama says he threatened her recently. Also, that there have been rumours of mysterious deaths.'

Theo flexed his mouth, one hand in the pocket of his white tuxedo. A good-looking guy. Penny felt her mouth go soft. It often did around men like Theo. Sometimes she wondered if she should see a doctor. She couldn't help noticing Theo'd noticed. 'Surely even Costas . . .' he said. He cleared his throat. 'Ever seen a little old lady with garbage dumped all over the porch and her cat lying on the kitchen floor with its neck broken, courtesy of the Kyriakou Foundation?'

'Not that I remember.'

'I have.'

'Wonder if he's ever considered working for the Salvation Army.'

'Trouble is, I kinda like the guy.'

Penny watched Sibylla Schumann cross the room and move Hector away from Costas. She had on a dress of kumquat silk chiffon and make-up like a wedding-cake has icing. 'Are you and Alexandra still thinking of getting hitched?'

The shoulders of Theo's loosely fitted jacket drooped. 'Thinking is all,' he said. 'Until he lets her loose. He says he can't do without her.'

'I hate to bring this up,' Penny said, 'but she's not exactly in kindergarten. Couldn't she go independent?'

'You could. My sister could. But it's a question of culture clash. Girls in her neck of the woods are brought up to feel second class. Even when they know the system stinks, it's difficult to shake. Besides, she's terrified of what he'd do if she left. Hell. Don't think I haven't suggested running off together, shacking up some place. She won't hear of it.'

'Her heart belongs to Daddy.'

'Not her heart,' Theo said. 'But everything else.' He looked rueful. 'One day she'll pluck up the courage to defy him. And then he'd just better watch out.'

'Sounds dangerous,' Penny said.

Theo shrugged.

Penny lifted the braids on her forehead and let them flop back again. 'How's your wicked stepmother?'

'A real pleasure, these days. Ever since—uh—what happened to Irene, she's been off my back.' Theo smiled down at her. 'I'll go find you some of that caviar.'

Penny worked the room a while. Sybilla had left Hector and was talking with Costas. Tonight her chilly beauty held an enigmatic ambivalence, as though the warm colour of her dress mirrored a hidden fire. Costas, definitely unambivalent, stared down it. Marty watched. As Penny passed them, several of the City men took her arm and told her how well her mother was looking.

Someone in a pale green shirt insisted he'd seen her somewhere before. She told him he most certainly hadn't.

Standing by the windows, a dark man stared at her. His dinner jacket had been tailored by someone who knew what he was doing. He wore his black tie outside a wing collar. Under deep brows, his eyes were hungry. If he was hoping for a midnight feast, he'd got the wrong girl. She'd seen him before, somewhere.

A cold hand fell suddenly on to her shoulder. The shock would have stopped a nosebleed in its tracks. She turned round. Hector Oakley, face as red as a douche bag. He seemed mad.

'I'm surprised to see you here,' he said.

'Why?'

'I was under the impression that this was a purely business do.'

'I'm here to do pure business, Mr Oakley.'

'I want to say something to you, Miss Wanawake, and now is as good a time as any.' Hector pushed his beard out and looked up at her meanly. His red-gold hair curled over his head like a pelt. 'You've been investigating me. Looking into my background.'

'Hell,' Penny said. 'You spotted me.'

'I don't like it.' Hector narrowed his eyes. 'It upsets me.' He moved his head slowly to one side so the muscle rolled.

'Try Pepto Bismol.'

'This intrusion into my private affairs is quite unwarranted. I must ask you to cease forthwith, Miss Wanawake. Otherwise I may be forced to talk to my solicitor.'

'You sound like you've been taking elocution lessons from the Lord Chief Justice.'

Oakley's expression changed. 'Get off my back, you interfering bitch.'

'Don't give me attitude, Mr Oakley,' Penny waited two beats. 'Or should I call you Mike?'

Silence. A dangerous one. Hector Oakley's big hands jerked. Champagne slopped over the edge of his glass. 'What did you say?' His voice had the menace of a rattlesnake. Minus the noise.

Penny stepped back. Ridiculous to feel threatened. Oakley couldn't pull anything. Not in a room full of people. She coughed. 'Michael Ashe,' she said. 'Isn't that what they call you, down Tufnell Park way?'

Until now, she hadn't spent a lot of time wondering what it would feel like to be caught in the kind of grip known as vice-like. Now she needn't spend any. Not the way Oakley grabbed her. He put his face very close to hers. He shifted his shoulders so his jacket bulged. 'Call me anything but Hector and you're in big trouble,' he said.

'Jesus. How will I sleep?' said Penny. She tried to pull away.

Oakley wasn't having it. He shook her. 'I mean it. I've come too far to be stopped now.'

'Where were you headed?'

'That's my business.'

'Maybe this is the end of the line,' Penny said.

'Not yet. Not just yet.'

Perhaps Tim Lampeter's suspicions about him were right. 'Irene's death was kind of convenient for you, wasn't it?' she said. She nodded significantly a couple of times. Sometimes you had to argue from a position of weakness. That was when significant nods could come in useful. She'd read somewhere that the weapon of the weak was the errors of the strong. But she wasn't real sure that Oakley had made any. She added another significant nod. 'You've been awful lucky with your wives, haven't you?' she said.

It was Oakley's turn to step back. 'What the hell do you mean?' he hissed. Hard to hiss without a sibilant, but he made it.

What *did* she mean? Had she stumbled across something? She wondered how easy it would be to get a flight to Athens. And, as if the stumble had somehow given her brain a kick in the crutch, it came to her what it might be that Hector Oakley did on the days he went up to London.

Nah.

Couldn't be.

Too kooky.

But definitely worth checking out. Which she'd do as soon as she could. If she was correct, it had damn-all to do with the Stock Market.

'I need a refill,' she said.

'What did you mean?' Oakley said again. 'Who've you been talking to?'

'I never reveal my sources,' Penny said.

'Interfere in my affairs, and you'll regret it,' Oakley said. 'You don't have the first idea what you're meddling with.'

'I think I'm beginning to.'

'Just leave me alone, girl, and Bob's your uncle.'

He walked away, insouciant as Lew Archer. There was a small hole in his black sock. 'Achilles your heel,' Penny said.

He looked back at her over his shoulder. 'Yes,' he said.

Penny wasn't sure what he meant. She joined Marty Schumann at the bar. He looked down on all fours. The way he and Alexandra were both eating their hearts out, they probably only had a whole one between them. 'Hi,' she said, 'Been here long?'

'We arrived this afternoon,' Marty said. 'Sibylla wanted Jason to show her over the place before this bunch arrived.'

'What did you think of it?'

'It's a terrific set-up he's got here,' Marty said. He lacked enthusiasm. He gestured with his glass. 'Nice place. Nice decor. Superior, you know what I mean?'

'World-class.'

'Thing is, how'm I supposed to compete?'

'You're a gold-medallist yourself, Marty.' Penny kissed the top of his head.

'Like all them antiques and stuff lying about. Fancy furniture. Or that old well in his own bit of the place, all gussied up with lighting and houseplants. Boy, that really tickled Sib's fancy.' He drank heavily from a half-empty glass and gloomily shook his head. 'Where'm I gonna find a well back home?'

114

'Give me running water every time.'

'I'm drunk,' said Marty. She could see he was trying not to look over at Costas, who seemed to be encouraging Sibylla to get inside his clothes. Nature wasn't really fair when it came to handing out life's goodies. If the Nazis were scouting the place for their breeding programme, Costas would have won every time over Marty. But geneticists couldn't judge soul. Wouldn't have known that despite his Beetle body, Marty had a Rolls Royce heart. Trouble was, he didn't improve his chances by dressing like he shopped at Togs for Hogs.

'A drink in the hand is worth two in the bottle,' Penny said.

'Look at him.'

'Who?'

'Zorba the friggin' Greek.'

'Costas?'

'Coming on like goddamned Anthony Quinn.'

'You don't sound drunk to me.'

'Don't I? I am, though. And mad. 'S matter of fact, I'm so goddamned drunk and so friggin' mad that any minute now I'm going to go over and give that bastard something he won't forget in a hurry.'

'A kiss, I'll bet.'

'A punch in the nose.' Marty watched as Penny filled his glass again. 'I just about had all I can take of him.' He passed a hand over his face. 'You know something, Penny. I'd give every cent I've got if I could have Beattie back again. Every last cent.'

'Theo's mother.'

'Best mother in the world, too. Until that piece of crap over there got hold of her. Just like he's got hold of Sibylla. And you know something else?'

'What?'

'If it wasn't for him, she'd be alive today. 'Sa fact. 'San absolute fact.' Now Marty did sound drunk.

'What'd he do?'

Across the room, the dark man who'd been standing by the windows was looking at her and pretending not to. Beside him stood Jasper. He seemed to be explaining

115

how the lighting system worked. She could tell he'd have preferred to be shown how Penny's system worked. It came to her where she'd seen him before. He was the man who'd been tailing her tailing Hector.

Marty's phlegm-coloured eyes filled suddenly with tears. 'How many wives've I had?' he said. His nose had gone red. 'Five? Six? Fact is, the only one I ever loved was old Beattie. That bastard killed her. And you know why? 'Cos she wouldn't let me go in with him on one of his deals. Said it was dirt and we weren't gonna be mixed up in no dirt. She was right, too.'

'What kind of dirt?'

'Porno stuff. For the goddamned flakeheads out there who like to make it with kids. Beattie wouldn't get mixed up in no crap like that. And 'cos she stood up to him, the bastard murdered her. Not only her, but his own wife too.'

Penny looked quickly behind her. 'Don't think I'd go round saying stuff like that, Mr Schumann. Man like Costas might take offence.'

'Screw that.'

'Does Theo know? Or Roxanne?'

'Never told either of 'em.'

'Why not?'

'Long time ago,' Marty said, staggering a little. ' 'Sides. I had to choose between God and—what the hell's the guy's name?'

'Mammon.'

'That's the one. I chose him. But you're right. Guess it's about time they knew.'

'Hey, I didn't say that.'

'Guess I'll go tell Theo right now. Tell the poor kid just what kind of a slob he's nurturing in his bosom.'

At that moment, a woman appeared at the main door of the room. Straps as thin as pencil lines anchored her black dress to her body. You couldn't help wondering what would happen if one of them broke. That was probably the idea. She wasn't anybody's idea of pretty. The face was too strong. The boobs were too small. Her big mouth slashed across her face, curving down at the edges like a scimitar. Yet she stopped the show. Everyone was still familiar with that ravaged face, even though she hadn't made a film for ten years. Katerina Tasso. Film actress. She made Sibylla look like something operating out of a hot-bed hotel.

'Well now,' Marty said. 'If that isn't some hot patootie.' He moved off through the crowd in Theo's direction. He steered his son into a corner between an inlaid commode and a green marble plinth with a bronze statue on it. Nearby, the dark-haired man began eating the earlobe of an ash-blonde.

Penny pushed her way towards the door. She saw Costas shrug off Sibylla as though she were an earwig who'd landed on his arm and limp over to where Katerina Tasso waited for him. The gold-headed cane tapped at the parquet flooring with each step. She kept one hip slightly raised. It was the pose of a model. Or a courtesan. Flecks of silver glinted as she breathed. Did anyone else notice the way she stiffened as Costas pulled her towards him and full-bloodedly kissed her? The way she tried to turn away her head? In Penny's experience, there were only two reasons a woman did that. Halitosis. Or hostility.

'Costas.' Tasso's voice was scratchy and full of sexual invitation.

'Katerina.'

'Are you not surprised to see me?'

'Not in the least. I knew you would return one day,' Costas said richly. He took Tasso by the arm. 'My dear, you came only just in time. I was about to cut my throat with boredom.'

Sibylla really loved it.

10

PENNY WAS UP EARLY THE NEXT MORNING. SHE WANTED to talk to Jason. Last night had been no good, since he was far too busy fussing round dining-tables and checking wines. The connecting door between the small dining-room and Jason's private quarters was locked. She stepped outside.

Over her head the exuberant roofs of the house were outlined against a sky as clear as the inside of a mussel-shell. For a moment, the silence stunned her. Then something cawed rudely in a tree; a rabbit bounced across the lawns which slid away from the foot of the hotel towards lush plantings; lilacs stirred beside the entrance. At an iron-barred basement window a man in a green apron was morosely cleaning shoes. He brightened at the sight of her legs. She walked round the side of the house and along a pleached avenue of some kind of sweet-smelling tree whose name escaped her.

At the end of it was a curlicued iron gate set in a stone wall. Through it she could see a dewy lawn, the maroon leaves of a copper beech, a bronze child peeing into the mouth of a carp. Unless the carp was spitting at the child.

She pushed open the gate. Jason's cottage had probably figured in a hundred British Tourist Board leaflets. It was thatched. It was half-timbered. Clematis rioted round the door. The garden was stuffed with cottagey flowers.

Once it had been the gamekeeper's cottage. These days it was linked to the hotel. Any gamekeeper unexpectedly finding himself in the long low living-room now wouldn't have known where to put himself for chintzy fabrics, stripped pine panelling and Constance Spry flower arrangements. Turning the handle of the French windows, Penny found they were open. She went in.

One hundred per cent pure wool carpeting mossed the room as far as the door. The hall beyond was mostly taken up with stairs. Long since stripped of gamekeeper varnish, they had been buffed to a sticky sheen with beeswax. A copper bowl of potpourri stood on an oak chest. Upstairs, the only sound was a drip from a bathroom.

She moved over hooked rugs and opened another door. The single large room that doubled as kitchen and dining-room had once been pantry, gamelarder, scullery and coal-shed. Jason had torn out the interior walls and painted them white, leaving the odd artful beam. The fittings were tasteful. Modern appliances hid behind antiqued walnut. One end of the room was taken up by a giant Welsh dresser of stripped pine, complete with coops underneath for the chickens. Dump a chicken inside today and it would keel over in ten seconds flat, asphyxiated by lavender polish fumes. In the centre of the stone flagged floor was a pane of thick greenish glass.

Was this the well that Sibylla had taken a shine to? Penny peered down. It must have been the water supply when gamekeepers really lived in the gamekeeper's cottage. Some fronds pressed themselves up against the glass, searching for light. On the nearest wall was a switch and she flicked it on. Hidden bulbs lit up the well-shaft, illuminating from below a variety of small ferns that clung to the smoothly rounded sides. Peering through the glass, Penny could see far below the dead glint of water, smooth and black as molasses.

And something else.

White, and black. A sleeve.

And fingers.

Oh, Jesus.

Set into one edge of the glass was a brass handle sunk flush with the floor. You didn't need brains to figure that the glass could be raised. But how? It must weigh, if not a ton, certainly a hundredweight. Pulley wheels were attached to the wall. There was another set into the ceiling directly overhead, but no ropes were threaded over them. She tried to lift the glass, hooking her finger through the handle. She might as well have tried to straighten up the Leaning Tower of Pisa.

Below, in the thick black water, the fingers hung without moving, manicured, elegant. Pale hands I loved. The white of a shirt cuff showed greenly in the water, fuzzed as though seen through a silk screen, edging from the sleeve of a jacket. No rings. For a single terrifying moment, Penny thought it might be her mother. They'd said goodbye the previous night but Penny hadn't watched her drive away. Suppose she'd come back for something. Suppose . . . But the shape of the hands was wrong. It had to be a man. If, indeed, the arm belonged to a torso and wasn't simply floating there, unbodied.

She took the polished oak stairs two at a time. At the top, a wide landing. A Chinese rug, exquisite in creamy rose and green. Doors. A half-open lavatory papered in a Lampeter design of forget-me-nots, to tone with the blue-lilied Victorian porcelain fittings.

'Jason,' Penny called.

Silence.

'Jason. Where are you? Wake up.'

Behind one of the doors there were stirrings. A croaky voice called. Penny pushed it open. Jason was trying to sit up in a carved bed shaped lke a giant peapod. The sheets matched his lime-green silk pyjamas. His curls were awry.

'What in God's name . . .' he said. He tried to squint at a bedside clock on the table beside him. Limply he batted at it. Some pills and a jar of face cream fell to the floor. He located a pair of glasses and put them on. 'Six bloody thirty,' he said. He took the glasses off again and collapsed back on to his pillows.

'Jason, there's something in your well.'

'I know there bloody is. It's called water.'

'A body,' Penny said.

'A what?'

'Or maybe it's just an arm. A man's arm.'

Jason began squawking. Penny would have done too, if she'd known how. Although it was early, the one thing she really wanted was a Jack Daniels.

Jason got out of bed. He found a lime-green robe and put it on. His dark green morocco slippers slapped indignantly against the wooden stairs as he bustled down to the kitchen.

'What are you doing here, anyway?' he said. 'These are my private quarters.'

'The door was open. So I came in.'

The two of them stood at the edge of the well and looked down through the glass. The ferns didn't move. The arm still lay there.

'Jesus Christ,' said Jason. 'This is too bizarre.'

'Do you recognise it?'

'The hand, do you mean? Or the sleeve? Are you asking me to suggest who tailored it, or guess the shirtmaker or what? Jesus God, how on earth did it get in there?'

'I thought you might know.'

'Me? *Me?* I hope you don't think I had anything to do with this.'

'Who is it?'

'How the hell should I know? You tell me.' Jason's skin matched his pyjamas now. He looked like a hungover snapbean.

'One of your guests?' Penny said. 'Marty Schumann? Theo? Costas?'

'What on earth would Costas be doing down there?' Jason's face faded suddenly into grey. He lurched against the table.

'You're in shock,' said Penny. 'Where's the brandy?'

'Brandy? God, yes. Over there, by that baster thing. Pour us both a big one. I feel as if I'm going to heave.'

'I shan't clean it up if you do.'

A baster with a red rubber bulb lay on the counter, next to a frosted green bottle of Armagnac. Penny poured two big measures. Jason slurped his into his mouth, spilling some on the velour lapels of his dressing-gown. 'Oh God,' he said, 'How did you find it?'

Penny told him.

'I should have known,' he said dramatically.

'How could you possibly?'

'I was warned.'

'By whom?'

'The stars. They said there would be a period of difficulty, commencing on the twelfth. But what's it doing there?' His voice started to climb. 'How did it get down my well?'

'Involuntarily,' Penny said. 'I guess we can count on that.'

Jason began to shake. 'The police,' he said. 'Someone better call the police.'

When it arrived, the fuzz didn't take to Jason. Maybe it didn't like hoteliers. Maybe it had a thing about guys with liquor on their breath at seven in the morning. Maybe it just hated lime green. Whatever, it had him tagged for the murderer from the word go. Pale as a nun's back, he kept on saying he hadn't done it. The fuzz kept on not believing him.

Once the pathologist had seen the body *in situ*, a species of block and tackle dragged it up out of the well for a further examination. Nobody had been surprised to find that the muddy face of the corpse belonged to Costas. Heads had already been counted and no one else's was missing. Once it had been removed to the mortuary in a white polythene body-bag, the questioning had begun. A team of CID men talked to everyone still in the hotel. It wasn't long before the scenes-of-crime officer had established that Jason worked out for a couple of hours every day in the hotel's gym. They eyed his muscles. They decided he could have pulled up the glass panel and dropped Costas down the well.

Jason had protested loudly. 'You think I wear my underpants over my tights or something?' he screamed. His mid-Atlantic accent had travelled. Now it was definitely trans. 'Leap tall buildings in a single bound?'

'Oh,' said the fuzz. It raised its eyebrows. 'Would those be women's tights?' It made a note.

'What I mean is, you're trying to make me out to be some kind of Superman,' screeched Jason. 'If I could lift that well-cover, do you seriously think I'd be running a hotel?'

The fuzz said it wasn't qualified to say what Mr Jackson would be doing if he wasn't running a hotel.

'I'd be digging the Channel Tunnel with my bare hands is what I'd be doing. Winning gold medals for weight-lifting. Do you know how much that glass weighs?'

The fuzz said it hadn't the faintest idea.

'Neither have I,' said Jason. 'All I do know is that without the pulley ropes, I couldn't begin to budge the damn thing.'

The fuzz remarked it was a funny thing about the pulley ropes, wasn't it? The way they'd gone missing.

'Whoever shoved Costas down the well took the ropes out to throw suspicion on me. Can't you see that?' demanded Jason.

Without saying as much, the police indicated that whoever shoved Costas down the well was standing right there in front of them in a pair of lime-green pyjamas that they personally wouldn't have been seen dead in.

'You have to be out of your tiny minds,' Jason said.

One thing really burns the fuzz up, it's being told its mind is tiny. It tightened its mouth and checked the pulley wheels attached to the wall. It came up with some dust on its forefinger. It got a man to climb up a stepladder and look at the wheel on the ceiling. That was dusty too. 'Long time since there were ropes on those wheels,' it said. It asked again how many hours a day Jason spent in the gym. The implication was clear. Anyone with hands could have lifted the glass panel using the pulley. Only a superfit one—the kind who worked out every day in a gym, for instance—could have managed without.

'Why?' Jason said.

'Someone managed to lift that glass panel in the last eight hours.'

'It certainly wasn't me.'

The fuzz bunched its lips together.

'Anyway, the ropes were there last night,' Jason said. 'They're always there.'

'How come the wheels are dusty?' asked the fuzz.

'I can't imagine. My housekeeper's probably got better things to do than go round dusting pulley wheels.'

'But the ropes went *over* the wheels, Mr Jackson. There couldn't have been dust on them if there were ropes over them too.'

'I didn't kill Costas. He might have been a bastard, but I didn't kill him,' insisted Jason.

'Funny that he was found in your personal kitchen, then.'

'All my friends knew about the well. It could have been anyone.'

'Perhaps you'd like to come down to the station and make a statement,' the fuzz said.

'I most certainly would not like,' Jason said.

The fuzz didn't give him a lot of choice.

Enquiries came up with a final sighting of Costas inserting the key into the door of his hotel room at around two o'clock in the morning. He'd been alone. How and why he had shown up in Jason's part of the building an hour or so later was a bit of a teaser. It wasn't the place a would-be murderer would choose for a rendezvous—unless the would-be murderer was Jason. But if the murderer had killed him elsewhere, the risk of being seen dragging him into Jason's place was enormous. Unless the well itself had determined the choice of meeting place. As Jason said, it hadn't been kept a secret. Death had later been confirmed as taking place around three o'clock. There was no water in the victim's lungs. He'd been drugged with some kind of tranquilliser and hit on the head before he was put down the well.

The police seemed to think that Jason had invited Costas for a late-night business discussion, that things had got heated and Jason had solved the dispute by bashing Costas on the head. Faced with a dead body, he had to dispose of it. What more suitable place than a handy well? According to the police theory, sooner or later the body would have settled completely under the water. It was just Jason's bad luck that P. Wanawake had come poking around before it could do so.

So far, all that stood between Jason and a murder rap was the fact that the only person the police had come up with who could single-handedly raise the glass floor panel was the Home Counties Heavyweight Boxing Champion who happened to be a sergeant on their own force. With ropes threaded back on to the wheels, and a hook through the floor-flush brass handle, it was easy. Not without. But by the time they'd checked with Jason's accountants that his financial position was kind of dicey, they had their motive. When they learned further that interest rates on the loan were being hiked, that one of the bankers involved was talking about unsound investments, that key staff were being bribed away and that Costas had been behind all three, they felt that their suspicions were justified. Although Jason hadn't been charged, things looked kind of black.

Interviewed in her turn, Penny had pointed out that he was far from being the only person at the Rockingham that night who might have a motive for knocking off Costas Kyriakou. Quite apart from sundry disgruntled business rivals, she could think of at least five. Marty Schumann, for instance. Sibylla had been all over Costas that evening and jealousy often leads to murder. Plus the fact that he seemed to think Costas had been responsible for his first wife's death. He might present an amiable face to the world, but he couldn't have got where he was unless there was a streak of ruthlessness in him. Or Sibylla herself. Admittedly they both seemed to have an alibi, she and Marty having stated that they went to their room at about twelve-thirty and stayed there together the rest of the night. But it could be broken: they hadn't stayed awake all night, had they? and Sibylla could be classed a woman scorned. A woman humiliated in the way Costas knew best. Onedownmanship. Even Patient Grizelda might have run amok at being publicly labelled a bore.

Or suppose Marty *had* told Theo that Costas had been responsible for his mother's death. Suppose Theo had suddenly gone crazy. Had lured Costas into the kitchen and killed him.

She couldn't say any of this to the cops. Not without feeling like a stoolie. So she didn't even mention Alexandra, who might have gotten sick of the meltdown of prospective husbands, of always playing second fiddle instead of the solo. Nor did she bring in Tim Lampeter, who lived only a walk away from the hotel. It would have been an easy matter for him to nobble Costas, arrange a meeting, knock him on the head and stuff him down the well. Hit an accountant in the wallet and you hit him where it hurts most. In the manoeuvres for control of the Lampeter Group, there was an awful lot of money at stake.

'From what I was told, half the guests there had some kind of grudge against Costas,' she said.

'You wouldn't be trying to teach us our own business, would you, Miss Wanawake?'

'Hell no. Just to broaden your mind.'

'Thought it was supposed to be travel did that.'

'Yes, but . . .'

'I went to Ibiza for my holidays,' the fuzz said, leaning back in its chair and fiddling with a ballpoint. He pronounced it Eye-beezer.

'Oh well, in that case . . .'

Ibiza, for chrissakes. Sometimes there was no talking to people.

As it happened, finding an available flight to Athens turned out to be easy. It was early in the season and there was still plenty of room on the scheduled airlines. The plane was barely a third full, the passengers predominantly businessmen in confidence-inspiring suits. There were a couple of women with blonde-streaked hair and fur coats. In June, yet. Obviously trying to prove something. Probably the size of their husbands' disposable assets.

Once they had taken off, the flight attendant announced

that since there was plenty of room, people were at liberty to move about the plane or change their seats as long as it was understood that the captain would have a stroke if they didn't observe the No Smoking and the Fasten Your Seat Belt signs if or when they showed.

Someone immediately took the seat across the aisle from her.

'Hello there. I'm Paul Leandro.' The man smiling at her was dark-eyed, dairk-haired, dazzlingly-shirted. He hadn't seen thirty-nine for some time, but was still fighting off forty. His accent was New England, his antecedents unmistakably Grecian. Second generation, Penny would have guessed.

'Fascinating,' she said.

'Are you going on holiday?'

'Why?'

'I wondered if you had visited Athens before.'

'I've been visiting Athens since they finished the Acropolis.'

'Do you speak Greek?'

'No.'

'Then I should be delighted to place myself at your disposal if you wished to sightsee. Also my car.'

'Nice try, fella. Afraid I'm heading for somewhere called Port Faros.'

'But how very fortunate,' said Leandro. 'So am I.'

'Since when?'

'A second ago.' Leandro smiled. Very smooth. Very confident. Probably very successful, too.

'Your routine needs a facelift,' Penny said. She leafed through *Time* magazine.

'I'd be happy to drive you wherever you wish to go.'

'Will you also be happy if I throw up on the upholstery?'

Leandro paused.

'See, I get awful carsick on long journeys,' said Penny.

'Of course I shouldn't mind,' Leandro said eventually. 'I fell in love with you the first minute I saw you.'

'The last minute I saw you, it looked like you were handing the same line to some blonde piece of fluff.'

'So you *did* notice me at Mr Kyriakou's reception.'

'I could hardly help it.'

'I noticed *you*. I told myself, "Paul, you will not be able to rest until you have made love to that *beautiful woman*." '

Penny laughed. 'You must think I just got off the bus,' she said.

'Don't you believe in love?'

'Love is what you just scored, wise guy. So beat it, before I call the attendant.'

'My card.' From a Gucci purse as soft as a sow's ear, Leandro pulled an embossed card and laid it gently on Penny's knee. 'If you should change your mind . . .'

'I won't.'

' . . . call me.'

Penny picked up the card. Without looking, she tore it in half. She dropped the two halves on the floor. 'Wake it, dude,' she said.

Smiling, he waked.

Penny went on reading *Time*. She got a global view of America's current financial situation. It seemed depressed. She read about giant long-term loans to emerging nations and the need for economic stability. Under 'Milestones,' she learned that an ageing blonde film actress had recently married, she for the eighth time, he for the seventh. Sounded like one of the ones made in heaven, all right. She read that some former sports star was seeking bankruptcy. Win a few, lose a lot.

She turned to a copy of *Vogue*. She liked keeping up with what was cooking in the fashion world. A double spread featured some etiolated women in a variety of jungle prints, gyrating along a catwalk with hibiscus blossoms behind their ears. *CASAUBON GO-GOES GAUGIN*, ran the shoutline. The models didn't seem to care much about anything. Neither did Penny. No way she was going to wear colours like that. Pixie Casaubon, the diminutive Washington-based designer, was a good friend of hers, but she only ever wore white. You got better vibes that way.

She tried to imagine who would look good in them. Someone with Katerina Tasso's dramatic colouring, per-

128

haps. Or someone young. The police investigating Kyriakou's murder had let Tasso go after the briefest of interrogations. They were basing their lack of suspicion on the fact that someone with bones like Tasso's couldn't have raised the well-cover. She wondered about Tasso and Kyriakou. Had they been an item? If so, it certainly hadn't hit the headlines the way Kyriakou's other affairs had. And anyway, what woman stiffened like that when the man she was screwing kissed her? It couldn't have been the fact that they'd had an audience. No actress undervalues publicity. Penny tried to think.

Say they were a number. And say they were on the outs. Or about to be. Could Tasso have rubbed Kyriakou out before he could give her the push?

Whichever way you looked at it, it seemed unlikely.

On the other hand, while she was in Greece, it wouldn't hurt to take a further look at Tasso. An in-depth profile. Just out of curiosity. Not that Kyriakou's death was anything to do with her. She was tracking Hector Oakley, that was all.

She turned her face against her seat and let the back down as far as it would go. She told herself to try to catch some sleep. Try not to think about the full white shirt front, the dangling fingers under the green water. Try not to remember a woman's body dressed for seduction, a woman's mouth fleetingly registering dislike and fear.

She remembered something else. She reached down. The two halves of Paul Leandro's card still lay on the floor. Picking them up, she stowed them in her bag. You never knew what would come in handy. Waste not, want not.

Besides, he had a terrific smile.

11

PENNY TOOK A BUS FROM THE TERMINAL AT KIFISSOU
Street in Athens. She was glad she was fit. A long
journey in a Greek bus probably equalled two weeks on
an Outward Bound course. Although the bus wasn't
crowded, a toothless lady shared her seat, along with
two small boys. Penny was a pushover for small boys.
Large or small. Especially the kind with big brown eyes
and skin the colour of fino sherry. It seemed dumb to let
a lap go begging.

The bus trundled through the early morning streets
and headed on out for the hills. Once the child on her
knee had fallen asleep, Penny did too. It wasn't easy.
The bus smelled of herbs and old clothes and motor-oil.
It bumped a lot. Not surprising, with the suspension
gone. Dawn came up over the skyline, pink and glittery.
There was mist down in the hollows under the olive
trees. Summer heat hadn't yet burned away the spring
flowers.

The driver saw dozing off as a comment on his ability.
A rude one. He took offence. As soon as anyone got
their head down, he sounded his horn, or shouted at
something in the road. Chickens, it might be, or a goat
tethered at the roadside. Once a donkey with a hearing
problem and a wooden saddle slowed them down to
walking pace for a half-mile, deaf to the honks and
curses behind him. No one in the bus was. Once, a
Bentley in two tones of brown overtook them in a spurt
of roadside gravel. The bus driver, piratic in a red knot-

ted scarf, immediately floorboarded and took off after it, leaning on his horn and peering through the distraction of pin-ups, saints and waving plastic hands which decorated his windscreen. Several of the passengers prayed.

Penny dozed and woke and dozed. The skies lightened. The sun hotted up. Outside, thistles flourished beside fruited lemon trees. A high-hatted black-skirted priest, long hair gathered at the neck, waved as they passed. From grilled windows dark faces peered between geraniums. Oranges grew. They came to Port Faros. Penny said goodbye to the little boy, the little boy's mother and the little boy's brother. She said goodbye to the people in the seat in front and the people in the seat behind. Also those on the other side of the aisle. Finally she said goodbye to the driver. He took it personally.

Out in the open air, it was already hot. She could feel the heat of the hardbaked earth through the soles of her white top-siders. There were yellow concrete hotels here, and even a triangle of municipal flower beds with a small statue of someone unmemorable standing among them. Outside one of the hotels stood a Bentley in two shades of brown. There was a strong smell of dead fish. Penny hefted her white leather grip and sauntered over to the quay. There wasn't much else to saunter over to. She hung about, admiring the yachts. Admiring, also, the boat bums doing nautical things to them in cut-offs. Most of the bums had once been white. Now they were the colour of heirloom cherrywood.

Penny strolled up and then down. It wouldn't take long. Eventually one of the bums, crouched over a hand-bearing compass, called out to her. She stopped.

'Looking for someone?' he said.

'Just a ride,' she said.

'Where to?'

'A place called Eufonia. Know it?'

'Sure. It's three hours' sail from here.'

'I'll pay.'

'Come aboard,' the bum said. He grinned. 'I've got some ouzo.'

She stepped on to the mooring warp to bring the yacht closer, then swung over the guard rail on to the deck.

'You've done that before,' the bum said. He stood with his back to the mast, watching her. He had pale blue eyes and a New Zealand accent. He was enjoying her white duck pants and halter top. So he should.

'Just a Sunday sailor,' Penny said. It seemed politic not to let on that he was right. Whatever they say, men don't like a woman who moves at the same speed they do. Anyway, sailing ranked as her least favourite activity, or close to it. She repressed a shudder. The Fastnet Race, crewing for Lady Helena. Gaahd. But it was either hitch a ride on a boat or wait around for the ferry, which she'd already learned wouldn't hit Eufonia until early evening.

'I'm Hans,' the bum said.

'Hi. I'm Penny Wanawake.'

'Welcome aboard, Penny.' Hans handed her a glass of ouzo and water. It had never been her favourite tipple. Anywhere else in Europe, it tasted like toothbrush rinsings. In Greece, it tasted like warm toothbrush rinsings. Before she drank, Penny poured some over the side. Here's looking at you, Poseidon. It was as good a way as any to ensure safe passage.

After a while, they cast off. Penny lifted the stern anchor, while Hans steered them out into the channel. As they headed towards the open water, he told her he was sailing his yacht round the world in easy stages before going back to his job as an accountant in Wellington. He said he'd be glad to sign her on as crew, for as many of the stages as she liked.

Penny said she'd raincheck that one, if he didn't mind. They tacked about a bit. All around them the islands humped out of the water, blue-misted, superimposed on each other so that sometimes they seemed one island, sometimes many, changing as the boat moved between them, looking for wind. After a while they found some. It took them six hours of hard beating to get to Eufonia. Above them, the pitiless sun. Below, the boundless sea. Great.

Eufonia was a few houses circling a small harbour. One arm gave way to rising dunes, topped by the ruins of a small castle. Through fields of spring flowers, it faced the great cliffs of Ithaca across a strip of blue-grey sea. The hinterland rose sharply behind the hamlet, olive-spotted and spiked with cypresses. Small white buildings gleamed in the sun. Men sat in tavernas under twined trellises of vine leaves. Beads clicked. Bouzouki music came softly from the bar five steps from their mooring.

'These people you're looking for,' said Hans. 'Ask Nikolas, in the bar. He knows everything.'

Money changed hands. Penny went ashore. She asked for Parfitt. Nikolas pointed to where the houses clustered midway along the little jetty. 'Behind,' he said. 'In restaurant.'

Black-clad women sat on hard wooden chairs knitting as Penny walked along the single cobbled street. They made comments as she passed. Some called after her. What they called sounded rude.

The restaurant looked like all the other houses in the street. A wooden chair was posted outside the door, flanked by geraniums in cut-down gasolene cans. A glazed tile in yellow and green was set into the stucco above the threshold. The door from the street opened into a room full of small tables. It could have doubled as a morgue. Light blue composition tiles covered the floor. The walls were high and white and stark. The lighting was merciless. A vast glass-fronted counter spread across one end of the room, filled with metal trays of stuffed courgettes and aubergines, round white plates of tomatoes cut up with pink onions, portions of moussaka.

Doors led out to a dusty courtyard full of orange trees, with tables set out underneath. Penny called. After a while a woman appeared in a checked apron. Under a wild bush of gingery hair she had the face of someone who'd lived with Excedrin headache No. 126 since childhood. She reminded Penny of rickets.

'Hi,' Penny said. She ordered a carafe of white wine. When the woman brought it, she asked her to sit down.

The woman cast a guilty look back at the door to the kitchens.

'Go on,' Penny said.

'Well . . . ' said the woman. 'Oh, all right. Just a glass, though. It's nice to hear an English accent. It's still early in the season for tourists.' She sat down.

'My name's Penny Wanawake,' Penny said. 'And you're Joan Parfitt, is that right?'

'How did you know?'

'Nikolas told me.'

'Oh, him. He knows everything.'

'Also,' said Penny, 'I was talking to your brother Hector.'

Joan put her glass down on the table with a small thud. She moved the headache an inch down her face. 'My brother's name is William Beech,' she said. She didn't look at Penny.

'Guess I must have meant Bill,' Penny said.

'Who are you? What do you want?'

'Your brother owes you some money, doesn't he?'

'Yes, but . . .'

'I've come to pay it back. With interest. Bill said to be sure to tell you he's real sorry he's taken so long about it.'

The woman visibly relaxed. Penny'd noticed before how visibly relaxing money could be. 'Well, fancy,' she said. 'After all this time. Jim and I had really given up hoping he'd ever . . .' She swallowed some wine. Delicately, not looking at Penny, she said, 'Are you—uh—*going* with Bill?'

'We're just good friends,' Penny said.

'How is he? It's ages since I heard from him.'

'How long?'

Joan frowned. She bit her lip, thinking about it. 'I hadn't realised. Over two years. Goodness. Is he all right?'

'Naturally he's kinda depressed at the minute,' Penny said. 'Being a widower and all.'

'But Delia died *years* ago,' Mrs Parfitt said. 'He can't still be—'

'Who the hell's Delia?'

'Hasn't he told you about her? She's his wife. Or she was. She died, what, it must be nine or ten years ago now.'

'Poor old Bill,' said Penny. 'And they say lightning never strikes twice.'

'Delia wasn't struck by—'

'It's awful bad luck to be widowed twice.'

'Twice? I didn't know Bill had married again,' said Mrs Parfitt. Her voice tailed off.

'*I* didn't know he'd been married before,' said Penny. So she'd been right. There'd been more than one wife. How many more?

'What happened to his—uh—second wife?' Mrs Parfitt asked. She looked as if she didn't really want to know the answer.

'They were on holiday, right here in Greece, as a matter of fact, and Irene—that was her name, Irene— and she just died.'

'Oh my God. How?'

'She had a heart attack.'

'Poor Bill,' said Mrs Parfitt.

'Kinda tough on Irene, too.'

'But to lose two wives,' Mrs Parfitt said. 'Both in the same way.'

'You mean Delia also had a heart attack?'

'They probably gave it some fancy medical name, but that's what it amounted to, yes.'

'Gee. That's some kind of coincidence, isn't it?'

'It was terrible,' said Mrs Parfitt. 'Really terrible. Jim—that's my hubby—and I were right there when it happened.' She shook her head, remembering.

'What *did* happen?'

'We'd come on a package holiday to this place called Port Faros,' Joan said. She poured more retsina. 'It was just after Delia's father died, and Bill—my brother— thought she could do with cheering up. And Jim'd been saying for years that we'd have a holiday in the sun one of these years, do a bit of sailing—he kept a little dinghy at Portsmouth that he used to potter about in—so we scraped the money together and came along too. And then Bill had this place he wanted Delia to see, that he'd read about in a book—always a great reader, was Bill—and he would have it we all had to sail off and find it.'

'A shrine, was it?'

'It might have been. I can't remember now. A shrine or a ruin or some such thing. Something to do with one of those old Greek goddesses we used to learn about in school. Who was the one who stood for wisdom? Aphrodite, was it? I can never remember.'

'Athena.'

'Something like that. Anyway, we sailed over to this little island. Well, more like a bit of rock, really, miles out in the sea. And we anchored just off-shore—ever so pretty—and had lunch.'

'Lots of wine, I expect,' Penny said, pouring some more into both glasses.

'Oh, I really shouldn't . . . Yes, well, we were younger then, didn't get hangovers and headaches and so on.'

'So you swam ashore or took the dinghy—'

'Jim and I swam. Bill brought Delia in the dinghy. She was terrified of the water, poor girl, not being able to swim. I remember he nearly capsized her, getting in. She screamed, went quite white and breathless. Poor Delia. She always hated to look silly in front of Bill, him being so sporty. Tennis and running and that.'

'And halfway up the hill, she suddenly had an attack, did she?'

'Yes. We didn't know what to do, miles away from anywhere, like that, and no one to help. By the time we got her back to the nearest inhabited place—which was here—she was dead. It was dreadful. Just dreadful.'

Penny nodded. 'I can imagine.'

'I'd never seen anyone dead before. Dead drunk,' Joan said, with a small dry laugh, 'but not actually dead. I've never forgotten it. And poor Bill was distraught. Ever so cut up about it. He kept blaming himself. Kept saying if only he'd known.'

'Known what?'

'About Delia's heart trouble. It turned out she'd been under the hospital for tests only a month or two before and they'd found out she had this weak heart. Only, by the time the results were sent out to her, she was already dead. Bill kicked up ever such a stink about it. But that couldn't bring her back, could it? Oh dear, the number of times I've heard him say he'd give it all away if that would only bring Delia back.'

'Give all what away?'

'Delia's money. That her dad left her in his will. What with that and the factory, it was quite a sizeable sum. Plus the insurance. All Bill's, of course. She left everything to him. Funny, really, the way things turned out.'

'Like?'

'Well, I mean, Bill went to work for Delia's dad straight from school. At sixteen. And then he ended up owning the whole place. Not to mention the way Jim and I finished up here, in spite of what happened. When Jim's asthma never seemed to get better, and the doctor started talking about a change of climate, we decided we'd sell up and come out here. Make a fresh start. And we'd never have seen it if it hadn't been for Delia dying like that. Funny really.'

'Deliriously.'

A man called out from somewhere behind the big counter.

'That's Jim,' said Joan. 'I'd better go and see what he wants.'

'Mrs Parfitt.'

The woman stood. 'Yes?'

'Why did you send letters to your brother addressed to someone called Michael Ashe?'

For a moment she rubbed her hands over her apron, staring at Penny's cheekbones. Behind her eyes, the headache shifted, changed number. Then she said, 'You know Bill. How secretive he is.'

She was certainly beginning to.

'He's always liked to have a bolt-hole, somewhere to run to. You can't blame him, brought up the way we

137

were.' She turned and walked across the big clean floor to the food counter.

'How was that?'

The woman didn't answer.

Penny looked out through the open doors to the orange trees. Everything that Joan had said seemed to confirm Hector's—Bill's—guilt. Had he done it twice? Committed a copy-cat killing, and both times ended up with a healthy bank balance? Had the death of Delia's father, and the resulting legacy, been the precipitating factor that turned him to murder? Or had it been the hospital results? The realisation of how little it would take to send Delia to join her father? Except Joan had said the test results had been delayed.

But suppose they hadn't been. Suppose Hector had seen them and kept quiet about them, seeing a way to turn things to his own advantage. Easy enough to fake a delay. Until his wife became a rich woman, he'd probably been a perfectly ordinary man with a perfectly ordinary marriage. But with a gambling habit to support, perhaps the temptation to bump off the wife for her inheritance proved too much. And how easy, having done it once and got away with it, to kill Irene in the same way for her holdings in the Lampeter Group. After all, he seemed to have effectively cut himself off from his sister, who was the only link between Hector Oakley and the former Bill. Penny wondered if Irene Lampeter too had been undergoing hospital tests. She must remember to ask Tim.

Joan was coming back across the bare blue tiles. Behind her was a smallish man with a head as bald as an acorn. Once it might have looked like a scalp. Exposure to the sun had mottled and blotched it so that now it resembled the egg of some exotic bird. He wore rimless bifocals and a collarless white shirt.

'Joan tells me you're a good friend of Bill's,' he said. He looked as if his face would break into shards if you told him to smile. Mr American Gothic, give or take the accent and a pitchfork.

'That's right,' Penny said. One day she'd convert.

Settle up with God. Make amends for all the lies she'd told.

'Joan says he's lost another loved one,' Jim said.

'His wife died, yeah,' said Penny. It wasn't necessarily the same thing.

'Poor old Bill.' Jim put his arm round his wife's thin shoulders.

Joan had tears in her eyes. 'Things never went right for Bill,' she said. 'Not after Nina moved away.'

'Nina?' Penny said.

'Nina Sibley.' Behind his eyeglasses, Jim's eyes reminisced. 'The girl next door. Devoted to each other, they were. Her parents emigrated when she was ten.'

'Where to?'

'Canada. Somewhere near Montreal, I seem to remember.'

'She was a pretty little thing,' said his wife. She laughed, thinking back. 'Do you remember, Jim? Wanted to be a film star. Always dressing up, she was. Remember how she made us sit and watch those plays she used to write?'

'Yes,' said Jim.

'It was one of those childhood romances,' said his wife. She drew in a long sad breath. 'And then we heard her parents were killed. A train crash, was it, Jim, or a car accident?'

'Something like that. All I remember now is hearing that the kids were sent away to foster homes.'

'Kids?' said Penny, razor-sharp mind missing nothing.

'Nina and her little brother,' Jim said. 'That's what made it even worse. They were separated, apparently. Bill was terribly upset about it. Even though he was so much older than the little boy—Nina's brother—he doted on him. They both did.'

'So sweet, wasn't he? Do you remember, Jim? In those funny round glasses he had to wear?'

Jim nodded. 'Nice-looking kid. But a nasty little temper to him. Bit too fond of his own way.'

'Bill took it terribly hard when the family left,' said Joan. 'You know how it is at that age. Everything larger

139

than life and twice as dramatic. You don't understand, he kept saying. I'll love her till I die. Our love will last to the end of time. That sort of thing. It seemed to take all the life right out of him.'

'Only for a while, dear.'

'Oh, he got over it eventually. Started going with some girl from school, as I recall.'

'Cliff Murray's sister,' said Jim.

'But he never really got himself right after that, somehow.'

'Until he met Delia.'

'Not even then. Not really. He just seemed to—I don't know—drift.'

'Straight into the arms of the boss's daughter,' said Penny.

'In a manner of speaking,' said Jim.

'Delia was a nice enough girl,' Joan said defensively.

'Not much to look at . . .' said her husband.

'But nice enough . . .'

'A bit long in the tooth . . .'

'Only eight years older . . .'

'No reason why they shouldn't have made a go of it . . .'

'Except she died,' said Penny. 'How long had they been married by then?'

Joan looked at Jim. 'Ten years, was it?'

'If it's not a rude question,' Penny said, 'why did he have to borrow £600 from you?'

Jim took off his glasses and rubbed them on the sleeve of his shirt. 'It *is* a rude question,' he said.

'But with his wife's money and everything . . .' Penny trailed the question like a fish head in front of a sea-lion.

'Bill was never much of one for holding on to money, was he, dear?' Joan said.

For a moment Jim's mouth went grim. Then he shook his head. 'No, he certainly wasn't.' He looked at Penny. 'To be frank, Bill had a bit of a problem.'

'Gambling?' said Penny. She raised knowing eyebrows.

'Yes,' Mrs Parfitt said. 'He always said it came of growing up so poor: he never got a chance to practise

140

saving.' She laughed. 'Remember how he used to say that, Jim?'

Jim did. He nodded without pleasure.

'If you don't have it to begin with, all the more reason to hang on to it when you get some,' Penny said.

'That's easy to say,' Joan said sharply. 'You don't look like someone who's ever had to go without.'

'Just because I was born with a silver credit card in my mouth doesn't mean I can't empathise with those who weren't,' said Penny.

'You may well empathise, as you call it. You probably do. But you don't under*stand*.' There was a flush along Joan's cheekbones. It wasn't just wine that had caused it. 'We grew up poor, my brother and I. Dirt poor. Our dad went off one day and never came back. Our mum was a drunk. The only good thing about that was we could search her bag for the welfare money when she'd passed out, and steal enough to buy something to eat. It was the public library kept us going. You could go down there and sit up in one of the reading rooms and keep warm all day, and no one would bother you. We read a lot in those days, Bill and me. And we talked a lot about what we'd do when we were old enough to get away from her. Bill always said that somehow or other he was going to be rich. Because if you had money, you never had to be dependent on someone else's whims again. You could be your own master, he said. You could be free. Well, I haven't ended up rich, but I've got Jim.'

'Yes, you have, dear.'

'We get by all right. If Bill's got money, it's up to him what he does with it. So what if he sometimes needs a loan?'

'What my wife is saying is that Bill and his money were soon parted.'

'Oh. Is that what she was saying?'

'It never surprised me when Bill came round begging for a loan,' Joan said. 'So he gambled. Horses, dogs, it was his way of forgetting the way we were raised. Our

141

mum. We let him have what we could. He'd always pay it back.'

'Eventually,' said Jim.

The door of the restaurant opened and three people in shorts and T-shirts came in. They sat down at one of the tables.

'We'll have to go now,' Joan said.

'We've got customers,' said Jim. Just in case anyone mistook them for urban guerrillas about to make a hit.

'Don't forget my bill,' Penny said.

'Have it on the house,' said Jim.

Penny poured the remains of the carafe into her glass. She speculated on the first Mrs Oakley/Beech/Ashe/ whatever. It sounded classic. The boy from the wrong side of the tracks. The poor little rich girl. Delia, older than Hector—Bill—and not a looker, probably jumped at the chance to marry him. It occurred to her that perhaps there was a grander scheme at work here. A natural law. Perhaps all bosses' daughters were naturally plain, to give the office boy a chance to make it in a cut-throat world. When you're hungry enough, any food looks good. Or was she being unnecessarily cynical? Maybe Hector/Bill had genuinely loved, genuinely grieved.

She wondered how Delia's father had reacted to the marriage. She wondered if the police records on the case of the English tourist were still extant. And how she could get a look at them. And if she could, what good it would do her. She didn't read Greek any better than she spoke it.

More people were coming in now. The tables were filling up. Jim and Joan had begun to scurry, rushing around with glasses and cutlery. In the kitchen doorway, a fat man in a chef's hat appeared, scratching the back of his neck with a long metal spoon. Unsanitised for your infection.

Penny put some drachs on the table. Outside, in the street, afternoon had dropped heavily over the place. Sun beat off the white houses with a cruel glare. The old women in black had gone inside. The purple flowers drooped over silent balconies. Cooking smells blew from doorways.

A donkey clicked daintily round a corner, eyes demure. Behind him came a priest, black-robed and dusty. Penny asked where the police station was. He pointed back along the shallow harbour wall. She followed the roadway round until she was almost opposite Nikolas's bar. The water which lapped against the jetty was swollen with polystyrene debris. A dead seagull floated among the plastic cups and rusting kerosene cans.

Behind ornate wrought-iron doors backed with patterned glass, the police occupied a room the size of a Betty Crocker cake-mix box. The floor was raw concrete. There was a desk. A filing cabinet. A coloured photograph of a martial gentleman. None of those sissy-type extras like carpeting or girlie calendars. Behind the desk a fat man leaned back against the wall, reading a newspaper. The underarms of his white shirt were yellowed with old sweat. The top of his trousers was undone. Modifying sentences from her three-language phrase book, Penny enquired about the death of an English tourist some ten years ago. The cop pointed out to sea. Perhaps she'd said the wrong thing. Asked where she could swim. She said Parfitt several times, giving it a heavy Mediterranean intonation. The cop said *ristorante* and pointed back towards where Penny had just come from.

'The brother of Mrs Parfitt,' Penny said. She resisted the temptation to recategorise him as a moron. Just because he couldn't speak English was no reason. 'Wife. Dead.' She mimed a heart attack. The cop watched, unmoved.

She pointed out the file cabinet. She mimed someone leafing through papers. The cop pointed once more out over the water. Then he shrugged and got up. He pulled open the drawers of the file cabinet. The two top ones were empty. The bottom one held a folded waterproof cape. 'Faros,' he said. He did some more pointing. She decided the records were kept at Port Faros. She went away.

She followed the waterfront round to Nikolas's bar. Hans was lounging at a table outside. His bare legs were bloomed with dust. There was a backgammon set in front of him. On one of the moored yachts, someone was playing a Mozart horn concerto. It sounded like Dennis Brain. Penny sat down.

'What'll you have?' Hans said.

'I'll play you best of three for a ride back to Port Faros,' said Penny.

'You'll lose,' Hans said. He didn't look up.

'I wouldn't bet on it.'

'Back home in New Zealand I was junior town champion,' Hans said. This time he did look up.

'I still wouldn't bet on it.'

Hans smiled disbelievingly. 'Oh yeah?' He shouted something in Greek. From the black interior of the café someone answered. Nikolas appeared with two bottles of warm beer and a dirty glass.

They played. Dennis swooped and soared. He made the horn sound as easy as humming. Penny won the first game. And the second. Hans couldn't believe it.

'You won,' he said.

'Hans down.'

Hans shook his head. 'Nobody's beaten me in years.'

'Spare the rod and spoil the child,' said Penny.

Hans grumbled all the way back to Port Faros. The sky was thickening with dark as they moored at the very end of the quay. But not so dark that Penny couldn't take note of the larger yacht they moored alongside. Name of *Alexandros*. Because of its position, she hadn't noticed it earlier that day. On shore, lights shone in waterfront cafés. The two-tone Bentley was still parked in front of the yellow hotel. The main drag was full of T-shirted kids on motor-scooters, chatting up the girls. Pair-bonded old folk tottered along in the dust with oilcloth shopping bags.

Penny thanked Hans for the trip. She asked where the police station was. He took her to it. The place was empty. Hans told her that the handwritten sign on the door said that someone would be back after dinner. He added that he was awfully sorry but he'd have to leave her since he had to get to the other side of the island.

She said that was fine. He said she played a pretty cool game of backgammon. She said yeah.

When he'd gone, she walked back to the mooring. Tugging at the lines, she stepped aboard his boat. No one seemed to be around. Touristy music came from among trees at the edge of the waterfront where the houses stopped.

Quickly she climbed aboard the *Alexandros*.

The yacht rocked a little as she stepped down into the cockpit. She couldn't resist a groan at the sight of the heavy padlock securing the duckboards. Why did everything always seem to come down to lock-picking? She took out the manicure-set that Barnaby had given her one Christmas. Although Asprey's had provided the basic equipment, he had had it customised for her by an ex-con he knew in the Seven Sisters Road. The tortoiseshell handles could now be removed to reveal miniaturised implements designed to assist in the business of unlawful entry. Lessons from a safe-cracker he'd met in Parkhurst prison had been part of the gift, but, in spite of them, Penny had never mastered the art. She removed one of the nail-files from its suede holder and unscrewed the tortoiseshell handle. Inside was a lock-pick of high-quality stainless steel. Trouble was, she could never remember exactly what she was supposed to do with it. She stuck it into the padlock and twisted it around. To her surprise, there was a sudden click. The padlock swung open. Amazing. It had never happened to her before. She listened. From the trees a throaty female crooner informed whoever was listening that she was never never available on Sundays.

The main cabin smelled of stale wine and must. There was some light from the jetty. Not enough to conduct a search by. From her manicure set Penny took out the chamois-covered nail-buffer. Touch one end and it produced a beam the width of a needle. Turn the other and the arc of light expanded to cover a twelve-inch radius. She flashed it carefully around. She wondered quite what she was hoping to find. The Greek police might well have made a thorough search of the boat already. On the other hand, Irene's death had been certified as natural. And Kyriakou had the kind of connections that could stop a search warrant in its tracks, if one had ever been issued. So there was a chance that something might have been overlooked. Something that could be incriminating.

She examined the lockers. The perishable food had been removed but a few tins remained. There were staples in the galley still: salt and sugar in tightly lidded plastic containers, olive oil, a squeezy bottle of wine vinegar. She removed the locker cushions, but there was nothing there. Poking around behind the plates and glasses she found two sugar cubes wrapped in paper. The paper had a Pan Am logo on it. Were they significant? She decided not. The chart table told her nothing, nor did the drawer beneath it. In the heads, there was a cabinet. Carefully she shone the flashlight on the contents. Talc. Deodorant. Toothpaste. A couple of long black hairs. Nothing else. The hanging locker was equally empty of anything incriminating. What had she expected? If Irene had indeed been murdered, it had been done with the kind of subtlety that would mean covered tracks, unleft traces.

Without any expectation she went into the forecabin. She lifted the long triangular cushions. Nothing. She peered down into the lockers underneath. Nothing but air. She ran her fingers along the inside edge of the teakwood ledge on the port side. Zilch. She did the same to the starboard, climbing along the cushions to reach right into the V-shape of the bow. Which was how she found what she hadn't really thought could possibly still be there.

Small. Plastic. Unmistakable. Stuck to the teak with a piece of Blutack was Irene's bottle of pills.

If there was one thing you didn't expect to find on board a yacht, it was Blutack. Someone had come prepared. Someone had expected Irene to die. Someone had known that the pills were the instrument of death.

Whoever it was had not dared remove them until the verdict had been returned. If questions were asked, searches made, nothing could be more incriminating than pills found in a pocket where they should not have been. On the other hand, throwing them over the side could be equally dangerous if someone should ask where they were. Whoever had come on board armed with a piece of sticky blue rubber compound must have hoped to return at some point and take them away.

Penny opened the bottle and shook a few of the pills on to her hand. At first glance they all seemed identical. Only someone looking for differences would spot that some of them were very slightly greyer than others. She picked one up and touched her tongue to it. It stuck momentarily, the chalky substance absorbing moisture. It tasted of nothing. She picked up the second kind and licked it. After a moment she emptied the pills from her palm back into the bottle. Thoughtfully, she screwed the lid back on and put the bottle into her bag. A professional analysis would be necessary but she was already pretty sure of what they would find. Salt. No question. Salt. Which explained Irene's excessive thirst. Also the sudden flushes, the palpitations, the incipient paranoia.

Only problem was, anything suspect about the pills would tend to prove that Hector was innocent. Because of the entire party present at Irene's death, he was the only one who could legitimately have taken the pills away with him.

Where did that leave her investigation now?

12

W<small>HEN THE</small> P<small>ORT</small> F<small>AROS</small> <small>POLICE RETURNED FROM THEIR</small> dinner, they were cooperative. One of them spoke meagre English. He said they had files going back over twenty years. He remembered the lady tourist dying a few weeks back. He remembered other tourists dying. He told her about them. His colleagues cleared a table and offered her a glass of wine while she looked for whatever it was she wanted.

It would have been useful if she'd been able to read the language. She recognised α and was working on β. Anything beyond and she was stymied. She'd come to the conclusion that she was out of luck. At which point the door opened and Paul Leandro came in. He grinned.

'Hi,' he said.

One day she'd meet a good-looking man who didn't know it. Or knew, and didn't care.

'I already caught your act,' she said coldly.

'And?'

'It got a C + rating.'

'What're you doing for dinner tonight?'

Must be one of those Neanderthal types who thought a girl didn't know her own mind when she told him to get lost. But the guy spoke Greek. She didn't. He might be able to make head or tail of the files she was currently being baffled by. Maybe both.

'What is it with you Greeks, anyway?' she said. She made a dimple appear in her cheek. Paul registered it.

148

'Isn't it time you wised up, got yourselves an alphabet the rest of us can follow?'

'Please don't use words like follow,' he said.

'I got some better ones if you want to hear them.'

'It's just, I've spent all day following you. There's not a man, woman or donkey in the entire Ionian Sea who hasn't heard about the big black lady who arrived by bus from Athens this morning.' Pulling out a chair, he sat down opposite her. 'You told me you were headed for Port Faros.'

'And here I am.'

'You didn't say you were spending the day on a sidetrip to Aghia Eufonia.'

Penny widened her eyes. 'Did I fall asleep and miss something?

'Why?'

'Since when did what I do become your business?'

'Since I made it my business.' Paul hung his eyelids over his eyes. It probably wowed them back home.

'Get off my case, Leandro.'

He stopped grinning. 'It's not your case I'm on,' he said.

'Whose, then?'

'The man who calls himself Hector Oakley.'

'Calls himself?'

'That's right.'

'And what exactly is your interest?'

'I work for Costas Kyriakou. He asked me to check out Oakley's background. Standard procedure. Before Mr Kyriakou does business, he likes to know who he's doing business with.'

'We're talking the Lampeter Group here, are we?'

'We are.' Paul tried not to look surprised.

'Costas is dead.'

'I am aware.'

'Are you a cop?'

'No.'

'A PI?'

'No.'

'What then?'

'A financial consultant. Boston-based. We do a lot of work for Kyriakou, Stateside. As a matter of fact, he was the one who got me my job.'

'Would I have heard of your firm?'

'We operate worldwide, naturally. But whether you'd know—'

'I'm reasonably clued up.'

'CBF,' Paul said. 'I'm in the insurance department.'

'Cotton, Bradshaw & Filos,' said Penny. 'Guess you must've been involved in renegotiating those Third World loans with Lloyds of London.' So much for the brief chronicles of the *Time* she'd read on the plane coming over.

'Very impressive,' said Paul.

'What'd you think, you were talking to some retard?'

'Absolutely not.'

'And you'll still carry on investigating Hector Oakley? Even though someone's helped Costas into early retirement?'

'Yeah. Until told not to.'

'So who'll pay you?'

'I'm not worried about that.' Paul smiled. 'If necessary, I'll authorise myself to pay myself.'

'What've you found out about Oakley so far?'

'Man's got pure eel blood running round his veins. Boy, what a slippery customer.'

'That right?'

'I can't trace him back more than a couple of years. He's covered his tracks like he knew someone would be after him one day.'

'Doesn't sound like you got much, Mr Financial Consultant.'

'I've also discovered I'm not the only one checking the guy out.' Paul leaned his elbows on the table. 'What's *your* interest?'

'I was asked to investigate him.'

'By?'

'That's privileged information. And before you try pulling my teeth out one by one, I should tell you I'm impervious to pain.'

'Damn. And I majored in sadism.' Paul grinned again at Penny. 'You ready to eat yet?'

'Maybe.'

'Why don't you eat with me?'

'And afterwards?'

'I drive you back to Athens. Introduce you to my dad.'

'Sounds like a fun evening.'

'Listen, when God was creating the animals, he modelled the pack rat on my dad. I mean, this guy's got information where other people've got dust. Any thing you want to know, he has a file on it.' Paul put his hand over Penny's. 'So how about it?'

'How about what?'

'What say we work together, huh? Do a deal?'

'You trying to take advantage, Leandro? Just 'cos I'm blood?'

Paul spread his wide shoulders. 'No one ever called me racially prejudiced before.'

'Oh yeah? I know how those honkie deals supposed to work out. You give me a boxful of buttons and I hand over Manhattan Island, right?'

'Do I look like a Dutch settler?'

'About as much as I look like a dope.' Penny shook her braids around so the beads smacked together. 'If I level with you, what's in it for me?'

'I'm great in bed.'

'Jesus Murphy. Don't you Latin types ever stop hustling?'

'If *that* isn't racially prejudiced . . .'

'What else you got to trade, 'side from your prick?'

Paul breathed gustily. 'I'll come clean. All I got so far is one piece of info.'

'Let's have it.'

'Oakley's wife died six weeks ago.'

'As I already know.'

'My father happened to read about it in the paper.'

'And I'm supposed to give you what I got in exchange for *that*?'

'No. For what's in my dad's files.'

151

'Which is?'

'I don't know. He rang the hotel in London where I was staying and said he'd turned up something on Oakley he thought I'd be interested in. That was before Kyriakou died, of course. But when my father says something's interesting, you better believe it.'

'Why?'

'Because he used to be a cop. Until he was hired by Kyriakou to head up his security.'

Penny nodded slowly. 'OK,' she said. 'I'm sold. But this'd better be good.'

'Guaranteed.'

Leandro Senior had once been a big man. Now his clothes seemed to have stretched in the wash. He toted the inevitable brigand's moustache, its pelt touched with grey. His white shirt glowed through the cigarette smoke that hung round him. The end of his narrow black tie was tucked into black trousers made of some material that shone when he moved. He embraced his son the way film producers like to believe that Greek fathers always embrace their sons. Penny hoped he wouldn't whip out a hanky and start dancing.

The handshake he offered her was grudging. Suspicious, even. He looked at his palm after it. He rubbed it over his buttock. She recognised the gesture. He looked like the kind of guy who prided himself on calling a spade a spade. He'd probably never shaken hands with one before.

His room was tiny. The decor leaned heavily towards metal filing cabinets. There were fourteen of them ranged round the walls, each four drawers deep. Three doors were set into two of the walls. One led to a kitchen the size of a closet, the other to a bathroom. Through the third, half-open, she could see a little bedroom and more filing cabinets.

There was just enough space left in the living-room for an armchair. A bottle and a glass stood on top of a small plastic-topped table on a pivoting metal leg. Also a lot of ash. The air was metaxa-flavoured, with a deep underlay of cheap cigarettes.

'Miss Wanawake is a friend of Mr Kyriakou's,' Paul said.

Leandro breathed heavily through his nose. Tears hovered behind thin-rimmed eyeglasses. 'This news was such a shock,' he said, moving his head from side to side in a gesture more comprehensive than a mere shake. 'To hear that he is dead. Such a good man.'

Somewhere, several dozen corpses turned in their graves. They were going to have to rewrite the dictionaries if good was what Costas had been. Paul looked at Penny and away. 'And like me, she is looking into Hector Oakley's background,' he said quickly. 'Which is why we have come to you.'

The old man brightened. He managed to look Penny in the eye. 'You are with the police?'

'Uh—sort of,' Penny said. She closed one eye. Body language could be a useful alternative to lying.

Leandro chuckled. 'I understand,' he said. Penny was glad about that. He tapped the side of his nose. 'And you come to Leandro for help, is that right?'

'We need a break,' Penny said.

'I hope I can help you.' He indicated the filing cabinets. 'I have information in there that the CIA itself does not possess. Nor MI5.'

'Then you already knew that the sister of the recently bereaved Mr Oakley is living at Eufonia?' Paul said.

The old man's cheeks dropped. His dark eyes bulged incredulously. 'Aghia Eufonia. On Kefallinía?'

'Yes.'

'Why was I not told? The man there—Milos Angeloglou—has orders to keep me informed. Why did he not do so?'

'Probably because he didn't know,' Penny said. She didn't want to be responsible for Milo's head rolling. She held out the bottle of cheapo brandy she'd brought with her. She smiled at the old man. One pro to another. 'He knew of the English lady running the restaurant with her husband, but not of her relationship to the man whose wife recently died on another island. It took a lot of routine work to uncover her.' To save Leandro's face, and Milo's head, she added: 'Work that could only be done in England.'

'Aha,' said Leandro. He leaned confidently towards her. 'Scotland Yard, yes?' He spoke out of the side of his face.

'Something like that,' said Penny. In the right mouth, truth had all the stretchability of bubble-gum. Once you knew how to work it, you could blow amazing bubbles.

'You must give me the details,' Leandro said busily. 'It is important that my files are kept up to date at all times.'

'I'll make some coffee,' Paul said.

'I'll be happy to update you on Oakley,' Penny said. She perched on the arm of the single chair. She gave him what she had. When he'd got it all down in careful old-person's writing, she said: 'But why I'm really here is, your son tells me you have discovered something interesting. So I have come to beg for your help.' She could brown-nose with the best of them when she had to.

The old man put his black fountain pen in the pocket of his shirt. He unclipped the eyeglasses from his ears and folded them carefully. He poured metaxa into the glass and swallowed some, looking pleased. 'Paul,' he called. 'Can you hear me?'

'Loud and clear,' Paul said. He backed into the room with a tray containing fresh coffee in a small copper pot, and three tiny cups. The smell of coffee fought with the metaxa fumes and lost. He put the tray down on the table, first moving his father's ashtray to the arm of his chair.

'Very well.' Leandro Senior settled himself in his chair and lit a cigarette. The corners of his mouth were stained with dark yellow nicotine. 'When I read about the tourist who died here—Mrs Hector Oakley—I was interested at first only because it resembled the death of another lady, who also died in the islands.'

'How long ago?' Penny said.

'I was still on the force then. Must have been—ten years?' A heavy puff on the cigarette left a length of ash which suddenly broke off. Before it reached his shirt-front, Leandro had cupped his hand under it and caught it. 'It was only later, when Paul asked me if I knew anything of this man, this Hector Oakley, that I made a few phone calls.' Leandro drew in a sharp breath and began to choke to death.

'And guess what he came up with,' said Paul. He put down his coffee cup and began thumping the old man's back.

'I never guess.'

'How tall you figure Oakley for?'

'Five four, five five, in there.'

'A dwarf, right?'

'What are you, Junior? A sizeist as well?'

'Come on, lady. Five five's not big. Not for a man.'

'So nobody's gonna recruit him for the Harlem Globe-trotters.'

'Five four, five five is *small*. Right, Dad?'

'Right.' Leandro Senior pulled a handkerchief from his trouser pocket and wiped his eyes. His face had turned a dusty purple. 'When the papers mentioned the tourist—this Mr Oakley—as being not very tall, I re-membered this other case. There, too, the husband of the dead tourist lady was small.' He began to cough again, dragging phlegm up from his chest and letting his head wag with each burst of activity.

'Guess what else,' Paul said quickly. The liquid sound of his father's battle with suffocation almost drowned him out.

'I don't usually,' Penny said. 'But I'll have a stab. Could it be that in both cases the lady had a heap of dough and had left it all to her grieving husband?'

'Her *pygmy* husband . . .'

'And in the first case, no one realised the lady had heart trouble because the hospital results had been de-layed. And the lady's name was Delia Beech.'

Leandro Senior lay back in his chair, gasping and speechless. One hand flapped at his heart, the other

155

scrabbled for a fresh cigarette. Penny lit a match and held it close. Apart from an undertaker, she couldn't think of anything that would be more help.

'Some smart guesser,' said Paul.

She smiled. 'Doesn't look like much of a trade, Leandro, does it? I come all the way back to Athens and you try to pass off some old shit I already got in exchange for my shiny new stuff.'

'How about this, then? Did you know where the first lady—Delia—was when she died?'

'Halfway up a hill.'

'Which is kind of odd.'

'It is?'

'Delia was on her way to visit a shrine, right?'

'Dedicated to Athena,' said Penny.

'Just like Wife Number Two.'

'A.k.a. Irene Lampeter.'

'Said shrine located on a bit of rock named Avrios,' Paul said. He pressed down the end of his nose.

'Check.'

Paul placed his palms flat on his knees and bent them at the elbow. 'Tell her, Dad,' he said.

Leandro *père* struggled to sit upright. One hand at his throat, he said in a strangled voice, 'There isn't one.'

'No shrine?'

'Uh-huh,' said Paul.

'Not to Athena?'

'Not to any damn one.'

'Not even a ruined temple? A sacred fountain?'

Leandro shook his head carefully, in case it set off another coughing fit. 'Not on Avrios there isn't.'

'Hot diggety dog.' Penny stared at her hands. Then she stared at a seagull beating its wings together on top of a roof across the street outside the window. Finally she said: 'OK. Bring out your button box.'

'Good stuff, huh?'

'I might even throw in Fire Island as well. Do you realise what this means?'

'Tell me.'

'Means that if we still had the death penalty, Hector

156

Oakley would have taken a giant leap towards the scaffold. Two wives dying of heart attacks might be coincidence. Two wives dying of heart attacks on their way to look at a non-existent shrine sounds an awful lot like murder.'

'What method are you suggesting he used?'

'Delia was known to be suffering from heart trouble of some kind. I'll bet that when I look into it Irene Lampeter had a heart problem too. Or the pills . . . ' Penny stopped. It was always a good idea to keep an ace up your sleeve.

'What pills?'

She rushed on. 'And the motive is obvious. They were both rich and Hector was first in line to inherit.'

'Right. But what—'

Frowning, Penny said, 'But suppose the women had gotten to the top without dropping dead. What you gonna do when they start looking round and saying stuff like, "Hey, man. Where be the shrine?" How you gonna explain when they looking at you sideways and asking theirselves if maybe you planning to do them some mischief?'

'Easy,' said Paul. 'You shrug. You look around a bit. You say, "Hey, sorry, gang. Guess I slipped up somewhere, got the wrong island or something, but isn't it a great view anyway?" '

'Yeah,' Penny said. 'I guess people buy that sort of bullshit all the time. Who's going to jump in and say you got murder in mind?'

Over his father's head, Paul said quietly, 'What I got in mind isn't murder.'

'We can discuss what you got in mind somewhere else. Right now I still want to talk to your father.'

'Are you reasonably certain that the late Delia Beech's husband and Hector Oakley are the same guy?' asked Paul.

'One hundred and two per cent,' Penny said. It looked like she might be about to pin Hector down. Put salt on his tail. Provided he let her get close enough. At the same time, it wasn't anything to celebrate. Oh, the venality of man. The murderous impulse overcoming the civilised veneer that centuries of polishing was supposed to impart. That was always the trouble, the veneer was only skin deep. She remembered Irene. The guilty little face she made as she popped prawns. The fold of skin over the eyelid that made her eyes so warm. The final ignominious ascension.

How had Hector set it up? If she was going to nail him for Irene's death, she'd have to find out. Maybes and mights tendrilled somewhere at the back of her brain, but she ignored them. Sit on the fence too long and you could finish being split right up the middle. Along with that thought came another. Suppose Costas had caught wind of the high mortality rate among Hector's wives. Had hired Paul to check it out. Suppose he'd told Hector. Threatened with exposure, might a man already murderous not be driven to further violence? The kind that ends in sudden death? The kind that knows just what to throw down a disused well?

She put a hand on the old man's shoulder. 'Mr Leandro,' she said. 'That was the most helpful piece of information I've had since I started looking at Hector Oakley. Is there any chance you might be prepared to tell me about someone else?'

'Anything.' The old man stabbed at the full ashtray with the carcass of his current cigarette. Half the yellow filter had already gone up in smoke. 'Who do you want to know about?'

'Katerina Tasso.'

'Tasso,' said the old man. His head moved up and down in a series of tiny nods. His eyes shifted.

'Yes.'

Leandro pushed his lower lip out. There was a line of brown staining along the inside of it. She could see that whatever truth he was going to tell her, it wouldn't be the whole.

'Do you wish to know of her childhood? Her early career as an actress?'

'I'm not interested in anything that's in the public domain. I was hoping you might be able to supply me with the intimate private information that only an expert like yourself might possess,' Penny said. Would intimate and private cover a relationship with Costas? She hoped so. If it had been public, it had slipped by her.

The old man thought about it. 'You know she is very superstitious?' he said. 'She used to consult a man in New York. He died back in 1984, I believe.' Leandro went over to his files and pulled out a drawer. He took out a dark green file and laid it on top of the cabinet. He leafed through it, feeling his moustache with the ends of his fingers. 'Yes. July 1984. After that she began using an English clairvoyant. She travels twice a year to London for a long-term horoscope, according to my sources.' Keeping one hand on the file, he turned back to Penny. 'As you know, actors are given to that kind of thing.'

Penny smiled at him. 'Let's get serious,' she said. 'My own *mother* reads her horoscope. I was hoping for whatever you got on Tasso and Kyriakou.'

Leandro snapped the file shut and put it into the drawer. He pushed the drawer back so that the metal cabinet clanged. 'I do not wish to talk about this,' he said. The colour of his face darkened.

'Why's that?'

In answer Leandro spoke some fast Greek to his son.

'Of course she's not,' Paul replied. To Penny, he said: 'My father thinks you are a reporter trying to dig out some scandal about Kyriakou now that he's dead.'

'Who needs to dig?' said Penny.

'This one is obviously buried deep,' said Paul.

The father spoke again, addressing the brandy.

'He's afraid that you have misrepresented yourself. That you are a blackmailer. That you have come to make him pay.'

'What the hell for?'

'It could be interesting to find out.'

'I'm only interested in the truth,' Penny said. 'And in Hector Oakley. It just happens that someone I know's been accused of murdering Costas, and while it's perfectly possible that he's guilty, I'd like to check whatever facts come my way. Especially as Oakley and Kyriakou seem linked together. I swear that nothing your father tells me will ever be told to anyone else.' Although she spoke to Paul, she knew the old man understood every word. She wasn't prepared for his reaction.

He began to weep. He groped his way to his armchair. Reaching blindly out, he took the top off the fresh bottle Penny had brought and poured a full glass of the brandy. The tears on his face were probably one hundred per cent proof too. When he'd swallowed half the glass, he spoke again, his voice vibrating like a guitar string.

'The gods have many faces,' he keened archaically. 'Who can escape the past?'

'What is this?' said Penny. 'A try-out for *Oedipus Rex*?'

'Drink always takes him like this.' Paul put a hand on his father's shoulder.

'Just so long as he doesn't start piercing any eyeballs.'

The father talked, mumbling at his glass. 'Kyriakou was a good man,' he said. 'At least, in the beginning. It was the money that turned him sour. So much money. He began to put himself above other men. Then above the gods. He couldn't bear to lose. And when he did, which was not very often, he decided it must have been through trickery. After that, it became logical to think that anyone who tricked him must be punished. That's what happened to Jay Pannis.'

'Who's he?' Penny said.

Paul shrugged.

'It was an oil deal with the Mexican government,' said Leandro. 'The big companies were tendering bids for drilling rights. The Pannis people got it, instead of Kyriakou. He was furious. He'd spent millions of drachmas on bribes, only to see Pannis walk away with the contracts. He called me to his office one evening and showed me a gun. He was very drunk. He said he would either use it on Pannis or himself.'

'Justifiable suicide,' said Penny.

'He said it was the first time anyone had beaten him in business for more than ten years.' Leandro sighed. 'I took the gun away from him, of course. I had to. He was wild, like an animal. Perhaps it would have been better if I had not.'

'What happened?' asked Paul.

'He said he would wait for his revenge. The time would come, he said.' The old man poured more brandy. When he drank, it missed his mouth and slopped on to his shirt. His skin was pink where the wet patch touched his chest.

'And did it?' asked Paul.

'Oh yes. Pannis got richer and richer. He went into film-making for a while—that's where he met his wife. Then he decided to go into politics. Over there, in the States, dealing in one kind of illusion seems to make you the ideal choice when it comes to dealing in another.' He got up and went to his filing cabinets again. He opened the tenth one along the wall and flipped through it.

He brought out a folder the size of a family Bible. 'Pannis,' he said. He showed them a photograph. A big glossy. 9″ x 10″. It looked like a publicity still. Pannis was young, maybe twenty years younger than Tasso. Yet his face was mature as well as handsome. It promised both level-headedness and boyish energy. A winning combination for a politico.

'Governor Pannis? President Pannis?' Penny said. 'Have I been reading the wrong papers? And what—excuse me—does this have to do with Katerina Tasso?'

'Kyriakou decided the time had come,' gusted the old man. He looked down at the wrinkles in his trouser thighs and moved a finger slowly along one. 'He started a whispering campaign. Irregularities in the way some of the Pannis concerns were run. Tax evasion. Rumours about his sex life.'

'Wouldn't you need proof to make charges like that stick?' asked Paul.

'For a would-be congressman, such rumours are death. Besides, proof isn't hard to manufacture.' Leandro groaned theatrically and buried his face in his hands. Ham of the year, maybe. An Oscar, definitely not.

'Then what?' Paul said.

'It was during his first campaign. Kyriakou knew which

161

hotel Pannis would be spending the night at. He managed, with—with my help, to set him up.'

'How?'

The father talked rapidly in Greek, biting his lip every now and then. The level in the brandy bottle descended.

'They bribed the hotel manager,' translated Paul. 'Some young guy all too ready to take the cash and let the credit card go. He got hold of two girls and arranged for a press photographer to discover this Pannis character dead drunk in bed between them.' Paul listened some more. 'Turns out one of them was only twelve. Result: Pannis's political career up the spout. Like Teddy Kennedy and Chappaquiddick, he'd never have gotten away from it.' He listened some more, his face changing. 'Not, apparently, that it mattered much. Less than a year later, one of the girls was found murdered in circumstances that pointed towards, though not directly at, Pannis. And then Kyriakou dug out her father, some wino with a pickled liver who'd have done anything for the next drink. Although he hadn't spoken to the girl for years, suddenly he got an acute attack of the outraged fathers and went after Pannis with a gun. Took a pot shot at him, and missed, but managed to lodge a bullet in his spine, which crippled him for life.'

The old man spoke again, hiccuping. He reached a hand out and dragged beseechingly at his son's coatsleeve.

'What's he saying?'

'That he had no idea what Kyriakou was up to. He says it was he who bought the gun but it wasn't until afterwards that he found out why. And he couldn't say anything.'

'Why not?'

'Loyalty.'

'Loyalty,' moaned the father.

'Who stays loyal to a rat?'

'My dad, apparently.' Paul had gone red. 'Because Kyriakou had paid for my education. Helped me along in my career.'

'Character assassination to order being the kickback,' said Penny.

'Looks like it. My father always wanted me to do well, do better than he did, get rich. Dammit. You've got to believe I didn't know any of this till right this minute.'

'Who's judging you?'

'It's bad enough I'm suddenly judging my own father. The man I admired more than anyone I know.'

Leandro's shoulders shook. So did Paul's.

Just another crime for which Costas wouldn't be brought to book. 'And this Pannis was innocent of all charges, was he?' Penny said. She'd already known Costas was the kind who spent his spare time putting horses' heads in people's beds. But while you could wash bloodied sheets, you couldn't restore shattered faith.

'According to my father, completely.'

'How long ago was all this?'

'About ten years,' said Paul.

'Where's Pannis now?'

'Dead,' said the old man. 'For nearly ten years he sat in that wheelchair, while his wife looked after everything. Everything, you understand. This man who might have ruled the United States of America, only a young man still, had to be wiped like a baby. No man could have borne it for long. In the end, he decided that enough was enough.'

'What did he do?' asked Penny.

Another burst of coughing. The old man trawled his lungs, dredging up gobs of slime. Tears squeezed out between his clenched eyelids. 'One night,' he said. 'One night . . .' His chest shook with another paroxysm. 'It was only a few weeks ago. He managed to get hold of some scissors. He cut his wrists open and bled to death while his wife slept. When she woke up, he was dead beside her.'

'I never heard any of this before,' Penny said.

'It was hushed up,' said the old man. 'But it's all in my files. All the proof.'

'Did Pannis have any other family?'

The old man shook his head.

'And where's the wife? What does she do?' Penny said.

'She used to be famous all over the world,' said the old man. He sighed at the temporality of worldly renown.

'Anyone we know?'

Leandro nodded. 'She was one of the great names in her time. And a Greek, too.'

'Not—'

'Tasso,' said the father. 'Katerina Tasso.'

13

DID YOU RECENTLY THROW YOUR LOVER DOWN A WELL? IT was the kind of question the famous have unlisted phones to avoid. Too bad for Katerina Tasso that Leandro Senior's files were so comprehensive. Too bad for Penelope Wanawake that nobody was home at either of Tasso's ex–directory numbers.

After her sixteenth try, she rang the Kyriakou head offices. The receptionist who answered either had a sore throat or was rehearsing for life in a Trappist monastery. When Penny wondered if Alexandra Kyriakou was back in Athens, she made a noise about as non as committal could get. When Penny offered the name of her laryngologist, she didn't answer.

The house of Kyriakou occupied five floors of a shiny building in Thalassa Street. The main entrance was manned by a paramilitary person. There was an offensive weapon on his hip. Another sat beside him, showing off a tooth-studded jaw. Penny didn't fool about trying to make friends with man or dog. For one thing, she hated uniforms, especially the martial kind. For another, the only wordless communication she'd ever wanted with a Doberman was the sort that came off the end of a foot. Preferably one encased in triple-strength steel.

She mentioned Alexandra's name. The paraperson was unimpressed. She mentioned Theo's. The lack of impression deepened. When she came to Marty's however, the paraperson softened round the edges. She deduced that money had changed hands. She allowed some of hers to. The paraperson opened the steel-grilled doors of the building and let her in. He even pointed out the floor she wanted.

The elevator opened into an area of crap-coloured carpeting dotted with plants in big pots. It could have been anywhere in the world. Especially *Dallas*. A girl with the expression of one who was not only at the bottom of the ladder but had already met up with several snakes moved a supercilious mouth around. Her lips seemed to have recently been painted with boat varnish. Penny asked for Alexandra. The girl touched a grey button on a flat beige keyboard and said something sprightly, tossing her hair about. Her eyes did some swift accounting. She came within $50 of the cost of Penny's short white skirt and matching long-line jacket. When she'd added in the white leather purse and Maude Frizon shoes, she smiled. Carefully.

Another girl appeared. She'd have walked through a Miss World contest. She gave Penny a come-on smile. Penny went. She was shown into an impressive room hung with the kind of artwork that MOMA spends years budgeting for. On a freestanding couch, Marty and Theo were looking at a ring-bound folder together. Opposite them, in a matching armchair, Sibylla was frowning over Pixie Casaubon's *Vogue* spread. She was watching Theo from under her eyelashes.

Alexandra was seated at a big desk, doing a business bitch number over the telephone. There was a cigarette in her mouth. Kyriakou would have died. If he hadn't already.

'No,' she was saying. 'Contracts were *not* signed. I therefore do not intend to honour the agreement.'

Someone quacked on the other end of the phone.

'I don't give a shit,' Alexandra said. 'That was something my father set up. I'm in charge now . . . No. I don't, I'm sorry . . . No, I'm sorry but . . .' She held the receiver away from her face and held her head on one side, shaking it slightly. After a moment, she spoke into it again. 'Film actress? Are you kidding?'

Penny flopped her braids about. She hoped it would hide the fact that her ears were out on stalks. Under the white beads, her brains intermeshed like tangled spaghetti. Film actress? Could that mean Tasso? Keeping it casual, she sat down beside Marty. She'd never been much on maths at school, but she knew the price of a canful of worms. Also, she could spot a significance at ten paces. She wasn't the only one. Although she was still looking at *Vogue*, Sibylla's eyes had stopped moving.

'Hi, honey,' Marty said. He put his hand on Penny's knee.

'Who?' Alexandra said into the phone. She looked thoughtful. 'No. I didn't know that. But it doesn't change anything. Whatever my father may have said, I'm in charge now . . . All right. Yes, I'll have a word. But I warn you not to expect any . . . I'm afraid I don't care what . . . Whoever the hell else pulls out if we do is your problem, not mine.'

Theo put a hand on Penny's other knee. She smiled at him. Sibylla glanced up. On Kyriakou's island she had looked all of her thirty-plus years. Here, away from the harsh sunlight, she could almost have passed for a schoolgirl. One with a lot of extra-curricular activities.

'You'll sort it out,' Alexandra said. She listened some more. 'And to you too,' she said. She put the phone down. Getting up from the desk, she stretched. It was a movement designed to relieve muscle-kink. It was also a movement that showed off a figure worth more than a quick glance. Theo gave it several. Sibylla did too. Then she frowned some more. She slapped over a page of the magazine. Diamonds sparked aggressively on six of her eight fingers. She picked up a piece of embroidery. She made three tiny stitches, adding to an intricately shaded yellow rose.

Alexandra joined them. Today she was in wide-shouldered royal blue. Probably the latest thing in designer mourning. She seemed as composed as a Beethoven string quartet. Not a bit like an orphan. Not a bit how Penny would be if *her* father had just died. Costas

Kyriakou's death seemed to have acted on his daughter like monkey glands. She touched Marty on the shoulder.

'I didn't know you were interested in the film industry,' she said. She nodded at Penny, as though she'd remember where she'd seen her before if you gave her a minute. Trés tycooness.

'I'm not,' Marty said. 'Except as a—'

'So how come you were in on this deal my father was setting up with the people at Paramount?'

'Ask my wife,' Marty said.

Instead Alexandra sat down beside Theo. She took his hand. 'Darling,' she said. 'Did you know your stepmother was going into the movies?'

'Going *back* into movies,' said Sibylla.

'Selling ice cream in the interval?' Theo said.

The paleness of Sibylla's face changed to pink. She cross-stitched the edge of a bud in lettuce green silk. 'I don't need that kind of shit from you,' she said.

'You'd have been great, honey,' said Marty. 'Wouldn't she just, Theo? You've seen some of the reruns. Wasn't she something?'

'Something,' agreed Theo.

'How do you mean, Martin?' Sibylla said.

'Huh?'

'Why do you say I *would* have been great?'

'Hell, honey. With Costas—uh—gone, looks like the deal's off.'

'What deal?' said Penny.

'Apparently my father was negotiating to buy a piece of film studio out in California,' said Alexandra.

'And, incredible as it may seem, the current Mrs Schumann was angling for a major part,' Theo said.

'What's so damn incredible?' demanded Sibylla.

Theo looked her up and down. 'Shirley Temple you're not,' he said.

'Don't kid yourself,' said Sibylla. 'I still got a lot of contacts out in Burbank.'

'So you must have been pretty steamed when Costas pulled out,' Theo said.

'How'd you know he did?' asked Penny.

'I heard him telling Sibylla the deal was off. The very same night that someone murdered him,' said Theo. He stared coldly at his stepmother.

'You really are a little creep,' Sibylla said.

'Costas sure didn't say nothing to me about pulling out,' said Marty. 'Way I saw it, what's a few hunnerd thousand here or there, make my little girl happy?'

His little girl looked like happiness cost a good deal more than that. She moved the diamonds on her fingers about a bit.

' 'S why I'd been hoping you 'n' me could still talk business,' Marty said to Alexandra. 'Spite of what's happened.'

'Mrs Schumann,' Alexandra said. She leaned towards Sibylla. 'Persuade me I won't be losing money if I go in on this.'

'Listen, lady. I was already on the climb in TV when I married Martin,' Sibylla said. 'And like I said, I've still got the contacts. That's what it's all about on the West Coast—contacts. And I made damn sure I kept mine up. There's no reason at all why I shouldn't make the jump into films if I wanted to.'

'What you say may well be true,' Alexandra said. She turned to Marty. 'You can't seriously expect me to underwrite a project that seems based on so many conjecturals, can you?'

'I guess not.' Marty looked defeated. Probably knew what Sibylla would say when she got him back to their hotel. 'Maybe if you took a look at the videos . . .'

'Daytime soaps,' Theo said in a hard voice. 'It's hardly acting. All you have to do to be in those is be able to breathe.'

Sibylla moved her teeth together as though she were grinding corn. She spoke through them. 'Why don't you go shit in your hat?' she said. 'Damn you. I've tried just about—' She stopped. She put another stitch into her embroidery.

'Costas thought he could make money out of a film with Sib in it,' Marty said quickly. 'And he was always one hell of a shrewd operator.'

'Besides, it was his damn suggestion, not mine,' said Sibylla.

'Except he backed off,' said Theo, implacable as fate.

'And died,' said Penny.

'Have you given any further thought to that scheme Theo and I prepared for you?' Alexandra said to Marty. She turned her wide shoulders away from Sibylla. 'Now that—now that things have changed, there's nothing to stop us going ahead on that if we want to.'

'I guess not,' Marty said. He glanced unhappily at his wife.

'My father would have been displeased, of course, but there aren't any further obstacles that I can see.' Alexandra touched her shoulder-pads as though to check they weren't chips.

Was it years of not being allowed to express her own feelings that made Alexandra's lack of them now seem so complete? Or had the repressive influence of her father been so great that his death could only be seen as the lifting of a heavy yoke? Penny had an urge to telephone her parents, tell them she loved them, would be devastated if anything happened to them. But her father was travelling round his homelands, and her mother was incommunicado somewhere on a boat.

'I guess there aren't,' Marty said. 'On the other hand, you're free to do what you like now. Don't need no help from me to get started.'

'Only up to a point,' Alexandra said. She picked up one of the binders on the low table in front of her. 'Without a name like yours to inspire confidence in investors, we aren't going to get very far, are we?'

'You telling me the Kyriakou name won't have them reaching for their chequebooks?'

'I don't have my father's track record,' Alexandra said. 'Not yet.' She turned to Penny. 'For instance, where your mother wouldn't have hesitated to work for my father, would she work for me?'

She probably didn't mean to make it sound as though she was offering Lady Helena a job as washerwoman.

'Why not?' said Penny. 'You money's as good as anyone else's.'

'How is your mom?' Marty said.

'I don't know. Haven't seen her since the night—since your father—uh—died. She's sailing somewhere with friends.'

'Sounds interesting,' Alexandra said. She turned over the pages of the file on her knee, about as interested as a teetotaller at a compulsory wine-tasting.

'Say, if Lady Helena comes in on the kids' idea, you can definitely count me in too,' Marty said. He turned to Alexandra. 'It's a real nice plan the two of you got worked out there. Real nice.'

'Are you dumping the film idea?' said Sibylla. Everyone looked at her. Today, she was in the palest of caramel linen worn with creamy pink. They weren't the kinds of colour that normally had you covering your head and checking the exits. But underneath her ice, something volcanic was happening.

Nervy as a bug on a cactus leaf, Marty said, 'Well, hon, I mean, with Costas gone and all, I mean, hell, I don't know beans about movies. Haven't been to one since I was a kid.'

'Remember those magic lanterns?' Penny said.

'Sure do.'

'They updated them,' said Penny. 'Got these nifty electric projectors and all.'

'Say, is that right?'

Sibylla stood up. 'I'm going back to our hotel, Martin,' she said. 'I'm expecting a call from New York.'

'Aw, honey . . .'

'You'd better not join me until you've worked out who matters most: me, or the daughter of the man who murdered your first wife.'

The silence was flabbergasted. In it, Sibylla picked up her embroidery and walked across the carpet. The heels of her shoes left dimples in the pile that tufted together again after she had passed. At the door she paused.

'And maybe you better think about this: if you don't

171

want to come up with the cash, I'll go find someone who will.'

'Jeez, honey,' Marty said. 'Just because you're mad's no reason to—'

'I'm not mad,' Sibylla said. 'Not in the slightest.'

All of them stared at the door as she shut it hard behind her.

'Wouldn't you hate to see her when she *is* mad?' Penny said.

Alexandra touched Marty's arm. 'I'm terribly sorry,' she said. 'I hadn't quite realised this meant so much to her. I'll put up some money for you, if you want. Especially since my father had already—'

'—pulled out,' Theo said. 'He pulled out of the scheme. I heard him tell her.'

'I wish she hadn't said that about your dad,' said Marty.

Theo leaned against his father's shoulder. 'Dad,' he said, 'that lady is real bad news.'

Marty didn't say anything. He put his fat little hands on his knees and shook his head.

'You'll be better off without her,' Theo said.

'Better off? Do you have any idea how much another divorce'll cost?' Marty's face was drawn.

'I won't let you starve,' said Theo.

'You know, son, sometimes I wish . . . I just wish . . .' Marty shook his head some more.

'Wish what?'

'That I could meet up with someone like your mother. Not interested in fancy clothes and fancy cars, not forever wanting diamonds and expensive trips, wanting to go fancy places. I'm too old for it. Want to stay home, enjoy my house, have my grandchildren over Sundays, make a buck or two. Reason I keep marrying these young kid's because that's what I meet. Young kids. And all on the make. Figure five years with Marty Schumann's paunch and the way his feet smell're worth it for what they can get out of him when the d-divorce settlement c-comes through.'

Penny put her face alongside his. 'Bet your feet don't smell,' she said.

'Dad, I really wish there was something I could do,' Theo said.

'Want me to go and rough the lady up for you, huh?' Penny asked. 'Want me to tell her she picked the wrong guy to mess with, 'cos he's got real good connections?'

Marty's lower lip quivered. He put his head on Penny's shoulder. 'Never been right since Beattie died,' he said. 'Just never been right.'

'There are plenty of other fish in the sea,' Alexandra said.

'Trouble is, Marty doesn't particularly want to spend the rest of his life with a fish,' Penny said. Perhaps she should introduce him to Miss Ivory. Or Katerina Tasso. Although she was getting bad vibrations from Tasso. Very bad. The terminal kind.

'What the hell did she mean, anyway?' Theo said. 'About my mother and Alexandra's father?'

'Didn't Marty tell you the other night? At the Rockingham?' said Penny.

'Tell me what?'

'Didn't say nothing about it,' mumbled Marty. 'I was going to, but it seemed kinda dumb. I got no proof nor nothing.'

'Proof of what, Dad?'

Marty twisted his hands together. 'Aw, hell,' he said. 'Can't talk about it. Not in front of Alex here.'

'Please go right ahead,' Alexandra said. 'I'm afraid there's very little I wouldn't believe my father capable of. Even murder.'

'I didn't say that,' Marty said.

'What exactly happened to Mom?' asked Theo. He held his father's hand very tightly. 'It's time I knew, don't you think? Especially if she didn't die the way you said. The way you told us when we were kids.'

'Say, do you have anything to drink around here?' Marty said. The thighs of his checked trousers tightened suddenly, as though he had steeled himself to something unpleasant.

'Whatever you want,' said Alexandra. She stood up. 'Bourbon, gin, whisky?' She moved gracefully over the rugs to a bookshelf shuttered in rosewood. Her blue dress whispered.

'Bourbon,' Marty said. 'On the rocks, if you got any.'

Alexandra brought him one, the ice cubes knocking against each other. Marty swallowed it like an engine out of gas. 'Aaah,' he said.

'What's all this about Costas and Mom?' repeated Theo.

'Costas wanted your father to come in on some deal that involved pornography,' Penny said. 'Using children.'

Alexandra filled her lungs with air and let some of it out through her nose. She didn't speak.

'Yeah,' said Marty. 'Only Beattie didn't want nothing to do with it. Not with filth like that.'

'So what happened?' said Theo.

'Well.' Marty looked apologetically at Alexandra. 'Gee, I hate to say these kinda things about your dad, you know.'

'I'm used to it,' Alexandra said.

'What happened was, he invited us to stay on that island of his. Guess you weren't no more than a baby then. Beattie didn't want to go, said she didn't trust him, didn't want to have nothing to do with some guy's in pornography, you know?'

'I know,' Alexandra said.

'I said she was being dumb, that a guy like Costas didn't hold grudges. Boy, how dumb can you get! So we went. And after a couple of days, he invites her to go sailing with him. Him and some other woman and Melissa—that's your mother, Alex.'

Alexandra nodded.

'Anyways, they didn't come back that night. There was a helluva storm going on out there on the water, wind howling, waves smashing against the island. I was real worried, but the others kept saying there wasn't nothing to worry about, Costas was a real good sailor.'

'Who were the others?' Penny said.

'I don't remember now,' Marty said. 'Business friends,

174

mostly. A couple of Japs. Some kind of a high-up from the Bank of England. The man who came with the other woman who went out on the boat with Costas. She was a film actress and I guess he was her lover, half her age, couldn'ta been more than twenty. Beattie and me thought he was much better looking than she was. Fact is, they was a much classier bunch than me'n'Beattie was used to.'

'This guy with the film star. Was his name Pannis?' asked Penny.

'Maybe. Coulda bin. Yeah, now you mention it . . .'

'What happened to Mom?' Theo said.

'Costas finally showed up the next day, round supper time. Him and the film star. By then the storm had blown itself out. They both looked kinda wild. Way they told it, wind'd got up, and they was all of them thrown overboard except for the film actress lady. Beattie and Melissa—we used to call her Mellie—they were swept away. The other two couldn't get to them.' Remembering, Marty gave a small watery sniff. 'I knew right then there was something funny going on. Costas musta done something. I mean, if he survived, and the other woman, Beattie woulda done too. She could swim like a fish. And she grew up around boats, up there in Maine. She knew all about the sea.'

'Didn't you say something?' Theo said.

'I—uh—no, guess I didn't.'

'Why the hell not?'

Marty knotted his fingers together. Little ridges of fat stood up on the backs of his hands. 'See, the thing was, sounds terrible, but we had a deal going down, me and Costas. I just couldn't afford to start throwing accusations round, louse the whole thing up.'

'Jesus, Dad.'

'I had you and Roxanne at home to think about,' Marty said miserably. 'So I told myself it was fate. Told myself Beattie'd just drowned. But I knew deep down it was him, it was Costas killed her.' He pressed his hands against each other. 'The bastard. The shitting *bastard*.'

Of the four people in the room, only Penny was uninvolved. She could feel the tensions between the other three as they reacted to what Marty had told them. Peripherally, she sensed the adjustments as they reperceived each other. And themselves.

Perhaps this wasn't a place she should be.

She stood up.

Motives. Marty's. Sibylla's. And it was odd how Tasso kept turning up. Right on the spot at the time Beattie and Melissa Kyriakou died. And again when Costas was killed.

Did it mean anything? And if so, what?

14

THE YOUNG MAN SPRINKLING THE GERANIUMS ADMITTED that Miss Tasso was staying there. He further grudgingly allowed as how she was in the house that very minute. Whether she would see visitors was another matter. Penny suggested that maybe Miss Tasso could be persuaded. The man intimated that he would need persuading to persuade Miss Tasso. Penny waved some persuasive drachmas around. The man let her into the garden.

Tasso's house was in a suburb of Athens. Red-tiled, surrounded by a white wall, shaded by dusty palms, there was nothing to set it apart from those on either side. You could tell that the suburb was not a slum by the type of car parked along the kerb. Also by the absence of obvious children. There was a baby, some way down the avenue, being pushed along in an English pram by a Greek nursemaid in a dark-blue uniform and shiny black shoes. Otherwise the street was empty.

The shutters of the house were pulled across the windows. From the outside, it looked unlived in. Inside, it looked the same. The walls were white-painted and roughcast. A simple open-tread staircase curved up to the first floor. There were two carved wooden tables on the bare tiled floor, heavy squat things that didn't pretend to be anything but tables. On one of them was a verdigrised bronze of a child's head, rounded with the ruthless innocence of the very young.

The man stopped at the front door. He didn't come in. He shouted. A white-aproned woman in a black dress

177

appeared. She listened with a frown to what the man said. She pointed Penny to a hard upright chair and went away. So did the man, quietly closing the front door behind him.

Penny sat. One thing you had to say about Katerina Tasso: she hadn't read *Better Homes* recently. This kind of minimalist chic went out in the 60s. It was curiously restful. Unjarring to the eye. Tasso obviously didn't care for decorator clutter. Penny reviewed what she knew about the woman. According to the official releases, she'd been discovered at a tender age in a mountain village in the north of Greece. Either milking goats or tending sheep. Or vice versa. Penny couldn't remember which. Something rural like that. Her mother had been a gypsy, her father farmed a couple of rugged acres and held the local kerosene franchise. After a couple of films in her own country, she'd been shipped to Hollywood. The mournful subtleties of her facial planes—the yearning glance, the unspoken hurt, the melancholy brush of eyelash on cheek—had been the paradigm of sorrow to an entire generation. She had been well served by black-and-white film. Aware of this, she had refused to make the move into colour. Ten years ago, she'd dropped out of sight. Since then, she'd maintained a profile lower than Howard Hughes. Even the press had given up trying to coax her out of reclusion. Were it not for the art theatres and the film clubs, Tasso might not have existed. Thanks to Paul Leandro's father, Penny now knew why.

She heard movement above. Tasso appeared at the top of the stairs. She walked down without looking at her feet, keeping one hand on the rail. Gloria Swanson in *Sunset Boulevard* couldn't have done it better. She was pale. Her black hair stretched back across her skull like a ballet-dancer's. Heavily outlined in kohl, her dark eyes were set deep in their sockets behind smoky sunglasses. With that well-known classic bone-structure, it was easy to see why the young husband hadn't noticed the years between them.

Tasso's face didn't change when she saw Penny. Except for the eyes. Even the shades couldn't hide their terror.

Interesting. Penny was used to a varied reaction from those she came into contact with. Terror was rarely one of them. Even when it was the one she hoped for.

'Hi,' she said. 'I'm Penny Wanawake. You probably don't remember me.'

'I remember.'

'The police let you go.'

'Of course.' The actress stood on the bottom step. It brought her level with Penny. She was wearing a black sweater and tight black trousers. Her mouth had been carelessly marked with lipstick the colour of meat. 'I told them I must return to Athens immediately. There was no reason for them to stop me.'

'They haven't pinned the murder on anyone yet.'

Tasso didn't answer. Every now and then her mouth shook. When it did, she placed a finger over her lips as though to calm them.

Penny waited a count of ten. 'But when I left England, an arrest was imminent,' she said.

'Good,' Tasso said. She paused. Touched her mouth. Said, 'Who?'

'Jason Jackson.'

'The owner of the hotel?'

'Yes.'

Tasso came down the last step. 'I need a cigarette,' she said. She walked across the hall and opened a door. Sunlight flooded in from a room that faced out over a tangled garden. Shrubs grew so close to the windows that their leaves pressed against the glass. Beyond them, scarlet and purple flowers shocked like sores. The actress went quickly to a low table topped with green marble and took a cigarette from a box. She used the lighter beside it, putting her head back and closing her eyes as she drew the first three drags deep into her lungs.

Penny followed her. 'Do you know him?' she said.

'Who?'

'Jason.'

With her eyes still closed, Tasso shook her head. 'No. Not at all. That is, I have stayed at his hotel in the past. I know who he is. But I would not say I knew him.'

'He's having hysterics, of course. Anyone would, faced with a charge of murder when they're entirely innocent.'

Behind the sunglasses, the eyes opened. The beautifully shaped head turned towards Penny. 'What makes you so sure he is innocent?'

Penny shrugged. 'Where's the motive?'

'I understood that he was in debt over his hotel,' Tasso said. 'I understood that he was experiencing financial difficulties.'

'Where did you understand that from?'

Tasso stilled her unruly mouth. 'I heard it.'

'It's an odd thing to remember about someone you don't know.'

'Not really. If you were told such a detail about the owner of the hotel where you were staying, you would naturally be interested.'

'Was the teller in your case called Kyriakou?'

Taking off her glasses, Tasso stared at Penny. 'I really don't remember.'

'You remember what the person said, but not who it was?'

'Exactly.'

'Did Costas invite you to his party, Miss Tasso?'

'No. But when I heard he was at the same hotel as I was, naturally I went to see him.'

'Dressed to kill.'

'He is an old friend from a long time ago. Naturally I was glad to see him again. As he was glad to see me.'

'A friend?' Penny said. She looked about her. The room was furnished as sparsely as the hall. Two sofas upholstered in green velvet were on either side of the marbled table. A further carved table stood against a wall. Above it were two paintings of a religious nature that could have been very Old Masters or very new fakes. That was it. On the table a photograph of a man was framed in silver.

'Yes.' Tasso lit another cigarette. 'A good friend.'

Penny picked up the photograph and held it at arm's length. 'Is this your husband?' she said. She knew the answer. She'd already seen it in Leandro's files.

'Yes.'

'He's a good-looking man.'

'Yes.'

'Too bad he was shot like that.'

The actress stood very still. Even the smoke seemed to hang for a moment around her without stirring. Only her mouth moved, shaking, as though it existed apart from the rest of her face. The terror that had been there when Tasso first saw Penny returned. She backed away towards the wilderness of the garden. Then she said, 'You seem to know a great deal about me.'

'Some.'

'I wish I knew as much about you.'

'From what I heard,' Penny said, 'your life has been a helluva sight more interesting than mine.'

'From what you heard.' Tasso stubbed out her cigarette in a jade ashtray. She took another one from the box and lit it. 'What do you want?' she said. Her voice broke as she said it.

Penny tried not to feel like a hunter about to trap a threatened species. 'Just the truth,' she said. 'And I don't think it's true that Jason killed Costas Kyriakou.'

'Do you think I did?'

'I think you had an excellent motive, Miss Tasso.'

'Which is?'

'Revenge.'

'For what?'

'The ruined political career of your husband, Jay Pannis. The fact that he spent ten years in a wheelchair as a result of being framed by Kyriakou. The fact that you gave up your own career to care for him.'

'I could have you thrown out,' Tasso said.

'I know. But you won't.'

'What makes you so sure?'

'You need to know what I know, and what I merely suspect. Besides, why should you? An innocent person, especially an old friend of Kyriakou's, should be happy to see justice done.'

Tasso's mouth hardened. 'Justice?' she said. 'If I talk to you at all, it's because now my . . . now both Pannis and Kyriakou are dead, I don't care who knows the truth.' She gave a long shuddering sigh. 'I knew you would come, Miss Wanawake. I was warned that soon I would have to face the past again.'

'Who warned you?'

'Someone I trust. Who tells me—what will be. Are you with a detective agency?'

'Just a gifted amateur.'

'Ah.' Tasso's huge eyes stared out into the garden. At a guess, she wasn't seeing flowers.

'I think that it wasn't until your husband finally died that you were free to go after Kyriakou. To plan your revenge,' Penny said. 'You'd probably discovered by then who was behind that frame-up with the under-age call girl.'

The downward curve of Tasso's mouth deepened into something that was half grimace, half smile. 'I was told,' she said. 'The person responsible made sure I knew.'

'I figured. And because he was so goddam conceited, Costas didn't see anything strange in your coming back to him after Pannis killed himself. In spite of the fact that he was responsible. After all, you and he had been pretty tight years ago, way I heard.'

'You seem to have heard such a lot, Miss Wanawake.'

'It was about a year ago that your husband died, wasn't it?'

'Ten months,' Tasso said. Her mouth moved again, as if in pain. 'And I'm sure you know how he died.'

'Yes.'

'He bled to death in the bed beside mine. I hope—I pray—that it didn't hurt. Even if it had, he would have made no sound. He wouldn't have wanted to wake me. He wouldn't have wanted me to stop him. I often wonder if I was cruel to prevent him from doing it before. He begged me so often.'

Rule Three of detective work: Don't Get Involved. Penny was being drawn in. Manipulated like a lump of clay. 'You can't ask another person to take your life for you,' she said. Dammit. The last thing she wanted was to end up feeling sympathy for the woman she was beginning to feel pretty certain had killed Costas. And left Jason to take the rap.

'But if that person is helpless,' Tasso said softly. 'If you are the only one who can release them from their suffering . . .'

'Even so . . .'

'When all they ask is that you leave the means within their reach, the pills, the knife, so that the decision to live or die is theirs, not yours?'

'You can't opt out of your own moral responsibility,' said Penny. Yet what moral responsibility was there in allowing a man to spend the rest of his life in such circumstances, over which he had no control? She thought of her mother. Lady Helena had often said that she would rather die than end up a vegetable attached to a life-support machine. And Penny had often sworn that she would see she didn't. Did she have a right to do that? Did her mother have the right to ask? 'In the end, you can only take responsibility for your own life, not for other people's.' She knew she didn't believe that, not if it was her mother helpless in a wheelchair. Or Barnaby . . .

'Would you like some coffee?' Tasso said. 'I'll call for Sofia.'

'No thank you. I'd rather get on with this.'

'Frankly, Miss Wanawake, I'd rather you didn't.'

'Afraid?'

Again Tasso gave that grim smile. Her long mouth curved like a scimitar. 'Not for myself,' she said. 'I've lived with the past for too many years to be afraid.' She looked out again at her wild garden. Perhaps she let it go where it would because of those years when her young husband could go nowhere except where others took him.

Somewhere at the back of her neck, Penny felt an

antique shiver. Just so must vengeful Clytemnestra have looked, barbed mouth, deep eyes, hunger for blood.

She coughed. 'I think you planned to kill Costas as soon as Pannis died,' she said. 'But you had to wait for the circumstances to be right. I think they were as right as they would ever be, that evening at the Rockingham. You knew about the well: you'd stayed at the hotel before. You probably got Costas to lift the glass for you—it was the sort of macho thing he'd have gone in for. Then you pushed him in, maybe without even bothering to bash him on the head, lowered the glass, perhaps even watched him drown.'

'Ingenious.'

'It was sheer bad luck that I get up so early. The body would eventually have sunk below the water level and might never have been discovered. It's not as if the well is used as a water supply.'

'A wise young judge.' Tasso narrowed her eyes behind the smoke that crawled up her face.

'I'm not judging anybody. Just don't want to sit by and see Jason get blamed for something he didn't do.'

'For something you think I did?' The actress gave a small laugh. She touched one eye behind the sunglasses. 'Would you not agree that the circumstances were extenuating?'

'This wasn't the first time you've been linked with Costas and sudden death.'

'How do you mean?'

'Remember Beattie Schumann and Melissa Kyriakou?' Penny said.

Tasso nodded a couple of times. 'You're very thorough.'

'Were those deaths—Melissa's and Beattie's—accidental?'

Tasso moved away from the window. 'You frighten me, Miss Wanawake.' She took another cigarette and lit it. Slowly she pulled in the smoke. 'You seem terrifyingly close to things I would rather keep secret. A secret shared is no longer a secret.'

'I know how to keep my mouth shut.'

'Good.' Slowly the actress sat down. She spread her

arms along the back of the sofa. 'Melissa,' she said. 'I haven't thought of her for years. There has been so much other . . .' She made a waving movement with one hand. She looked back into the past.

'Think of her now.'

'Poor little Melissa.'

'How old was she when she died?'

'Sixteen.'

'Is that all?' Somehow Penny had pictured Alexandra's mother as older than that, a woman heading towards middle age.

'Such a pretty child,' Tasso said.

'Go on.'

'Costas always prided himself on his sailing,' Tasso said.

'Yeah.'

'Doesn't it strike you as odd that such a brilliant yachtsman has such a small boat?'

'A 42-footer's plenty big enough for me.'

'And kept it in the Ionian? Hardly the world's most dangerous waters. The truth is, he's scared of the sea. It's easy to fiddle about with a tiller and study a compass when you never lose sight of land. Even when a squall comes up, it doesn't last for very long.'

'Frankly, I'm with Costas on that one. Did Mr Pannis sail?'

'Until his accident, Mr Pannis loved sailing. Especially long-distance sailing.'

'Did Melissa enjoy it?'

'Melissa enjoyed only what Costas said she could. She didn't dare to have ideas of her own. Costas married her when she was only fourteen.'

'Was that legal?'

'In Greece, at that time, yes. Besides, who would question what Costas Kyriakou did? Even then he was already powerful. He liked them young in those days, untouched, vulnerable. He would use them sexually as though they were part of a circus act, until they were afraid of sex, of men, afraid of a kiss or a touch. Then he'd get rid of them, knowing they would never look at

185

another man without fear.' Tasso threw her head back again and squinted at the ceiling through narrowed eyes. 'Melissa was by no means the first. She might have grown up to rebel against him, but he didn't give her the chance. She was very beautiful. That's what he liked: the spoiling of beauty, of innocence. Perhaps it was for the best that she died when she did.'

'How exactly did she die?'

'I think she probably drowned.'

'You don't know?'

'Not for certain. Costas took three of us out for that day. Me, Melissa and Beattie Schumann. It was fine until late in the afternoon. Then a squall blew up. He sent Beattie and me below, and kept Melissa up in the cockpit with him although she was terrified. *Because* she was terrified.'

'Beattie knew a lot about boats, didn't she?'

'Yes. Which was a fatal mistake on her part.'

'Why?'

'Because instead of lying down on a bunk, the way I did, she stood at the chart table, checking our course. I think she must have looked up into the cockpit at the wrong time.'

'And seen what?'

'I'm not sure. As I said, I was lying down. I wasn't a good sailor in those days. I'd never have gone on the trip if I'd thought the wind would get up like that.' Tasso blew smoke about. 'I thought about it so often afterwards. I think she must have seen Costas attack Melissa in some way. Perhaps with the winch handle. Whatever she saw, Beattie was out in the cockpit faster than you can imagine.'

'Did she say anything?'

'I didn't take it in at the time. I felt too ill. I've tried to reconstruct it since in my mind, her shout, the sounds she made. Maybe she said, "Murderer." Maybe, "He's murdered her." Maybe something else. It wasn't until it was all over that I remembered. That I thought about any of it.'

'What happened then?'

'After a while, I heard Costas shouting. Screaming. I got myself up on to the deck, though if you've ever been seasick you will know what I mean when I say that I would infinitely have preferred to die there and then. There was no one else on board. It was almost dark. I looked over the side, but there was nothing. No Beattie. No Melissa. I found Costas down in the water, hanging on to the dinghy line at the stern. The wind had died by then. Somehow I managed to help him back on board.' The long eyelashes swept down over the cheek. 'I should have left him there.'

'And he told you that both Beattie and Melissa had gone over the side and he'd gone over himself to try and help them.'

'Something like that. It wasn't until later that I realised he'd probably killed them both. When I knew exactly what he was capable of.'

'Why would he kill his own wife?'

'Because he was bored with her. He couldn't divorce her: she was the mother of his daughter.'

'And Beattie Schumann?'

'Because she'd seen something she shouldn't have done.'

'Or prevented her husband from coming in on a deal with Costas that she disapproved of.'

This time Tasso smiled a real smile. 'That fat little husband of hers. How she adored him.'

'You didn't confront Costas with it?'

'I had other things on my mind. Heavy things.'

There was a faint tap at the window. An insect, maybe. Or a leaf. Tasso whirled round. One hand touched her heart. 'I keep forgetting,' she said. 'He's dead.'

'You hated him, didn't you?' Penny said.

'Totally. I spent most of my life hating him. I hate him now.'

'I can see where you'd want revenge.' What it was boiling down to was whether Tasso could have lifted the glass covering Jason's designer-chic well. Extreme emotion bred extreme strength, didn't it? Which she'd have needed if the pulley ropes had gone.

'Maybe you can. I doubt if you see what for,' Tasso said.

Maybe the ropes *had* been there originally. Maybe someone had removed them after replacing the well-cover, in order to throw suspicion on to someone else. Or remove it from themselves.

'What he did to your husband is reason enough.'

'I hated Costas a long time before Pannis was shot. A long time.'

Bells clanged somewhere inside Penny's head. Sirens. 'When you said Melissa wasn't the first young girl that Costas had—uh—had . . .'

'He was forty-two when he married Melissa,' Tasso said. 'He'd decided he needed an heir.'

'And you were discovered when you were sixteen, is that right?'

'No,' Tasso said.

'No?'

'I was fourteen, like Melissa. Another virgin. Another innocent.'

'And the discoverer was Costas?'

'Yes.'

There was no need for her to say more. No wonder she had stiffened when he touched her. To take from a woman the joy of sexual love was a cruelty that might well madden into murder. Of course there *were* such things as extenuating circumstances. Some people didn't deserve to live.

'I see,' Penny said again.

'I'm afraid you don't see half of it, Miss Wanawake. Not even a quarter. You came here today to accuse me of killing Costas. I don't deny that I wanted revenge for the things he had done to me. I wanted him to suffer the way I had done. But you've got it all wrong. I had every reason in the world to want Costas alive. I'd have risked my own neck to rescue him from his murderer, just so he could live with what I told him that night.'

'Which was?' Penny shifted on the green velvet cushions. In front of her, Tasso's cruel passionate face hung like a shield, an insufficient protection for the secrets it was designed to defend. Mrs Macbeth, alive and well and raging for revenge.

'The truth about Pannis.' Tasso banged another cigarette in between her lips like a poisoned blow-dart. 'Costas had seen to it that his life was ruined, partly because of the oil deal in Mexico, partly because Pannis was mine. Costas never forgave me for running out on him before he could run out on me.'

'When was that?'

'When I was sixteen. While I was still able to salvage something of my life.'

'And then you met Mr Pannis.'

'I don't know whether Costas was aware of it, but Pannis was everything he was not. Idealistic. Generous. Lovable and loving. That's why he wanted to go into politics. He saw people like Costas, the powerful unscrupulous rich, as the real evil in the world. He thought that political legislation was the best way of combating them.'

She laughed, a creaking sound that broke somewhere in the middle. 'When I told Costas what he'd done, I watched him grow old in front of me. When he realised that all the money in the world wasn't going to bring Pannis back again.' The actress bent her head and raised both hands to her face. She breathed in, deep and slow. 'Oh, my God. My God,' she said, her voice aching with pain. She looked across at Penny and said quietly: 'It was the most triumphant moment of my life. And the most terrible.'

'What did you tell him?'

Tasso jabbed her cigarette into the ashtray. She paused with the lid of the cigarette box in her hand, hand hovering over the contents. 'With a man like Costas, daughters don't count. Have you noticed how his boat is called after the son he didn't have, rather than the daughter he did?'

'I have,' said Penny.

'So, no doubt, has Alexandra. Have you seen him tap his cane on the ground when he wants something? As though she were a trained dog? He did the same thing

189

with her mother. To a man like Costas, a son was everything. The fact that he never had one made him a failure in his own eyes.'

'What was it you told him, the night he was killed?'

'That Pannis wasn't my husband.'

'What, then?'

'My son, Miss Wanawake.' Again the terrible smile. 'And his.'

15

'Lucas?'

'Ye—?'

'It's Penny.'

'Wha—?'

'Penny Wanawake.'

'I know which Penny, for God's sake,' Lucas snapped. 'What other Penny would have the nerve to ring up at this hour?' A pause. 'You do *know*, what time it is, don't you?'

Penny looked at her watch. The tiny diamonds on the face twinkled infinitesimally as the hands moved. 'Two thirty-one,' she said.

'What the hell do you want?' said Lucas.

'A fortune-teller.'

'At two fucking thirty in the morning.'

'Two thirty-one.'

'I've got a pregnant wife, Penelope.'

'I know that. But it's literally life and death.'

'Added to which, by the time I've finished cleaning the shit out of the rich folks' houses, I am dead beat.'

'It's, I only just got back from Greece, see. I'd have asked my mother, except she's away. Thing is, I really need to know where to get hold of a clairvoyant.'

'And I need to sleep.'

'Don't be mean, Lucas. I brought you back a sponge.'

'A sponge! A *sponge*? Hold on a minute, will you?'

'Why?'

'I want to break it to my heavily pregnant wife. She is

191

not going to be able to contain herself when I tell her the good news, however badly she needs her sleep. As does the child in her womb who is probably curled up with its little foetal fingers in its rudimentary ears, trying to catch some rest in preparation for its big entrance scene.'

'This is a natural sponge I'm talking here,' Penny said. 'None of your cheap rubbish.'

'There is a special hell for people who bring other people sponges back from abroad,' Lucas said coldly. 'Also for people who bring lamps made out of shells, and ashtrays with some cute local proverb handpainted on them.'

'What kind of asshole you think I am, Lucas?'

'Also for idiots who ring up in the—'

'Is there a hell for people who bring back duty-free for other people?'

Pause. 'A clairvoyant, you said?'

'Yeah. You actors are supposed to be a superstitious lot. Thought you'd know how I'd set about finding one.'

'Look in the back pages of the monthly women's magazines,' said Lucas. 'Can I go now?'

'Sorry,' Penny said. 'You know how it is.'

'I know how it is to be woken from a deep sleep,' Lucas said.

'Grovel. Bootlick.'

'As long as you realise that just because I clean your house in between rôles it doesn't mean you own me body and soul.'

'I'll really try to remember that,' Penny said.

She was smiling as she put down the telephone.

The small ads pages of the magazine she found downstairs were a new class of reading. The clairvoyant section came right after an ad promising permanent low-cost contraception in the form of a vasectomy, and right before another offering to reveal her true sexual nature through an analysis of her handwriting. Of the clairvoyants, she straight off benched Aswaz, fresh from triumphs in Delhi and Calcutta, who assured potential clients that he could read their characters as easily as most people read a book. With illiteracy on the rise, it wasn't a promise that thrilled. Nor did she pay much mind to Sister Lucille, who offered help with any problems Penny might have, such as divorce, alcoholism or lost loved ones. The ad that grabbed her said simply:

ANTHONY PYNE: Confidentail postal readings. FEE £10. Personal consultations: FEE £120. Full horoscope included.
Complete confidentiality assured.

She dialled the number provided. The Ansafone had a number of things to tell her. She listened to them. It invited her to leave her own message after the bleep. She declined to do so. She put down the receiver. Gaahd. How she hated being patronised by a machine. She'd call again in the morning.

She picked up the postcard that had been waiting when she returned from Athens:

Having an idyllic time tracing Odysseus's voyage home. Luckily it isn't taking us as long as it took him. Hope all is well. I'm arriving at Heathrow 19.06 Thursday. Please meet.

Love, Muth.

Did her mother even know that Kyriakou was dead? People in sailing boats usually find newspapers superfluous. They limit their radio-listening to weather reports. The news could come as a rude shock.

There was a note on the pillow on her side of the big double bed. Barnaby had gone to Oxford on business. She stared at the Georgia O'Keefe on the wall and wondered what kind of business. Although he was safely back from South Africa, he was talking wild. About ways of getting famine supplies into areas behind battlelines in other poorer African nations. About the possibilities of recruiting mercenaries. It didn't sound like a recipe for longevity. 'I like it that the diamonds I

193

smuggle out of the country go back to help alleviate some of the problems created by people like my father,' he'd said. She missed him.

It takes two to tango. It takes two to make a murder. What would it be like to be struck down in the prime of life because of another's whim? She thought herself into a wheelchair. Being dressed, being fed, being toileted, her body out of her own control. She clenched her fists. Impotence. Rage, scalding as tar. And fear. If the hand that fed you were to decide enough was enough, what then? You'd be alone. Or institutionalised. How much better the sharp blade, the bloodstained sheet, life ebbing as the woman who loved you so fiercely she wouldn't let you die slept in the next bed.

Some woman. The smell of Tasso's hatred had grown as she spoke on into the evening in her harshly accented voice. Outside, the wild plants pressed at the window. Inside, the room seemed like a time capsule unearthed, free-falling through the years as long-ago events came cruelly to life again. She told how she had run from Costas on finding she was pregnant, determined that he would never get his hand on the child. How she'd left the baby with her mother, while she went to Hollywood to earn the money to bring him up. She'd seen him frequently, her reputation as a recluse beginning then when, still a girl, she had disappeared sometimes for days to be with her child.

'If Costas heard that I had a son,' she said, 'and how old that son was, he would know it was his. Even though Pannis was born in the U.S.A., was an American citizen. A son is the one thing he has not been able to buy. He'd have tried everything to take mine away from me.' Stubbing out a cigarette, she had added, 'I *would* have killed him if he had.'

Costas's lessons had been too deeply ingrained for her ever to be able to bear the caress of a man again. She lived alone, until Pannis was almost eighteen. It was then that a stringer for a German scandal-sheet had turned in the story of reclusive screen idol Katerina Tasso and her young husband. She hadn't bothered to deny it. She had thought it would make Pannis safe. Costas couldn't possibly suspect. Leandro Senior's information-gathering service had filed the story without checking.

Pannis proved to have a business brain at least as keen as his father's.

'Do you know the word *decoro*?' Tasso said. It was the only time she looked at Penny. 'The art historian Vasari uses it to describe appropriateness in a work of art. I felt there was *decoro* in the way Pannis pulled that Mexican oil deal from under his father's nose. And the father didn't even know.'

She had reckoned without Costas's ruthless need to get back at those who had done him down, however long it took. When she told Costas just what he'd done by destroying Pannis, just whose life he had ruined, it was as pure and terrible a revenge as the one the Fates had meted out to Oedipus, with as little regard for those closest to him.

She had wept, once. 'Oh, my son,' she had said. 'My beautiful, talented son.'

She was totally convincing.

Now, lying in the darkness of Chelsea, Penny asked herself one question. If the murder of Costas Kyriakou had nothing to do with Tasso, did it have anything to do with Hector?

Maybe she'd find out in the morning.

It wasn't morning when she woke again. In fact, it was pitchy black night. Carefully she manoeuvred her watch so she could catch the tiny diamonds. 4.24. Odd how humans need the time dimension to add solidity to their realities. 4.24. With the thick curtains closed to keep out the orange neon street-lamps, it made no difference what time it was. What had woken her? Why was she checking her watch as cautiously as if it was attached to the tail of a tiger?

She sat up. Sniffed. Smelled sweetness on the air. Listened. Heard the tiny puff of lungs, the little thud of adrenalined pulse. Where? Not close, not in the bedroom. Carefully she pushed back the duvet. Swung her long legs to the carpet, black invisible in the blackness. Stood. Listened again.

Someone was downstairs. Almost certainly at the big desk in the window overlooking the street. Padding across the rugs, Penny stood at the open bedroom door. From below, a faint orange glow tinged the darkness of the hall. Someone had pulled back the curtains in the drawing-room. She could smell the night, too, from the front door, left on the latch and half-open. Forward planning for a speedy departure.

She started down the stairs. Halfway up was a tread that creaked. The tenth from the bottom. But what was it coming down? Were there sixteen or seventeen steps? Before she could remember, the tread creaked. The stillness of the downstairs stiffened. The someone at her desk moved like a reflection across the floor. As Penny reached the bottom of the stairs, leaping them three at a time, fingers sliding down the banister, the someone was at the front door and running.

Penny ran too. At the front door, she stopped. There are places where six feet of naked black lady are a privilege. Streaking up a desirable SW10 street at 4.27 a.m. is almost certainly not one of them. Some distance away, the intruder was turning the corner into the King's Road. Penny had time only to register dark clothes and slimmish build. No other distinguishing marks. The only thing she could have said for certain was that the intruder was not Marty Schumann.

If not him, then who? What had she got that was worth stealing? Or what did the intruder think she had? What did she know that someone else wanted to know? It didn't take long to establish that the intruder had only been at her desk. Nothing else seemed to have been touched. Easy enough to get in, if you had a key. Or knew how to pick locks.

She bolted the front door. Walking back into the drawing room, she stared down at the papers on her desk. The likelihood was that the break-in had something to do with either Hector Oakley or Costas Kyriakou. But which one?

                              *   *   *

In the next morning's newspapers, she read that the man
who had been helping police with their enquiries into the
death of Greek millionaire Costas Kyriakou had been
allowed to return to his home pending further investiga-
tions. A reprieve for Jason. That was something. One of
the tabloids brought up Irene Lampeter's death and the
earlier death of her first husband, James Lampeter, a
cousin of the Greek tycoon. A crime correspondent speculated on a possible link.

Penny didn't ring the number given in Mr Anthony
Pyne's advertisement until ten o'clock. Give him time to
arrive, open his briefcase, flex his muscles. She timed it
right. When she rang, Pyne himself picked up. He said
so straight out.

'Anthony Pyne here.'

She recognised the voice. 'I am desperate, Mr Pyne,'
she said. She Frenched her voice, gutturalising the 'r',
nasaling the 'n's.

'We can't have that, can we?' he said. The voice was
smooth as an avocado, comforting as the womb.

'May I see you? As soon as possible?' begged Penny.
'I 'ave important things to decide, but I cannot wizzout
your 'elp.' She hoped the French accent would make it
clear why she wasn't consulting her regular clairvoyant.
If it occurred to him to wonder.

'Let me see.' She heard him riffle through the pages
of an engagement diary. 'I'll be on holiday tomorrow,
for a week. How about a week the day after tomorrow?
Shall we say four-thirty?'

'Ah non, non,' she cried. 'Zat is too long. Let us say
today. Please, Monsieur Pyne.'

'I don't believe you've consulted me before,' Pyne
said. 'May I ask how you got my name?'

'It was recommended to me,' Penny said. 'By a very
dear friend.'

'Yes?'

Time for a shot in the dark. 'Uh—Katerina Tasso.'

'You're a friend of Miss Tasso's are you?'

'Oh yes,' breathed Penny. 'Ever since I was a little girl.'

'Very well. For a friend of Miss Tasso's . . . How about during the lunch hour today? Could you manage that?'

'Yes, yes,' said Penny. 'I have rehearsals until twelve, but after zat . . .'

'You're an actress, are you?'

'I am trying to be,' Penny said. Keep blowing truth bubbles and they might explode in your face.

'And your name?'

Name, name. 'Uh—Caresse.'

'Caresse who?'

'Just Caresse.'

'Do you know what my fees are?'

'It doesn't matter. I have plenty of money. *Grandmère*— my gran'muzzer, she left me everysing.' Was it imagination, or did she hear Pyne's ears prick up?

'I'm looking forward to meeting you, Caresse,' he said, creamier than sachertorte. 'Until lunchtime, then.'

'Monsieur Pyne?'

'Yes?'

'Where do you live?'

The address he gave her was in one of the big blocks of flats overlooking Regent's Park. Cars parked outside reflected the owners inside: a Mercedes, four BMWs, a dark blue Jag with leather upholstery. The grilles of the Snowdon aviary hung above nearby greenery. Tropical efflations from the Zoo sounded above the noise of traffic as she mounted the steps to the front door and pressed the buzzer.

Tinny syllables asked who she was.

'Cassette,' she said.

'Who?'

Damn. Rule One when using an alias: Remember it.

'Caresse,' she said. 'I rang you zis morning.' She leaned hard on the 'r's.

'Ah yes.' Beside her, the buzzer sounded and the front door opened. 'I'm on the fifth floor,' clanged the voice from the intercom. 'Flat 5B.'

Inside, mock marble spread towards a bank of lifts. Beside them was a rise of green-carpeted steps. The

foyer was glassed on two sides, its Michelangelian stark-
ness relieved by a dead tree stuck into a pot full of
marcasite chips. Penny took the stairs. She figured Anthony Pyne might come out to meet the lift. One look at
her face, and he'd be back inside his apartment before
she could say 'Whoopee Goldberg'.

Coming by stair, she might take him by surprise. And
she could out-stick anyone on the foot-in-the-door routine. Rounding the last curve of the lift-housing, she
stopped. There was no sound from above. If Anthony
Pyne was waiting for her, he must be dead. Or else as
suspicious as she was. Softly she went up the last four steps.
The hallway was empty. Two antique side tables stood
against the walls. Both were fakes. One held an arrange-
ment of dead twigs. The sound-proofing was high class.
Not a sound anywhere. Navy carpet, three inches high.
Navy doors, four inches thick. Number 5B had an Eye of
God painted on it in gold. It didn't conceal the peephole.

Penny pressed the bell of the door. Immediately she
stood well to one side. If Anthony peeped, he'd assume
the desperate Carette—no, *Caresse*— was a midget. Or
else that she was standing well to one side of the door.

She made her move as soon as the door began to
open. By the time it was wide enough to reveal Anthony
Pyne, all lit up, she was over the threshold.

'You!' he said. She'd known he would.

'You,' she said. He might have guessed she would.

'I thought you were an actress,' he said. Never mind
Europe: the lights were going out all over Anthony.

'And I thought Machiavelli was a Scotsman,' Penny
said. 'Just shows how wrong you can be, sometimes.'

He stepped back. He pushed at the door. She got in
the way. 'Move it, short stuff,' she said.

'Go away,' Oakley said. For, as she had suspected, it
was he.

'Dabbling in futures,' she said. 'I should have worked
it out sooner.'

'Piss off.' He leaned hard on the door.

'And at the same time assuring your own,' Penny
leaned harder.

'What?'

'Come on, Hec. You can level with me. How many of your customers have you married?'

'I don't know what—'

'I only know about Irene and Delia,' said Penny. 'So far. My guess is that's just for starters.'

'Delia? Who's De—'

'You can't have forgotten,' Penny said. 'Delia's the one whose hospital records got held up in the mail. The one whose money got you started.'

'My God. You've really been scraping the bottom of the barrel for dirt, haven't you? Who put you up to this? Lampeter?'

'No.'

'For your information, I loved Delia. Her death was exactly as reported.'

'And Irene's?'

'A tragic coincidence. Nothing more.'

Penny walked across the wide hall to a half-open door and pushed it open. A spread of glass looked out across the park to where the golden dome of the mosque gleamed like an inflatable onion. 'If you'd made it to the top of Avrios, what would Irene have seen?'

'The ruins of a shrine. And a spectacular view.'

'What would you say if I told you that there is no shrine on Avrios? And never has been.'

'I know there is.' Over his beard, Hector stared at her belligerently.

'How?'

'I read about it. Years ago, when I was still a kid, I found a book, a travel book, about the Greek Islands, and it mentioned it in there. Not just mentioned, enthused. I was young and impressionable. Reading about it in a North Country public library, with rain beating at the windows and a view of factory chimneys, it seemed a magic kind of place. Naturally I wanted to share it with my wife. I remembered it when I went back with Irene.'

'Hoping the gods would come to the rescue again, were you?'

Oakley set his jaw. 'What exactly do you want?'

'A cup of tea, please,' Penny said.

'Are you bloody jok—'

'And after that, a confession.'

'Of what?' Oakley retreated into his hall. Penny followed, shutting the door behind her. Ahead of her, a large Buddha squatted between two man-sized candle-holders of vaguely Eastern design.

'How about murder?'

'I could throw you out,' Oakley said. He was dressed in a brown robe that Thomas à Becket wouldn't have scrupled to wear. His work clothes. Designed to impress the punters. Something in the cabalistic line was slung round his neck on a heavy bronze chain.

'Hell. I know that,' Penny said. 'But you won't.'

'What's to stop me?'

'Simple curiosity. The desire to know what I know.'

'Listen, you fucking black bitch. You've been bugging me for a long time. I'm sick and tired of it.'

'Oh, my Gaahd.'

Squaring up to her, Hector fisted his hands. 'You may be taller than I am, but I can take you any time, any-where.' Under the loose sleeves of the robe, his biceps swelled.

'Which airline you working for, Hector?'

'And don't think I'm afraid to hit a woman. I've got no inhibitions about that sort of thing.'

'Way I've been hearing it, you got no inhibitions, period.'

'What have you heard? If anything.' Hector bounced on his feet a couple of times. He lowered himself by bending his knees. Like a pair of too-big pants, his centre of gravity hung below his crotch. 'Or is it all one big sodding bluff? Some amateur attempt at blackmail. You probably don't know a bloody thing about any-thing, do you?' It was amazing how people reverted to type when threatened.

'You're wrong,' said Penny. 'Jim and his wife were both quite helpful.'

'Jim who?'

'Parfitt.'

Backing up against one of the two closed doors, Oakley stared at Penny.

'His asthma's improved no end since he's been out there in Agia Eufonia,' she said.

'You cunt. What right do you have to spy on me?' Hector half lunged at her, then held back. Penny stepped back and sideways. If there was one thing she hated, it was that kind of talk. Not that she had anything against lively language. But she objected to the way men tried to reduce women to the sum of their sexual parts, as if those were the only female identifier, and then to use those parts as insults.

'What beats me is how you were able to remember all those aliases of yours,' she said. 'And there I was having trouble with just one.' She had expected violence, but not so soon. Not until she'd passed on enough to Hector to make him realise he'd been rumbled.

'Go back and tell Lampeter he can't prove a thing.'

'Wanna bet?'

Hector shifted his muscles about. He rolled the upper part of his body as though he had a cactus in each armpit. 'You've made a hell of a mistake, trying to put the frighteners on me,' he said, mastodon-grim. He stretched his fingers. She could see dark roots under his red curls.

'Did Irene come to you for reassurance? For a quick peep into the future, to see if it was going to improve or was going to stay bloody awful?' Behind Penny was another closed door. She felt for the handle. She turned it. If he made a move, so would she. Not that she was worried. Hector might—*might*, because she didn't really know anything for sure—be a murderer, but he had nothing to gain from beating her up. 'Did you check her credit rating before you proposed? Go through her medical records, calculate the odds on how long she'd last?'

Hector gritted his teeth. 'I loved her,' he said.

'What did you give her? I figure it must have been salt pills, the way she was always so thirsty. And of course, not only is salt definitely not recommended for high blood pressure, but she was also missing out on the real medication, wasn't she? Though by the time anyone thought to check, you'd have seen to it that the proper pills were back in the bottle, and her death was put down as due to natural causes.'

He looked outraged. In a choking voice, he said, 'I loved Irene, dammit.'

'Is that why you dragged her up a hill in the heat?'

'I knew she wasn't well. But she tried to hide any illnesses from me, and I played along with it where I could. And also—I know it sounds odd—I wanted her to make it to the top just because Delia hadn't. I can't describe what I felt like when it happened a second time. It was as though the fates had marked me down.'

Penny hesitated. Darn it. The man sounded as if he meant every word. Maybe he had loved Irene. There was quite a bit of *decoro* in the fact that because your mother had been a dead loss, you ended up marrying a woman who looked like everybody's mother. Motherliness had been Irene's unique selling-point.

'She was always so worried about the difference in age between us,' Hector said. 'It never bothered me. I told her so a thousand times, but in her heart she couldn't believe it. We'd have been perfectly happy if it hadn't been for those damn sons of hers. Especially Christopher. Obnoxious little sod. You'd have thought he'd been sleeping with her himself, the way he behaved when we started sharing a bedroom.'

'Yeah, yeah,' Penny said. 'If you're so white bread, how come you got so many pseudonyms? By the time I've finished delivering the rollcall of your aliases to the fuzz, they'll be round here quicker than a rat up a drainpipe.' She tried to sound like a force to be reckoned with but her heart wasn't really in it. Part of Hector's stock-in-trade must be to sound believable. Knowing that, why did she believe him? Almost.

'What exactly are you going to the police for?'

'I found Irene's pill bottle on board the *Alexandros*. You must have left them behind in the confusion over her death.'

203

'I know,' Hector said. 'I couldn't get back for them although I wanted to. They're the only proof there is.'

Behind him, across the passage, was another door. Plain wood, stripped pine, with an ornate brass handle. Nothing odd about that. Except that it was opening. Very slowly.

'Who's your company?' Penny said, watching the widening gap.

Oof! Wrong again. Hector *was* violent. He went for her knees. His arms closed round them like handcuffs. Together they fell into the room against whose door she'd been standing. They landed on the carpet with a painful crash. The room was dark except for a strip of light from the passage. Hector placed a fist at the side of her head with all the delicacy of a pile-driver. She saw stars. The ceiling was covered with them, huge gold ones. When you wish upon a star, makes no difference where you are. Especially if where you are is underneath a person trying hard to hurt you.

'Where?' he said, his mouth very close to her ear.

'Where what?'

'Are those pills?'

'Aha,' said Penny. Not very nonchalantly.

'Where are they?' He hit her again, on the side of the jaw.

'Boy. Bet nobody kicks sand in your face,' she whispered through one side of a mouth that felt the size of a puffball. Hector didn't answer. Too busy crashing sledgehammers at her. Her face was swelling like a soufflé. She'd gone deaf in one ear.

Somehow she scrambled to her feet. She made for the door. Before she reached it, Hector had grabbed her wrists and swung her round so she had her back to it. 'It's vital evidence,' he said into her face. 'Where are they?'

'Quite safe.' At least, that's what she tried to say.

'Where. Are. Those. Pills?'

If something didn't happen soon, she'd tell him. Because he might not be very tall, but he packed a mean wallop. A wallop that hurt. Just as she was about to say that she'd sent them to a lab to be analysed, something *did* happen.

Hector's eyes suddenly focussed beyond her. They widened. 'No,' he said. 'Don't.' She twisted, to see who was behind her. The back of her head crunched. Silvery darkness ran like fire across her skull. She wondered if she'd remembered to renew her BUPA subscription. She blacked out.

Years passed. When she came to, she was centuries old. Must have been. Only someone very antique would feel like she did. And very sick. As if the life-support machine had just been switched off. She wished she could see. Oh, Jesus Christ. Had she gone blind? Had Hector or his accomplice damaged the optic nerve? Her heart creaked into top gear. She could hear it beating. She began to sweat. She could stand anything, as long as she could see. But she couldn't. There was blood inside her nose. She touched the back of her head. It was still there. If her skull was fracture-free, it wasn't from want of trying. Well done, you guys. A for effort.

She tried to stand, using the wall for leverage. She couldn't. Under her palms, the wall seemed fuzzy. Christ, had he shattered something vital? Like her nervous system? Would she ever walk again? She could smell blood. Also something cheaply perfumed, sweetish and floury like spilled face-powder. It made her retch. Neatly she puked in the corner. A present for a good boy. Beyond the vomit smell was the other one. What was it? Incense? Joss-sticks? Midnight intruder? Midni—that was the scent that had woken her the night before. It had been Hector, had it? Looking for the pills?

Once again she tried to stand. This time she made it.

Feeling along the walls, she found a switch. She pushed it down. And there was light. Thank God. It clutched her eyes. Pink wasn't her favourite colour but better pink light than no light at all. She could see. The room was lined with cloth in a rich paisley pattern. All the woodwork was red. It made her very nervous. Over the marble fireplace a Chiricoesque painting showed a piazza under a pale sun, neatly gravelled walks leading to metaphysical infinity past shadowed arcades full of mystery.

Witch balls hung from the ceiling. So did a giant watch, suspended from a trail of gold links. When it moved, it glistered. It probably wasn't gold. A series of charts painted with zodiacal symbols were stuck to the walls. There was a life-sized stuffed goat in one corner, a pointed hat on its brow. A dead owl stood on a bit of driftwood on the mantelpiece. A wooden pentangle framed a convex distorting mirror. A huge hand of white porcelain, its palm marked with black squiggles, stood on a table near the door.

It was the room of a man who believed in giving his customers what they thought they wanted. A man who told lies in a warm voice. A man as smooth as snake oil, working hand in glove with someone else, someone as violent and unprincipled as he. Someone who'd hit her on the head with a very blunt instrument.

Who? In that last split second before she'd lost awareness, had she seen the person behind her? Was there anything in Hector's voice that could have given away the identity? She couldn't remember.

She tried the door. It was locked. Either they expected her to be out for a while longer, or they'd left the flat. Quietly, she opened the drawers in the desk. Stationery, headed with the Eye of God, and underneath it, *Anthony Pyne, Clairvoyant*. Papers. Bills. Letters. She read through a couple. '*Dear Mr Pyne, Thank you, thank you . . .*' '*Your skilful diagnosis has restored my faith in my fellow human beings and, more importantly, in myself . . .*' '*Once again you were right! I got the job. And the salary increase! Thank you so much . . .*'

In the bottom drawer, memorabilia. A birth certificate for William Hector Anthony Beech. A couple of school reports from Bartledale Grammar School. The young Beech/Oakley/Pyne did well in Maths and French. History left something to be desired. In English, they felt he spent too much time daydreaming. A brown envelope of poor-quality black-and-white snaps. Hector and his mother. Hector and his sister. His sister and a younger but unmistakable Jim Parfitt. A pretty girl of about ten: Nina Sibley, long-lost love? Hector holding the girl's hand. The girl standing ankle-deep in cold-looking sea holding the hand of a little boy. The girl holding the little boy upright on the crossbar of a bike. Hector on a sloping beach with his arms round them both.

Penny didn't believe in coincidences. Only patterns. Sometimes the patterns were so unexpected they took your breath away. Staring at the photograph of a far-off summer day, she began to see a design. The seaweed on the shingle was dead long ago. The sea had come in and gone out a thousand, thousand times since then. The three children in their woollen bathing suits had grown up in an era before the rise of leisure fashion. They smiled unself-consciously, the girl with her hair in tight plaits, the little boy with his round-rimmed National Health specs, Hector, still Bill at that stage, with his curls close to his head, as if he had just been swimming. All three of them were years older now, and very different. What led a man to change his identity? Or to run several at once? Was he looking for one he never had? Or did he feel uneasy with the one he'd been landed with? Had his own been taken away too young, and was the rest of his life a search for it? She'd have to track him down and ask.

The children in the photographs no longer existed. Twenty-five years ago they'd gone their separate ways, made separate lives, the pattern flinging them away from each other then curving back until they'd been brought together again a generation later, changed but still the same.

Only difference was, this time one of them was probably a murderer.

16

No one had mowed the lawn at the Lampeter house for quite a while. Weeds grew unchecked among the roses. At the upper windows, the curtains were still drawn shut although it was close to lunchtime.

Penny pulled her Porsche in behind a dark green Mercedes. A wide rockery led down to the herb garden which had always featured in the picture credits for *Pick and Choose*. With Irene gone, it was losing its definition. Sage ran riot, unkempt fennel towered among clumps of pennyroyal and thyme. Wan wistlessness was definitely the keynote. The old order changeth, giving place to nothing very much.

She banged the door-knocker. The porch needed sweeping. The door was half-glazed, not a front but a garden entrance. She was looking up a narrow stone-flagged passage to what was probably a big country kitchen. She banged again. Someone appeared against the door of the kitchen and came towards her. Orange and lemon striped pyjamas. Leather slippers. On the other side of the glass, Christopher Lampeter stared at her. He looked surprised.

Opening the door, he said, 'I thought you were in Greece.'

'I came back.'

'You'd better come in.'

Penny followed him into the kitchen. It smelled of fresh-baked bread and just-fried bacon. 'We were about to have breakfast,' Christopher said, 'Tim and I. Want some?'

'Thank you.'

Christopher neatly removed rolls from the oven. 'And one of these,' he said, 'I insist. The dough was one of my mother's specialities. She gave me the recipe.' He spoke as if asserting a proprietorial right. As though someone might otherwise snatch it from him. His way of coping with bereavement?

'In that case.' Penny sat down at the table. Scrubbed pine. Earthenware pots on the counter containing raisins and oatmeal and stone-ground flour. Naturally. What else in a place like this, with people like these? There was a pot of Lampeter's bramble jelly in a cut-glass bowl, and butter so pale you knew it had barely paused at the churn on the way to the butter-dish.

'It's lovely to see you,' Christopher said. 'Is there any particular reason?' Domesticity emphasised his likeness to Irene: full cheeks, round eyes under fleshy lids, smooth jaw.

'I was hoping to catch Hector.' As Penny spoke, she realised the futility. Might as well try to get with child a mandrake root. Hector was an escaper. From the past. From responsibility. Maybe even from justice.

'He's not here.'

'Where's he gone?'

Christopher shrugged. The movement dragged his pyjama jacket upwards. His lower chest was pink. 'I wasn't paying a lot of attention, to be honest. To stay with friends, I think he said.'

'Did he say who?'

Christopher shrugged again. 'Hector and I don't talk a lot. He's probably trying to find another buyer for his shares in my mother's business.'

'Any ideas?'

'How about my cousin, Alexandra Kyriakou? Presumably, unlike Tim and me, she's inherited the commitments—and the goods, of course—now her parent is dead.'

Jesus. Talk about cynical. 'If you have tears, I take it you're not prepared to shed them now,' Penny said.

Christopher stared at her without expression. 'Do you want an egg as well?'

'Please.' What she really wanted was to kick his ass all around the kitchen. Beat some feeling into him. She hoicked the butter towards her and spread some on a hot roll. Delicious. There's a lot to be said for a low-fat diet, but a lot more for a high-fat one. The best things in life are bad for you.

'You enjoy cooking,' Penny said, mouth full.

'Of course. Who do you think wrote *Lovesome Things*?'

'I rather thought your mother did.'

'My mother and *I*,' Christopher said. 'It was my idea, originally.'

'Really?'

'You seem surprised. But there're more ways than one to be a whizz kid.'

'How did whizz kids get into this?'

'Whenever anyone does a write-up of my mother and the business they refer to Timothy as a financial whizz kid. As if *I* didn't exist.'

'I'm sure that's not—'

'They'll realise the truth one day.'

'What truth?'

'That my contribution to the Lampeter Group was every bit as important as Tim's.'

'Has any one suggested differently?'

'I'm just never mentioned, that's all.'

Sounded like a bad case of ego-bruise. Penny hoped it wasn't the terminal kind. 'Come on,' she said. 'Those features always give you credit.'

'Big deal.'

'And say it was your artwork that put Lampeter designs on the map.'

Christopher slid mushrooms out of a saucepan and on to a plate. He put them into the oven to keep warm. 'Well, anyway. I'll show them,' he said.

'Attaboy.'

'When I start my restaurant.'

Gaahd. Another one. Sometimes it felt like she was the only person in the entire country who didn't want to go into the catering trade. 'When's that?' she said.

'I'd rather hoped it would be early next year. But with

210

this sudden reversal of fortune, it looks as though it'll have to be postponed.'

'Reversal of fortune?'

'My mother dying, I mean.'

'That's what I was afraid you meant.'

Opening a door that enclosed the back stairs, Christopher bawled Tim's name. 'I know my brother'll hate to miss you,' he said.

'I'm not going anywhere,' Penny said. Not until she could figure out where to go. Kyriakou's murder seemed to be scrambled in with Irene's death, yet she was nowhere nearer proving anything against Hector than she had been when Tim first asked her to investigate him. The reverse, if anything.

Tim arrived. Christopher was able to transcend his pyjamas. Tim wasn't. Although rounder than when she had last met him, he seemed oddly diminished, defeated by his towelling bathrobe. In this anachronistic kitchen, Christopher was definitely in charge, as Tim had been in the Covent Garden offices. He orchestrated food in a flurry of warm plates. He poured tea and passed salt. Under his direction, breakfast assumed a gloss that Penny hadn't realised it could possess. As he worked, he talked. Gentle beauty-parlour patter, soothing as rain on a summer afternoon and requiring as little response.

Just as well. Tim made none, staring miserably down at his plate. Every now and then he raised his fork and put whatever was on the end of it into his mouth. Had Irene ever made any distinction between her sons? Were the two brothers even aware that one was not the natural son of Irene and James? If they weren't, telling them could come as a shock. Might be better not to bring the matter up.

Penny reached for another of the rolls and more butter. Yesterday, there had been times she thought she might never eat again. Getting out of Hector's place had taken her longer than expected. Even after she'd liberated herself from the womb-like consulting-room, she still had to negotiate two more doors. The phone had been wrenched from its socket, so telephoning for help was out. As was screaming for it. With that thick-carpeted corridor, and the width of the doors, a person could shout her lungs to shreds and not be heard. Once she'd realised that, a person had been forced to concentrate on serious lock-picking.

Fiddling about with the tools from her personalised manicure-set, her fingers felt as big as bananas. She sighed. Hector's locks had been particularly intricate, designed to foil more able lock-pickers than she. Dealing with them was the kind of finicky job she hated. Like embroidery. Or like— She paused. Like setting up a murder with infinite care to point away from the culprit.

She stared down the passage. From the other end, the Buddha had stared back. She shook her head. Very clever, Miss Van Snoop. Just one question. Who exactly *was* the goddamned culprit?

It had been well after midnight by the time she emerged into the passage outside Hector's apartment. Or was it Anthony Pyne's? She was too hungry to care which. Having been there since lunchtime, she was about ready to eat her own arm. As she drove through the empty streets, she knew what she would find when she got home to Chelsea. After being interrupted the night before, her midnight visitor almost certainly wanted time to search again, at his leisure, for the pill bottle she'd removed from the *Alexandros*.

Even so, she wasn't entirely prepared for the mess. At least he hadn't vandalised the place. Scrambling some eggs, she decided two things. The first was, whatever she personally felt about dogs, she would have to get one. A vicious one. One that would tear the seat out of anyone's pants without fear or favour. The second was that next time she caught up with Hector she wouldn't stand on ceremony. There she'd been feeling almost sorry for him. At least he hadn't broken anything in his search.

Early next morning, she gave Lucas a call. He said he couldn't talk. He was busy doing ante-natal exercises with his wife, he said. She pointed out that a man in his position needed every spare penny he could lay his hands on. He said *she* might be spare but *he* was spoken for. He added that what a man in the position he'd just been in needed was to refrain from sex. He asked if any baby was worth it. Penny said definitely. Which was exactly why she was putting extra work his way, at double the normal rate of pay. He said God. He said he was too kindhearted for his own good. He said he'd be round after breakfast.

She'd then driven down here to confront Hector. To ask him what the hell. Only to find he'd gone. Why did that make her hair start doing a fretful porpentine number? It seemed important to know where. And who with.

'Neither of you has any idea where Hector might be?' she said.

Christopher stuck a pair of quilted gloves on his hands and took a baking tray out of the oven. 'No.'

'No,' Tim said. He swallowed the food in his mouth. 'By the way, I shan't do anything about the helicopters. Recall them, or anything, when the six months is up. Let Hector deal with it.'

'Come on, Timbo.' Christopher rested a hand briefly on his brother's shoulder. 'Don't be so defeatist. We'll sort it out. Maybe Hector will never have the chance. The dotted lines haven't been signed on yet, you know.'

'What's the point?' Timothy said. He fixed a red-eyed gaze on Penny. 'I mean, what's the point? With Mother gone . . .' Opening his mouth wider, he slipped in a button mushroom neatly skewered to a square of bacon.

Christopher ignored him. 'How's *your* mother?' he said. 'I suppose she's missed all the excitement, being away.'

'By excitement, you mean—'

'Kyriakou dying and everything,' Christopher said.

The guy was all heart. Honestly. 'She'll be back on Thursday evening, actually,' said Penny. She used her cold voice.

'You're lucky,' Tim said chokingly.

'I, for one, don't intend to mope,' said Christopher. 'She wouldn't have wanted us to.'

'What happens if Hector dies?' Penny asked.

'The shares revert to Timothy and myself,' Christopher said.

'He's not going to die,' Tim said, cheery as Cassandra. 'People like that never do.'

'Maybe we'll get lucky,' said his brother. 'Or Hector'll get unlucky.' He grinned widely at Penny to show he didn't mean it. Underlining how much he did. 'Or maybe Cousin Alexandra won't match the offer her father made for the shares. Or maybe she'll at least drop her price to a level we can meet.' He shoved the bread basket towards his brother. 'Go on,' he said.

'I'm not hungry.'

'Go on,' Christopher said forcefully. 'You're hardly eating a thing these days.'

That depended on your definition of thing. Penny had already seen Tim put away enough food to keep hunger at bay for a week. He must have added ten pounds to his weight since she'd last seen him. The extra poundage made the resemblance between the two brothers seem much stronger.

She coughed. 'Well, now,' she said. 'Want to hear what I got on Hector?'

'Yes, please,' said Christopher. Tim didn't speak. Cheeks bulging again, he nodded instead.

Penny told them. It took a while. Christopher whipped up a batch of scones while she did. When she'd finished, she showed them the bump on her head. 'If it weren't for my braids,' she said, 'I could be dead.' They didn't seem to care much.

'Even if the pills turn out to be something they shouldn't be,' said Christopher, 'it's hardly conclusive proof that Hector put them in the bottle.'

'Who else would have done?' asked Tim.

'You, for a start,' said his brother.

'Me? Don't be ridiculous.'

'Or me. Or Mother herself. Or Kyriakou. Or, if it comes to that, anyone who was at his place when she died.'

'Or anyone,' Penny said, 'who'd ever been near enough

to the bottle of pills to substitute something lethal for your mother's medication. Opportunity's not a problem. Do you know what they were for?'

'High blood pressure,' said Christopher. He opened a cook book lying on the counter and squinted at it, holding it close to his face then further away like someone wearing the wrong glasses. 'Hypertension. And I believe there was something slightly iffy about her heart. It runs in the family.'

'Ah,' Penny said. Something else that seemed to run in the family was a fair amount of indifference to major bereavement. Christopher sounded as cut up about the loss of his mother as his cousin, Alexandra, had about her father.

'We found a hospital report on her desk after she'd —uh—died,' explained Tim.

'Opened?'

'Yes.'

'So she knew about it before she went to Greece?'

'So did Hector,' said Tim. 'He's the obvious suspect.'

'He also,' Penny said, 'genuinely seems to have loved Irene.'

Tim shook his head several times. 'Why all those false names? There was definitely something fishy about the man.'

'Perhaps he wanted to get away from what sound like unfortunate beginnings,' Penny said.

Tim scowled at his empty plate. Christopher popped another bread roll on to it.

'Talking of mothers,' he said, 'when does yours get back?'

'She flies into Heathrow next Thursday evening. At 7.06 pee-em precisely.'

'Marvellous the way they can time these things to the minute, isn't it?' Christopher said.

'We live in an age of miracles,' Penny stood up. 'Could I use the bathroom?'

'There's a cloakroom along the passage,' Christopher said, opening the door into the rest of the house. 'Unless you actually want a bath. In which case it's upstairs.

215

Second on the right.' He laughed. So did Penny. Upstairs was where she wanted to go. Sneak around. Poke her nose into a few private pies. See what she could see.

The window at the top of the stairs was stained glass, crimson roses among green and yellow leaves. Predictably, the bathroom could have come straight out of the Lampeter Designs catalogue. She washed her hands, ran water, flushed the loo. During the running and flushing, she pushed open bedroom doors, keeping to the middle of the thick Wilton which ran down the middle of polished oak boards. Two of them recognisably belonged to the brothers. Timothy's held a smell of old perspiration that came almost visibly from the checked shirts on the floor behind the door. Christopher's had high-tech musical equipment on a wall-long shelf, and a contact-lens box beside the bed, next to a pornographic novel. Penny flipped through it. Tut tut. To do that with a piece of steak you'd need a digestive system like a steam engine's.

Across from the bathroom was what must have been Irene's room. More Lampeter Design prettiness. Diamonded windows swathed in yards of flower-sprigged cotton. Four-poster hung with matching drapes. Pastel pink carpet. Good furniture. And photographs. Hector, smiling and un-. The boys, endlessly. Irene herself, a girl, a bride, a mother. Irene thin and Quanted, black bangs on either side of her face. Irene with Kyriakou, squinting against an unseen sun. Irene with what must have been James. Tall, bespectacled, unflattered by the khaki uniform he wore. The same toothy overbite as Tim's, that stopped just short of buck. The same air of chinlessness. No wonder Kyriakou was enraged by Irene's defection. Any hawk, rejected for a worm, might feel the same.

She opened the drawers in the bedside tables. Irene's side first. She found creams, both hand and cleansing. She found a hair-grip. She found a brown bottle of pills. On Hector's side, she found a pamphlet advertising a course of body-building with a man built like a Dumpster truck. There was a paperback by Jim Fixx. A watch without a strap. Tranquillisers, newly prescribed. A small rectangle of pasteboard covered in blue fuzz with gold-colored copperplate in one corner. The copperplate spelled out the word Bucknall's and a telephone number.

Tiptoeing back across the pink carpet, Penny frowned. Christopher's resemblance to Irene was very strong. Yet so was Timothy's to James. Which of the two was the adopted one? And how could she have been so dumb as not to check it with her mother? She'd just assumed it was Tim. That was the general pattern, wasn't it? A couple found they couldn't conceive, they adopted, and six months later discovered they were pregnant. Release of tension, or something. Could the adoptee after all have been Christopher? He was the one who came after Irene with her pills, the day she left for Greece. And death. He was the one now stuffing his brother with food. Had he stuffed his mother too?

As she left the room, there was movement at the head of the stairs. One of the brothers. Against the light coming in through stained glass she couldn't tell at first which one. He stepped forward on the half-landing. Christopher. He wasn't smiling.

'Did you find what you wanted?' he said.

'The loo? Yes, thanks,' said Penny.

'But that's my mother's room.'

'I do hope you don't mind,' Penny said. She pushed the 'Gracious' button. 'I just wanted to see Irene's space, how she lived. After being there at the—when she—uh— . . .'

Christopher didn't say anything. The light from the small stained-glass window caught his face. She wished the red didn't fall straight across his mouth. He looked as if he'd been drinking blood.

17

FOG IS A FAVOURITE DEVICE OF THE SUSPENSE NOVELIST. It symbolises confusion. It shows that the dick hero hasn't a clue. Dump him in the middle of a good thick fog, and you know exactly where you are. So does he. Lost.

Driving back to Chelsea, Penny decided she had news for Chandler et al. You didn't need fog. You could be lost with the temperature in the seventies and the sky clear. Completely in the dark. She was living proof. She knew a killer was on the loose, but she didn't know where. She knew another murder was on the cards, but she didn't know whose. All she was sure of was that it was up to her to stop it. And even that was only pretty.

Back home, she sat on the white suede sofa and stared out of the window at the houses opposite.

'Can you really change identities that easily?' she said. Next to her, Barnaby refilled their glasses with Salon le Mesnil. He pushed one in her direction.

'Sure you can. Simple,' he said. 'You come, you go. Stay loose. Hang free.' His hand waved the air. It brushed her leg. Accidentally. Kind of.

'As long as you pay your way?'

'Right.'

'No bills.'

'And no debts.'

'No friends, either,' said Penny.

'Because, that way, who's to notice when you come or when you go? Transients—every big city's full of

218

them. Remember that guy in California who offed twenty or thirty migrant workers? No one missed them.'

'Juan Corona,' Penny said.

'Or the English one—Denis Nilsen. Only reason they ever got on to *him* was the drains started to smell. Not because anyone was out there wondering what the hell happened to Joe or whatever.'

'I don't see Hector Oakley as a mass murderer,' said Penny. Sad. All the lonely people. Existing in limbo, singular, no one to care whether they lived or horribly died.

'No one ever sees anyone as a murderer.'

'I still can't work out why he'd want to set up so many different identities.'

'Maybe he was trying to avoid some woman. He seems to have whatever it takes to turn the ladies on.'

'Not this lady.'

'You're no lady, you're my life.'

Penny leaned forward until her nose touched his. 'Sweet thing,' she said. 'Though even Sibylla melted when he opened his baby blues at her. Unless it was Jason Jackson she was high on.' She thought back to an Ionian sunset, and Sibylla, excitement palpable as silicone all round her.

'By the way, I meant to tell you I saw him last night,' Barnaby said.

'Who?'

'Jackson. At Bucknalls. With your friend Hector. If he's still calling himself that.'

'Jason and Hector,' said Penny. She drew her feet up under her. 'Was Hector winning?'

'For once.'

'And you're sure it isn't illegal to operate so many identities?'

'Not unless you do it with intent to defraud. Companies do it all the time, for perfectly innocent reasons. So do individuals. 'Specially the self-employed.'

'Like you?'

'Exactly like me, sweetheart. I can assume as many names as I like. Even buy houses or open bank accounts.'

219

If it wasn't fraudulent, it looked like the Lampeter sons weren't going to get their company back from Hector. She'd done what she could to track him for them. It wasn't a whole hell of a lot. Too often she'd found herself bogged down in the past, in other people's sadnesses. What would her own be, twenty-five years on?

She got up and went over to her desk. Lucas had straightened up with his usual efficiency, even moving the marker on her desk calendar. The twenty-third. The day her mother flew back. She riffled through the papers, looking for the postcard from Greece. Her mother's ETA had been 19.06, hadn't it? She riffled some more. The postcard from Greece wasn't there. Penny shook off the twinge of fear that shivered in and out of her vertebrae. She searched more thoroughly. The card had gone.

She dialled Lucas's number. There was no answer. She looked at her watch. By now her mother should already be on her way back to London.

'I'm worried,' she said.

'Why?'

'That break-in the other day.'

'So?'

'There was a postcard on my desk,' Penny said. 'From my mother.'

'I read it.'

'It's gone.'

'And you think the breaker-in took it.'

Penny did. She found herself unable to say so. She watched the bubbles at the bottom of her glass. Through them, she could see her fingers, the knuckles bone-brown round the stem.

'Why would anyone?' Barnaby said quietly.

'Suppose she saw something that night, as she was leaving. Something that didn't seem that significant at the time, but which she'll realise is, the minute she learns about Costas.'

Barnaby poured more champagne. 'Like someone coming out of the wrong room?'

220

'Exactly,' said Penny. 'And suppose whoever it was saw her seeing. Suppose that person and the breaker-in are one and the same.'

'That person now knows when she's due back in England.'

'Yes,' Penny said. Mother, she thought, you can spill ash all over the whole damn house if you want. Just don't get tangled up with whoever it is behind all this. Just don't get yourself killed for something you maybe saw and didn't tell.

Barnaby reached out and hugged her to him. 'We'll leave for Heathrow right now, if you like,' he said.

'Please.'

Out on the streets there still wasn't any fog. What there was was rain. Lots of it. It dropped out of the sky, grey and heavy as a portcullis. It bounced on car roofs. It blackened the hardtop on the roads, made it slick under the early-shining neon lights. Turning out of the King's Road, Barnaby's BMW skidded. Briefly, he swore.

Beside him, Penny stared ahead. She wished she could stop hearing her mother's voice inside her head. Danger for Leos in the third week of the month. She didn't believe in that kind of stuff. So why was she so worried?

On the Fulham Road, cars crawled westwards. A set of traffic lights had gone out. Water was rushing down the gutters on the left-hand side of the road, causing big pools that drivers were trying to avoid. They moved slowly towards the airport. The rain fell.

She shook her braids about, feeling the beads heavy on her neck. Not nearly as heavy as her heart. She was being stupid. There was absolutely no reason to think that the murderer was after her mother. Except for the missing postcard. Why would anyone want to take that, except to remind themselves of a flight's ETA? A dark blue Jaguar overtook them, orange light sliding across its polish. Up ahead, a car hooted in a sharp angry burst. Others joined in for a moment then stopped.

It took them an hour to get to the airport's perimeter. Which was where they found themselves slowing down to a stop. Ahead was a long queue of stationary cars.

Blue strobe-flashes indicated a police presence. Some-where an ambulance whined. Barnaby didn't speak. He wore pigskin driving gloves, taut and shiny over the grip of his hands on the steering wheel. Penny fidgeted around for a while. She pressed the button that opened the windows. Then the one that closed them. She opened the door. Rain spattered. She got out.

'I'm going to go see what's up ahead,' she said.

'How wise is that?' asked Barnaby.

'I'm not thinking wise, I'm thinking gut,' Penny said.

'That's what worries me.'

Standing in the rain, Penny put her head back into the car. 'We're going to get there too late, aren't we?' she said.

'Not necessarily.'

'We're going to miss her,' Penny said. She shut the door quietly, leaning on it to click it into the lock. She started walking along the hard shoulder towards the traffic obstruction.

A car-transporter was slewed across the lines. Beyond, the road to the airport was clear, shining with water under the lamps. Behind the transporter, something that had once been a car. Beside it, his head turned away so he wouldn't have to see, a man in a leather jerkin, checked shirt sleeves rolled up above his elbows, talked to a WPC. Rain had greased his hair flat on to his skull and soaked the shoulders of his jerkin dark. He didn't seem to notice the water that dripped from his hair down on to his face.

' . . . like I said, I feel this thump, like a giant kick in the . . .' he said. He leaned on an arm held rigid against the back of his vehicle. 'First I think, Christ, summink's fallen off the back, the load's slipping. It was all so fast. The whole thing starts drifting, out of control, so I pulls up. Moves on to the shoulder, dunneye? Gets out to take a look.' He swallowed. 'Which is when I see—that.' He jerked his head over his shoulder at the car.

Penny looked. The front of it was crumpled flat, the paintwork flaked, the windows shattered. Beneath what had once been the right front wing was a pool of something dark. Rain splashed steadily, spreading it. The back of the car was undamaged. Was dark green. Was all that remained of a Mercedes. One she'd seen before. Already men in hard hats and donkey jackets with water-proofed shoulders were trying to pull the shattered front of the car apart, in order to get at whatever was inside. She didn't need anyone to tell her who it was. A victim of fate as surely as Oedipus had been. And equally powerless to change the course of events.

'Course, I knew there wasn't nuffink I could do,' said the transporter-driver. 'Then this uvver geezer in the car behind comes over, says he saw it all . . .'

The other geezer was telling another police-person what had happened. He'd been cruising at around sixty-five m.p.h., with the Mercedes some two hundred feet up ahead, when a big Jag had overtaken first him, then the Merc. For a few seconds the two cars had raced along side by side, then the Jag had pulled ahead. The Merc had suddenly gathered speed. He'd assumed the driver was one of those idiots who can't bear to be overtaken. Microseconds later, he'd seen that the car was going straight into the back of the transporter if it didn't swerve immediately. He'd realised, with horror, that it wasn't going to. 'He was bent over, as if he was trying to reach something on the floor,' he said. 'I could see his shoulders moving. I suppose the accelerator must have jammed.' He watched as the cop wrote it down. 'Or the brakes.' His voice was unsteady with shock.

Lights glinted in the grey sky. Landing lights, red and green, flicking on and off as they raced towards earth. Away to the left, in the grey wetness, jet-engines screamed. A group of police cars had angled together on the other side of the transporter. In one of them, a grey-haired man sat talking steadily into a receiver. A motorcycle traffic cop wheeled out from among the cars streaming into London on the other side of the road. The cop reared back on his machine to bring the parking stand into play. His crash helmet flashed in time with the swirling lights on the police cars. A flat-bed truck

223

with traffic cones tumbled in the back pulled in from the other lane. Penny went over.

'Sorry, miss. You can't—'

'I have to get to the airport,' Penny said crisply. 'It's an emergency.'

'So's this,' said the grey-haired man frowning.

'I am Dr Leo Mulholland's receptionist,' Penny said. The cops looked blank. 'The laryngologist,' she said impatiently. 'From Wimpole Street,'

'Look, miss, if you don't mind—'

'It's absolutely vital that I get to the airport to pick up a shipment of blood plasma,' Penny said. She moved so that her white dress showed under her raincoat. A touch of the Nightingales never came amiss. 'Dr—uh—Mulholland has a patient waiting for an emergency operation which can't take place until we have it. Please, could someone get me to the airport? I can take a cab back into London. The sooner I get back, the sooner the doctor can operate.'

The cops looked at each other.

'This kid only has a fifty-fifty chance as it is,' Penny said quietly. She saw their faces soften in the rain and resisted the temptation to throw in a widowed mother, a father on the dole, a hole in the heart. When telling lies, keep it simple. She hated herself. But she had to get to the airport before her mother could be intercepted.

'It's only a mile or two down the road,' said the motorcycle cop to the grey-haired man. He tightened his chinstrap. 'And I've got a spare crash.' He twisted on his seat and tugged at a red helmet strapped behind him.

'For God's sake, get out of here,' said the grey-haired man. He looked at Penny. 'Remember, I've never seen you.'

It was 19.36 when they reached the terminal. Digitally the twenty-four clocks emphasised the fact. Tearing off the helmet, she thanked the cop and raced for the escalators. 19.37. People were trickling through from Customs, carrying their luggage. Penny stopped one of them, a fair-headed kid in a backpack.

'Where've you just come from?' she said. 19.39. Her

224

mother's flight was scheduled to arrive over half an hour ago. Her eyes scanned the crowd of meeters. Parents waiting to be reunited with children. Children impatient for parents. Limo drivers in peaked caps holding home-made signs saying TEXACO or HERR LIMBERGER. Lovers. All of them halves, waiting for the other.

'Munich,' he said.

'You didn't come via Athens?'

'Of course not.' His accent was teutonic.

'I didn't really think you had,' said Penny. Her face was hot with rage and fear. Inside her chest, her heart pumped overtime. Her white shirt was wet under the arms. 19.40.

A woman emerged in a pink dress that was just an oversized T-shirt. She couldn't have got her tan in Munich. Over her shoulder was a white straw bag with ITHAKA plaited into it in black raffia.

'Were you on the flight from Athens?' Penny de-manded, standing in front of her. Maybe there was still hope.

'Please?'

'Have you come from Athens?'

'No. I have just come from Germany, from near Munich.'

'Your tan,' Penny said.

The woman looked down at it. 'I have a sun-lamp, yes?' She grinned.

It wasn't something Penny felt able to do. She turned and ran for the bar. Idiot woman. Travelling from Mu-nich to London with a bag from Greece. Raising peo-ple's hopes like that. Dammit.

19.43. She scanned the drinkers in the bar. No Lady Helena. None in the restaurant, nor in the snack bars. None in the loos. None buying books at the newsstand nor face-creams in the pharmacy. She checked that the flight had arrived on time. It had. She had her mother paged. Her mother didn't show. If she'd ever been at the airport, she was not there now. Which meant decid-ing where she *was* at.

But though she couldn't see her mother, she could

plainly see the scenario that had lured her away. Lady Helena, Penny asked me to come and meet you. Her car broke down/her house fell over/she's in hospital. And her mother, grateful, believing it, going off with a murderer.

The German woman was crossing the concourse as Penny took the escalators at speed. Ithaka. You thought Ithaka, you couldn't help thinking Odysseus too. The man of many wiles. She needed a few of those herself. Barnaby was waiting outside the terminal in a no-parking zone. She knew he would be. She got in beside him and told him where to go. She tried not to shake. 'Step on it,' she said.

He did.

When they reached the Lampeter house, there were several cars already parked. One was a dark blue Jaguar.

In the damp dark, leaves dripped on to other leaves. There was a sharp smell of fresh-turned earth. Wet fronds brushed their faces as they walked round the side of the house. Lights burned in the kitchen windows. Penny leaned across unpruned rosebushes to look inside. It mattered who was in there. It mattered a lot. Also, what condition they were in. She couldn't see much. A table with people seated at it. Sibylla Schumann. One of the Lampeter boys. Alexandra Kyriakou. Hector Oakley. On the floor, a body.

She'd expected to see two of them. The rest were a surprise. They'd complicate things. Behind her, Barnaby whispered.

'Lady H there?'

'No.'

'Is that good or bad?'

'I don't know.'

'She could be asleep at home.'

'She's here somewhere,' Penny said. 'I'm sure of it.' She didn't tell him about the person on the floor. Nor that there was a jacket slung over one of the chairs. An unstructured jacket, loosely woven in some fashionable non-colour. There was a gun in the pocket. She could see its outline clear as spit.

226

'Want me to check the place out?' whispered Barnaby.

'Yeah.' Penny pushed herself upright. Invisible thorns caught at her clothes. Barnaby took hold of her. She rested her cheek against his face. His hand hesitated on her hip. Big hand. And warm. It felt good.

'Wait here,' he said.

'Be careful.' They both spoke together.

She didn't want him to leave her. But if he stayed, he'd be protective. Cramp her style. Try to stop her from going inside and confronting the person who'd met her mother off the plane and driven her back here. And then—what? She looked away from the gun in the jacket. The thought of Lady Helena's body filled her head. She saw wet fields and rain-blackened hedges and somewhere her mother, neatly dead, a bullet in brain or heart. She scrunched panic down like cellophane. Like cellophane, it went on crackling. It wouldn't stay quiet. If she didn't believe her mother was still alive, she would begin howling like a wolf. She told herself that howling wasn't her scene.

Once Barnaby had gone, she moved along the wall to the side door. A PVC roller-blind sprigged with rosebuds had been pulled down to cover the glass. Where it bulged away, she could see the light from the kitchen.

She took hold of the handle. The door wasn't even on the latch. She pushed it inwards. Carefully. On the inside, something swung against the panels, making a small wooden noise. The acorn on the end of the blind pull. She stopped pushing. It continued to swing, making a slight bumpy sound.

She could hear a voice.

'—all I've worked for,' it was saying. 'You take advantage of a menopausal woman, and suddenly everything's gone. All my plans, my future. Years of my life wasted. It doesn't seem fair.'

Nobody answered. Penny walked quietly towards the inner door into the kitchen. It was half-open. The passage was full of the smell of roasting meat.

'Does it seem fair to you, Hector?' The voice seriously wanted to know.

Peering through the gap, Penny looked to her left. At the pine table, hands clasped in front of him, Hector swallowed. Opposite him sat Alexandra. Their eyes were on the Lampeter boy who was watching them all from the end of the table. Behind them, in a glass-fronted oven, a large piece of meat was roasting.

'Irene did leave the shares to me,' Hector said. He sounded carefully reasoned. As a rabbit might, trying to persuade a snake to dine on something else. The bright strip-lighting broadened his squat torso. Penny watched him try to turn on his own incandescence and fail. 'But I'll sell them to you, if you want.'

'For how much?'

'A price you can afford.'

'Irene would never have left them to you if she'd thought you'd try to destroy the Lampeter Group.'

'I had no intention of doing that.'

'Accepting that offer from Kyriakou. Taking them out of the family. That would have destroyed us.'

Alexandra, sitting across the table from him, spoke. Her voice was quiet, businesslike. 'Kyriakou is dead,' she said. 'There is no offer.'

Hector licked his lips and glanced at the door which shut off the back stairs leading to the upper floor.

'Last time we spoke,' the Lampeter boy said to Hector, 'you mentioned another offer you'd have to take up if the Kyriakou one fell through. What's happened to that?'

Nervously Hector looked around the table. 'I—I'm not quite sure.'

'Of course, I can't really see why I should have to pay anything for what is rightfully mine.' The Lampeter boy shifted position slightly. In the stark light, Penny could see the scoremarks on the blade of the Sabatier carving knife in his right hand. It looked very sharp. It looked as if it could slice through flesh as easily as through yoghourt. No wonder Hector was showing the whites of his eyes.

'I could make the shares over to you,' he said.

Beside him, Sibylla Schumann shook her head slowly. 'Dumb,' she said. 'Real dumb.'

228

'Who?' said the Lampeter boy.

'You, kid.' Sibylla supported her head on her hand and stared down the table at him. 'You seriously think you're gonna get away with this kind of junk?'

'You're a businesswoman yourself, Mrs Schumann. Surely you can see that my request is perfectly fair.'

'I can't see anything of the goddamned kind, you flakehead,' Sibylla said aggressively. Her mouth creased with contempt. Hector lifted a hand and fingered the bridge of his nose.

Penny pushed the door a little wider. She could see the body on the floor. It belonged to Marty Schumann. The antiseptic light greyed the skin round his nose. He lay on his side with his eyes closed. One thing Penny picked up on fast; he wasn't taking a nap. Someone had zapped him. Already the bruise was turning blue on his cheek.

'But Irene agreed that as long I carried on—'

'You already told us,' said Sibylla.

'—the business the same way—'

'Irene is dead,' Sibylla said loudly. 'In my book, that renders the agreement null and void.' She looked down at her husband on the floor. 'And speaking of business agreements, I made one not too long ago and I'd like to check out my partner in it, if you don't mind. The one you slugged, remember?'

'I do mind.' The blade of the carving knife gleamed.

'Tough shit,' Sibylla said. She swung out of her chair. From the door, Penny could see the strain round her eyes.

'Sit down,' said the Lampeter boy, his voice somewhere near falsetto.

Sibylla ignored him. She knelt beside Marty. She put her hand inside his shirt. 'His heart's beating OK,' she said. She took in a deep breath. 'Gee, it's gonna beat ten times faster when I tell him the news.'

'What news?' said Alexandra. She looked sideways at the Lampeter boy and quickly away.

It was obvious Sibylla was only talking as a distraction. 'Funny thing is, I was trying to persuade Marty to go in with Jason,' she said.

'Will you be quiet?' The Lampeter boy half rose, holding the knife towards them. For a moment there was complete silence except for the spitting of the meat in the oven.

Alexandra spoke very quietly, not looking at the end of the table. 'Why in the world would you want to go in with Jason?'

'Everyone knows he wants to expand,' Sibylla said. 'Also that he's having a hard time raising the dough. Which is where Marty and me would have come in. I may look like a dumb broad, but I'm quite a sharp cookie. Also, I know about the hotel trade.' For a moment she looked wistful. 'Boy. I could just have done with something like the Rockingham to keep my hand in. I've been going crazy with boredom.' She touched her husband's recumbent form. 'Marty and his weird ideas about working wives.'

'I was under the impression you wanted to make a comeback in films,' Alexandra said.

'That was your father's idea, not mine. I never really thought it'd get off the ground,' Sibylla said. 'Though I have to say I was kinda mad at Marty when he made it so goddamned clear he didn't think I had what it takes.' She smoothed Marty's forehead and smiled. 'Now I guess I don't really care too much.'

'Why's that?' said Alexandra. She wore a dove-coloured silk dress of almost the same colour as the jacket slung over the chair.

'Can't you tell?'

'You're going to have a baby.' Alexandra looked down at her ringless hands.

'Right,' Sibylla laughed. 'I'm thirty-six and this is the very first time I've gotten pregnant, even though I'm on my third husband. Two of them were real studs, too. Real hunky types. Too busy studying their profiles in the goddam mirror to make babies. The jerks.'

'Pregnant?' The figure at the end of the table sat up.

'That's utterly disgusting. Mr Schumann must be nearly sixty.'

'So what? Charlie Chaplin was seventy-five. No one called him disgusting.'

'Congratulations,' Hector said.

'That's why I wanted to spend a few extra days at Jason's glitzy hotel,' said Sibylla. 'To celebrate. Not that Marty knows—not for sure—yet. I was going to tell him tonight, when we got back after dinner here.' She gave a snorting sort of laugh. 'Some dinner this has turned out to be.'

'That's wonderful news,' said Alexandra. She glanced at the knife.

'I guess I'm kind of long in the tooth for motherhood,' said Sibylla, 'but so what.' She looked round at them all. The same excitement bubbled in her that Penny had seen on Kyriakou's island. 'I'm gonna be the best god-dam mother in the business.' The meat in the oven spat and sizzled.

Someone would have to tell her Lady Helena Hurley had already won the title. For life. Penny pushed the door open a little wider. Behind her, outside in the drive, she heard the surreptitious noise of footsteps tip-toeing across damp gravel. Barnaby, searching for her mother. Or so she hoped. She ignored the prickle of apprehension that suddenly tightened her scalp.

The Lampeter boy was several feet away from her. He was rubbing the back of his neck. It was a fattish neck, cut into by the collar of his white shirt. Was he the natural son or the adopted one? Did it matter? She tried to work him into Irene's murder, considered bluff and double-bluff, motive, the opportunities for pill substitution that he had had. She moved quietly into the room. The people at the table looked at her and quickly away. He saw them doing it. As he turned his head, Penny moved. Fast. She fetched up against his back. She reached over his right shoulder and clamped her hand to his right wrist, forcing it to the table top.

'Please don't get up,' she said. The knife clattered.

He tried to twist round. He couldn't. Penny had his

head clenched between her upper arm and her neck. She could smell whisky on his breath. She squeezed. Hard. Against her neck, his jaw sounded as if it had cracked.

'Whatcha doin', boy?' she said.

The tension drained soundlessly from the room.

'Jesus,' said Sibylla. 'What a fruitcake.'

'You can't have thought he'd hurt you,' Penny said.

'Why the hell not? Waving that friggin' knife around. And then he just hauled off and decked Marty one right in the—'

'Because he wouldn't *listen*.' Timothy Lampeter's face, clamped close to Penny's, was slimy with tears. She released her pressure on his neck.

'Why'd you do it?' she said.

Tim sat slumped at the table, running one finger over and over along the grain in the scrubbed wood. 'All Christopher and I ever wanted was the Lampeter Group's shares,' he said. 'I was forced to give up any idea of being a barrister because of the Group. We spent most of our lives building it up. Why should someone like Hector just walk in and take it away from us?'

'I never intended—' began Hector.

The timer on the oven pinged.

There was a silence. Then Tim said, 'I suppose someone ought to take that joint out. Christopher says meat has to sit for half an hour after it's finished cooking.'

The domesticity of the remark dissipated whatever might have been left of uneasiness.

Obediently Alexandra pushed back her chair. She seemed to have reverted to the dutiful daughter rôle played so often with her father. She found a pair of oven gloves and opened the oven door. Taking out the meat, she set it down on the tiled counter next to a cylindrical baster with a blue rubber bulb on the end. Penny had an identical one in her kitchen. As Jason Jackson did in his.

'Someone ought to drain off the fat,' Tim said. 'I wonder where Chris can have got to.' Tears suddenly gathered in his eyes and moved steadily down his face to fall onto his shirt. Talk about wets. Penny moved away from him and sat down on a chair with the jacket slung over it.

'All right,' Alexandra said. She opened cupboard doors, searching for a bowl.

Penny reached her arm down into the jacket pocket. The gun was slightly warm, not very heavy. She palmed it. Everyone was watching Alexandra. She slipped it into her own pocket.

'How about a drink, folks?' she said. 'The evening so far doesn't seem to have been a terrific success, but I'm sure we're all prepared to forget this whole crummy scene ever happened.'

'I sure as hell am not,' Sibylla said. 'And what the hell do you know about it, anyway? You weren't even here. Christ. The guy invites us over for dinner with his brother, then shows up stinking drunk, minus brother and waving a knife about, just because we were a little late.'

'That wasn't why,' Tim said.

'Not only that, he starts laying into my husband. And you want me to forget it?'

'Be reasonable, Mrs Schumann,' Penny said. 'If your dinner guests arrived late, and you'd been hitting the bottle, you'd probably have done the same.'

'Wasn't my fault we were late,' Sibylla said. 'Marty couldn't find the Jag. Some dope had moved it round to the back of the hotel.'

'How recently?' Penny said.

Sibylla thought back. 'Yeah. Marty said something about the engine being warm. And I could still smell the guy's aftershave.' She wrinkled her pretty nose. 'Brothel-keeper's Sunday best, if you ask me.'

Penny nodded. Things were getting clearer by the minute. She moved so that she was standing with her back to the big pine dresser. That way, no one could creep up unexpectedly and plunge a dagger into it.

'Just one thing,' she said.

They all looked at her. Hector's mouth hung open with apprehension, his beard hiding the green tie he wore. 'Yes?' he said.

'Where's my mother?' said Penny.

'Don't ask me,' said Tim.

'If she's been hurt, I'll personally take whoever's responsible to pieces.'

Sibylla narrowed her eyes. 'Who would want to hurt your mother?' she said.

'Probably the same person who killed Irene Lampeter.'

'But why?'

'To stop her saying what she saw.'

'When?'

'The night of Costas Kyriakou's murder.'

There was a sudden eruption of noise. Alexandra stiffened. The door covering the back stairs opened suddenly and was flung back against the wall with a thumping crash. Jason Jackson stood there. He was wearing black velvet trousers and a shirt of white silk with full sleeves and rows of small self-covered buttons. Très dramatique. Très Hamlet. Any minute now he'd start in on a soliloquy. To be or not to be? With a knife and a gun already in the room, that really seemed to be the question.

'What *did* she see?' he said. He stepped off the bottom stair and into the room. 'My dear, do tell.'

18

'ALL RIGHT, JASON,' PENNY SAID. 'WHAT'VE YOU DONE with her?'

'Moi?' Jason said. He grinned. 'Why should I—'

Timothy leaped up from his chair. He grabbed the knife from the table and lunged at Jason, holding it with both hands.

'*You* killed her?' he said. Behind his glasses his eyes stared wildly.

'Of course I didn't,' said Jason. Hummingbird-quick, he darted out of Tim's way, both hands up in front of him, warding off danger. A ridge of light lay along the greased smoothness of his hair. Penny could see the throb of adrenalin pulsing in his jaw.

'But Penny said . . .'

Jason's eyes met Penny's. They were dangerous. 'Why in the world would *I* kill Irene?' he said. His breathing was uneven. 'That jerk brother of yours, yes. But not me.'

'Christopher? He'd never . . .' Timothy looked at the knife in his hand and frowned. He put it down on the table. 'He'd never . . .' he said.

'Don't you believe it,' Jason said. 'That kid is absolutely ruthless.'

Tim looked around. 'I wonder where he is. He should be back from your place by now, Jason.'

'Ruthless,' Jason said again. 'He'd have done just about anything to get that restaurant of his.' He leaned back against the counter. 'I'll say one thing for him,

235

when he thinks, he really thinks big. Such a pity his plans didn't include you.'

'What do you mean?' Tim said.

What the smile on Jason's face lacked in humour it more than made up for in malice. 'Surely you knew he hated you.'

'But he's my brother.'

'In a manner of speaking,' Jason said.

'How do you mean?'

'Didn't your mother ever tell you?' said Jason.

'Tell us what?'

'That one of you was adopted? Why should he have any kind of feeling for you?'

Timothy stared at him disbelievingly. His mouth opened but he didn't speak. He took his glasses off and rubbed them up and down the cloth of his shirt. 'Which one?' he said finally.

'Does it matter?' Jason looked round at the others. They were staring at him with varying expressions.

'Knock it off, Jase.' Penny took a step forward. The gun in her pocket swung against her hip. 'What have you done with my mother?' Never mind her mother: what about Barnaby? She knew she had to provoke him in some way. She kicked out, landing a blow on the side of his thigh that must have hurt like hell. It certainly didn't do her foot any good.

Jason brought up his fists and clenched his teeth together in a fighter's snarl. Then, as if sensing what she was trying to do, he relaxed both jaw and arms. 'When all else fails, resort to violence, huh?' he said sneeringly. 'That's how you Brits got your Empire in the first place, isn't it?'

'*Us* Brits?' Penny said.

'Right.'

'You sound as if you aren't one yourself,' said Penny.

Jason's small round eyes blinked. 'I'm as English as you are,' he said.

'But brought up somewhere else,' Penny said. 'Somewhere like—for instance—Canada?'

'What?' said Jason.

'Canada,' said Penny. 'From the accent, I'd guess somewhere near Montreal.'

Hector made a small noise. It could have been a blocked drain unblocking.

Jason spun round in his direction. 'I thought I told you,' he said. His voice was quiet and full of menace.

'I've not said a single word,' said Hector. He shrank inside himself like a turtle backing into its shell.

The weight of the gun was dragging Penny's pocket to one side. She hoped she wouldn't have to fire it from there. Apart from anything else, it'd ruin the jacket.

'I suppose you killed Irene so you'd have Hector even tighter by the balls,' she said.

They all stared at her.

'I should have remembered much earlier that you had the opportunity to doctor Irene's pills when she left them at your house, a couple days before she arrived at Kyriakou's place. Perhaps you deliberately hid them so she *would* forget.'

'What the fuck are you—'

'It *had* to be someone who'd had access to them before she left for Greece,' Penny said. 'She was constantly thirsty. While we were waiting to have our passports checked, she kept pressing her hand to her chest. I should have realised what it meant.'

'You're talking crap.'

'One wife dead was nothing much,' Penny said softly. 'But two of them, both dead in the same spot, in the same sort of way, would be something of a clincher. If anyone started making waves, it could look awful bad for Hector. Especially when there isn't a shrine where he thought there was. So you killed Irene and made him pay for your silence, didn't you?'

Timothy screamed. He threw the knife. They heard the split of silk as the blade went through Jason's shirt sleeve. Blood appeared, glueing the thin material to the arm inside.

'Jesus,' said Sibylla. She crouched over Marty. 'Jesus Christ.'

'What the hell did you do that for?' Jason stared down

at the widening patch of blood, then suddenly whirled and smashed a fist into Tim's stomach. Through the torn material, they could seen the gym-trained muscles bulge. Tim collapsed on to the floor. Viciously, Jason lifted his foot and kicked the side of Tim's head. Tim's face smacked against the kitchen tiles with a sound like snapping twigs.

The room was absolutely still. No one seemed even to breathe. Jason glared round at them. Were his eyes really growing bloodshot while she watched?

'It was silly of me not to check the name of Nina Sibley's younger brother when I was speaking with Joan and Jim Parfitt,' Penny said rapidly.

Jason said nothing. He didn't need to. Penny could have etched glass with the look he gave her.

'A spoiled kid, Jim called him,' she said. 'With a nasty temper when he didn't get his own way.'

This time Jason did react. 'I warned you,' he said. He reached suddenly behind him, his hand closing round one of the earthenware pots on the counter. He flung it hard across the table, catching Hector on the side of the head. For a moment Hector stared stupidly at him. He started to lift his hand towards his face. Then he slumped to the floor, his chair clattering down on top of him.

'A very palpable hit,' Penny said.

'I *told* him,' said Jason.

Penny held tightly to the gun. Theoretically it gave her an advantage. In practice, the advantage was so last-resort that she'd be better off without it. Guns kill. Everyone knew that. Which was why, unless she absolutely had to, she wasn't going to use it. Probably not even then. So figuring out the if and the when was a major occupation. One that, if she wasn't careful, could cause her to miss out on the opposition's next trick. And that could be dangerous, because one thing she was sure of: Jason had more moves than a square-dancer. 'Before or after you started to blackmail him?' she said.

'Blackmail? Why would I blackmail Hector?' Jason said. His eyes reflected no light at all.

'Maybe the whole thing started out as a major coincidence,' Penny said. 'You came back to this country, consulted a clairvoyant as you were used to doing, and by cracky the guy you picked turned out to be your old childhood chum William Beech.'

Jason began to move towards her round the table. Penny backed away.

'What made you realise there was lettuce to be picked from this particular patch?' she said. 'The fact that old Bill Beech was now calling himself Michael Ashe?'

Jason was measuring the distance between himself and the chair with the jacket. Behind him she could see Alexandra doing the same thing with the telephone. With the men all out for the count, that left three women. And of those, she reckoned Sibylla would be too busy protecting Marty to want to waste time protecting Penny.

'Or,' she said, 'did you just come back on some kind of nostalgia kick and decide to look up old friends like the Parfitts? They wouldn't have moved out to Greece by then. Was it hearing from them about Delia's sudden death and Hector's jump into the heavy money that gave you the idea?'

'I've never heard such a load of bullshit in my life,' Jason said.

'People always wondered where you got the down-payment on the Rockingham.'

'It certainly wasn't from blackmailing Hector, dear. All that gambling. The guy's practically bankrupt.'

'The shares Irene left him must have been a marvellous bonus,' Penny said. 'But my guess is, your first big piece of luck was being in the right place at the right time.' She could feel her biceps trembling. Any minute he would attack, and, if she wasn't ready, might kill. Her entire body felt like a tourniquet, wound as tightly as it would go.

'And where was that?' Jason asked. He spoke as if he could care less but his fists were slowly bunching together. He took a step forward. Another one. Blood still seeped from the nick on his arm.

Penny took a deep breath. 'Managing the hotel where Jay Pannis stopped over during his preliminary campaigning for the Presidential nomination. When Costas

239

Kyriakou paid you to find those two under-age hookers and have a photographer ready to burst in and record the scene.'

Jason had gone pale. 'Bullshit,' he said.

'Bull's eye,' said Penny.

He made his move, leaping like a ballet-dancer, grabbing for the jacket over the chair. As soon as he lifted it he realised the gun had gone. He also realised where. He sprang at Penny, hands chopping the air. One caught her on the side of the neck. For a moment blackness filled her eyes. Vaguely she saw Alexandra cower against the counter, one hand lifted to her mouth.

Jason chopped again, hands like blocks of wood. Penny's head snapped sideways. Her neck was the only thing that kept it anchored. She tried to kick, but he was too near, almost on top of her. How the hell had he got so close to her so fast? She tried to pull out the gun but he smashed at the top of her right arm, numbing it. The air hissed as his hands cut through it. Why in God's name had she dropped out of her T'ai Chi classes?

'And then you decided to kill Kyriakou,' she said, pushing the words out with effort. Alexandra had to be brought in somehow or they could all end up on the wrong side of dead.

The Greek girl stood up straighter. She began to frown. 'Why would he kill my father?' she said.

'Because he was terrified of losing the Rockingham.' Penny backed away along the dresser. Jason kept coming, jabbing at her. Another blow landed, this time just below the rib-cage. It felt as though she'd just been smashed with a piece of two by four.

'He didn't have to sell to my father.'

'Maybe not.' Penny wished Alexandra would stop talking and go call the police. Or better still, exterminate Jason. She knew she couldn't have everything. 'Except I'd guess that a few weeks back a whole bunch of chickens finally came home to roost.'

Jason laughed. It struck a chill note in the warm meat-scented air. 'Chickens?' he said.

'Yeah. Just as you were squeezing Hector, so Costas began squeezing you.'

'Why should he suddenly do that now? Why not earlier? I've known him for years.'

'Perhaps because before, he hadn't wanted the Rockingham. Now he did. So he told you he'd blow the gaff on your involvement in the Pannis affair if you didn't sell it.'

'The Pannis aff—' began Alexandra.

'Ancient history,' said Penny. 'But none the less bloody. I don't suppose at the time our friend here was even aware that Costas was behind it. Even so, putting the squeeze on Jason was probably not a good move on your father's part. Especially when it was obvious from the start that the Rockingham meant more to him than anything else in the world.'

She had stopped trying to get at the gun. Stopped even backing away from Jason. Standing still seemed to calm him down. She wondered if he were insane. Was any killer conceivably not? Her eyes ranged the kitchen, assessing what weapons there were to hand. Knives, of course. She didn't think there was any way she could ever attack someone with a knife. Not ever. What else was there?

Alexandra's eyebrows had drawn together in a way Penny remembered from school. Alexandra hadn't liked people fooling with her things then and she sure didn't like it any better now. Whatever she may have felt about her father, Penny could tell she wasn't going to stand for some punk pushing him down a well. Things were looking up. If Alexandra was about to make a move, the two of them might have a chance.

She made one herself. Sideways and backwards, bending in the middle to offer less of a target. As she expected, Jason immediately came after her. The side of his hand connected with her shoulder. It would have been the side of her neck if she hadn't seen the blow coming and tucked her head in. It would have been curtains.

'Stop it!' Alexandra suddenly shrieked, as though some-

241

thing inside her had broken. She sprang forward. There was a rolling pin in her hand. She thumped at Jason's shoulders with it. 'You murdering bastard. Stop it.' She lifted the pin to hit him over the head.

Jason whirled. One of his swinging hands caught her on the nose. She reeled backwards. Jason smashed at her again. Blood spurted from her face. She went down, hitting her head against the edge of a chair. Beyond her, Sibylla had dragged Marty under the big table. Penny could hear her panting, crouched over him like an Eskimo woman giving birth.

In the single second that Jason's attention had been occupied with Alexandra, Penny dashed across the kitchen. She held tightly to her upper arm. It pulsed with pins and needles, no longer completely numb. She flexed her fingers against it, trying to work the blood back into it. Nothing happened. It still felt as if it would never work again. She tried to stretch her other arm across her body to reach the gun. The jacket swung away. That was the trouble with dressing in drop-dead glitz: it didn't allow for emergencies like attack from murderous schizoids. Where the hell was Barnaby?

Half crouching, Jason came towards her. He was swinging the rolling pin loosely in one hand.

'Too many witnesses, Jason,' she said. Her fingers were at last starting to tingle as the blood slowly began to return. 'You may have gotten rid of Kyriakou and Irene, but you can't kill us all.'

'I can try,' Jason said. 'What's to lose? I'm already in way over my head.'

'Returning were as tedious as go o'er, huh?'

'You could say.' Jason struck out at her again. 'Give me that damn gun.'

She dodged, swinging her body away from him. 'You may be crazy, but I'm not,' she said. She knew that if he got hold of it, someone would die. If not right there, then later. First he'd use the gun to get away.

He stood in front of her, tapping one hand with the rolling pin held in the other.

On the floor, Hector groaned, drawing in a long snoring breath. For a moment Jason half turned, thinking the sound had come from behind. Breathing hard, Penny tugged at her pocket. This was probably the last chance she had. The pocket ripped. The gun finally pulled out.

Phew. She pointed it at him. 'I think you ought to know that I'll use this,' she said. 'If I have to.'

'Oh sure.' Jason grinned at her. There were flecks of spittle on his lower lip. He lifted his arm. The one holding the rolling pin.

As sharply as a photograph, Penny saw it connect with her head, saw herself stagger, hesitate, fall to her knees, hit the floor. The image terrified her. He wouldn't leave her alive, of that she was sure. *BLOODBATH IN COTSWOLD KITCHEN*: the headline pulsed in neon on a ridge of her brain.

'I can see why you felt like that,' Penny said. 'It was your one possession. As a child you'd been uprooted from home. Then your parents were killed. Then you were separated from your sister—from Joan—and sent to live with strangers. Costas taking over the Rockingham meant you would be kissing goodbye the one thing that was truly yours.'

'You and Mrs Freud,' said Jason.

She saw his arm begin to descend. She felt very tired. Her arm hurt. Her neck ached. The thing about people who erred and strayed from their ways was that they didn't do it one bit like lost sheep. Raging tigers would be nearer the mark. She pressed slowly on the trigger of the gun. At this distance, she couldn't miss. The bullet would rip into Jason's body, through the blood-stained white shirt and on into the vital organs, tearing them apart.

With the rolling pin, Jason smashed the gun out of her hand.

Not even thinking about it, Penny reached for the roasting pan on the counter behind her. It was still hot enough to burn her fingers. She swung it off and straight into Jason's face. Hot fat poured over his cheeks and chin. The edge of the pan cut into the side of his jaw-bone. The joint slid down his body, leaving a snail-wake of glistening fat, and skittered off along the kitchen tiles like a puck in an ice-hockey game. Jason flung his hands up to his face and screeched. The gun dropped.

Penny dropped too, scrabbling for it. She got hold of it and tried to stand up. One knee slipped in the congealing fat. Jason, hands still up to his face, began to run. Half-kneeling, Penny pulled the trigger. Around the deafening noise of the explosion a smell of fireworks drifted. Unhurt, Jason found the open kitchen door. She heard his footsteps in the flagged passage and the slow swing of the acorn backwards and forwards on the back door. A car revved. By the time she got outside, he was gone. She stood in the drive watching the tail-lights vanish. The sound of its engine died damply among the trees.

Sibylla came out and stood beside her. 'My God,' she said. 'He must be stark staring crazy.'

'Yeah.' It was all Penny could manage.

'Shouldn't someone follow him?'

'Who?'

'Uh . . . I'll call the police.'

'Great,' said Penny.

She knew she was a big girl now. Independent. Free-thinking. Able to take care of herself. But right this very minute, what she wanted more than anything else in the world was her mother.

19

JASON GOT NO FURTHER THAN THE RIVER. THE POLICE found his car early the next morning, nosedived into the water, its back wheels still on the bank. Suicide or accident: no one would ever know. Jason was at the wheel, face pressed up against the windscreen. His eyes were full of mud. You might wonder if metaphorically they hadn't always been, were you given to such thoughts. Penny wasn't.

'If I hadn't seen him in his glasses when I was in his bedroom after finding Kyriakou in the well,' she said later, 'I wouldn't have recognised him when I saw those photographs in Hector's apartment. He doesn't look anything like he did when he was a little kid.'

Later was back in her house, drinking tea in the drawing-room. A log fire burned in the grate. Outside, rain slashed at the windows. The English summer was going full swing.

'It was him who recommended Irene to me in the first place,' Hector said.

'And encouraged you to court her, I'll bet,' said Penny.

'That's right. A woman like Irene—a national figure—I didn't think I stood much of a chance. But Jason kept telling me I was just right for her.'

'And then came out with the revelations once the knot was safely tied.'

'That's right. My goodness, I was staggered when he let on who he was. Jason Sibley, as was.' Hector moved his head from side to side in a marvelling kind of way.

245

'Though he'd taken the name of his foster-parents by then.'

'And it was him who zonked me the day I came to see you,' Penny said.

'I'm right sorry about that.'

'Thank God he only zonked, as you call it, me,' said Lady Helena, 'before dumping me in that frightful shed place behind his hotel.'

'Saving you for later, Mother. Like a spider. He was desperate to know what you'd seen, but he couldn't risk asking you on the way back from the airport because you'd have suspected something and tried to attract attention.'

'As you can see,' Lady Helena said, holding out her arms, 'I am somewhat immobilised. Otherwise I shouldn't have to ask you to get me a cheroot from my bag.'

Penny ignored her.

Hector said embarrassedly, 'Look, I'm ever so sorry I hit you like that. It was those pills. I thought if I could just get hold of them they'd prove that Kyriakou had killed Irene.' He looked round at them. 'I loved her, you know.'

'I know,' Penny said.

'And that day I met you, that evening after Irene's little . . . outburst, he'd been so—so vicious about her. When she died, I was sure he was behind it. It wasn't until later I realised it must have been Jason.'

'When he started putting the pressure on?'

'Yes.'

Sibylla and Marty were sitting side by side. Marty was holding Sibylla's hand and looking as though someone had just crowned him king.

'For a while there, I thought you must be Nina Sibley, come back to claim Hector, your long-lost love,' Penny said to her. 'Especially that evening Theo and I found you gawping at the sunset, all lit up like a carnival, and Hector acting like he'd recently been declared clinically dead.'

'Jason had just told me how much of a percentage he was expecting when I sold my Lampeter shares to Kyriakou,' Hector said.

Sibylla smiled. 'And I'd just put a call through to my gynaecologist in New York,' she said. 'We were cut off while his assistant went to get the results of the test, but she'd already said that she was pretty sure they were positive. I couldn't get through again.'

'Greek phones,' Hector said. 'What can you expect?'

'Aw hell, honey,' said Marty. His plain face was bright. 'Why you didn't tell me earlier . . .'

'I didn't want to get your hopes up,' said Sibylla.

'Geez, ain't that something?' Marty said. 'Marty Schumann having a baby.'

'Right,' Sibylla said.

'It certainly is,' Lady Helena said. Both her wrists were in plaster. 'Could I possibly bum a cigarette from someone?'

'I wanna tell you,' Marty said, leaning forward with his hands on his knees, 'Theo was real excited when I told him.'

'Sure he was,' said Sibylla. Her tone was dry. 'I don't know what's with that damn kid. I've been trying to get close to him for three years but he just doesn't want to know.'

'He'll come round,' Penny said. 'Once they get back from honeymoon, Alexandra'll see to that. He's only jealous.'

'Seemed to think I was after his goddamned ass the whole time,' said Sibylla. 'Only ass I wanted was Marty's.'

'Hey, honey . . .' Marty's eyes bugged with embarrassment. And lust.

'As if I hadn't already had a gutful of dudes like that,' Sibylla said.

'Like what, exactly?' said Lady Helena.

'You know,' Sibylla said. 'One crook of the finger, and the girls are supposed to go for them like they're a cancer cure. And be grateful if they're stuck with the cheque afterwards.'

'I do know exactly what you mean,' Lady Helen said.

'At your age, you shouldn't,' said Penny. She looked at the door. Barnaby ought to be back any minute.

'The sad thing is Christopher Lampeter being killed,' said Lady Helena.

'At least they'll be able to pin that one on Jason,' Penny said.

'It sure takes nerve to shoot someone through the head at sixty-five m.p.h.,' Sibylla said.

'Or desperation,' said Hector.

'And using our damned car to do it, too.'

'Can you beat the guy's nerve?' Marty said.

'He was cutting it pretty close,' Penny said. 'And he didn't want to use his own car in case someone remembered it later.'

'What was the big rush?' Marty said. He gazed at Sibylla as though she were a diamond choker from Van Cleef & Arpels.

'Jason had to stop Christopher getting to Heathrow to meet Lady H,' Penny said. 'Poor Christopher. He was so much brighter than his brother. No wonder he got mad when people talked about whizz kids. He figured out that Jason had some kind of connection with Hector a long time ago. So when Kyriakou was murdered he didn't have too much of a problem working out that it was to stop the Rockingham being taken over. And also that my mother could probably provide the final clincher. She was the only person present at the reception that the police hadn't interviewed.'

'Listen,' her mother said. 'Be an angel and let me have a cheroot. You know I can't light it for myself with these damn broken wrists.'

'Uh-uh.' Penny shook her head. 'I just had the carpet shampooed.'

'You can be very cruel sometimes, Penelope.'

'I know.'

'The bum deserved everything he got,' Marty said.

'What exactly did you see, Lady Helena, that was so important?' Hector said.

'Just Jason and Costas sitting in Jason's kitchen around two-thirty, two-forty, in the morning,' said Lady Helena. 'We had a quick brandy together before I dashed off for the airport to catch my flight for Greece. I'd no idea until you told me that Costas was supposed to have been tucked up in bed at two.'

'Christopher cottoned on to something,' Penny said. 'And Jason must have realised.'

'So the cops were right about him all along,' said Sibylla. She shuddered. 'I thought he was kinda nice.'

'I don't think he was ever that,' said Penny.

'He sure ran a tight plantation,' Marty said. 'Everything taken care of, down to the tiniest detail.' He looked wistful. 'Wouldn't have minded setting up a deal with a guy like that.'

'It was attention to detail that got him arrested,' Penny said. 'Taking the ropes off the pulley wheels was one thing. Using a baster to blow dust over them was something else. There just wasn't any point to it, except to fudge the issue. I should have realised that the reason he came over all pale and pea green when he saw the body wasn't from shock, it was because he had a hangover. He knew already it was there.'

'God. I'm desperate for a smoke,' Lady Helena said. No one seemed to hear her.

'One thing I still want to know,' Penny said. 'Which of the Lampeter boys was adopted?'

There was a long pause. Lady Helena screwed up her face as though trying to recall something. 'Which of them was it?' she said slowly.

'I'll let you have a cheroot,' said Penny.

Lady Helena sighed. 'Does it make any difference?' she said.

'In the interests of truth.'

'There are different truths.'

Penny heard the front door open. Barnaby was home. If you wanted a self-evident truth, it was the way her heart lurched at the sound. 'Which?' she said. She wasn't going to get no satisfaction, she knew that already.

'I honestly can't remember,' said Lady Helena.

'Honestly?'

Her mother smiled.

About the Author

Susan Moody ws born in Oxford and after leaving school lived for a long time in the States. Eventually she returned to England and now lives in Bedford. Her previous novels are PENNY BLACK, PENNY POST, PENNY DREADFUL, and PENNY ROYAL.